W9-BTL-210

LOVE, HATE & OTHER FILTERS

LOVE,

HATE & OTHER

FILTERS.

SAMIRA AHMED

SOHO
TEEN

Published in the United States by Soho Teen an imprint of Soho Press, Inc.
853 Broadway
New York, NY 10003

Library of Congress Cataloging-in-Publication Data

Ahmed, Samira.
Love, hate & other filters / Samira Ahmed.

ISBN 978-1-61695-847-3
eISBN 978-1-61695-848-0

International edition
ISBN 978-1-61695-955-5

1. Muslims—Fiction. 2. East Indian Americans—Fiction. Dating (Social
customs)—Fiction. 3. High schools—Fiction. 4. Schools—Fiction.
5. Terrorism—Fiction. 6. Family life—Illinois—Chicago—Fiction.
7. Chicago (Ill.)—Fiction. I. Title.
PZ7.1.A345 Lov 2018 DDC [Fic]—dc23 2017021616

Interior design by Janine Agro, Soho Press, Inc.

Printed in the United States of America

10 9 8 7 6 5 4 3 2 1

For Lena & Noah,
Meri aankhon ke taare ho tum.

And for Thomas, who always believed.

His mind wanders back six months to a fetid basement. Window-less, lit by a solitary bulb; empty except for sweaty bodies. Meeting and sanctuary. There was arguing, then a loosely drawn plan, and a call for volunteers. They laughed when he raised his hand. Someone said, Can't send a boy to do a man's job.

CHAPTER 1

Destiny sucks.

Sure, it can be all heart bursting and undeniable and Bollywood dance numbers and *meet me at the Empire State Building*. Except when someone else wants to decide who I'm going to sleep with for the rest of my life. Then destiny is a bloodsucker, and not the swoony, sparkly vampire kind.

The night is beautiful, clear and bright with silvery stars. But I'm walking across a noxious parking lot with my parents toward a wedding where a well-meaning auntie will certainly pinch my cheeks like I'm two years old, and a kindly uncle will corner me about my college plans with the inevitable question: premed or prelaw? In other words, it's time for me to wear a beauty-pageant smile while keeping a very stiff upper lip. It would be helpful if I could grow a thicker skin, too—armor, perhaps—but we're almost at the door.

My purse vibrates. I dig around for my phone. A text from Violet: **You should be here!**

Another buzz, and a picture of Violet appears, decorated in streamers, dancing in the gym. Jeans skinny, lips glossed. Everyone is at MORP without me. It's bad enough I can't go to the actual prom, but missing MORP, too, is death by paper cuts. MORP is the informal prom send-up where everyone goes stag and dances their faces off. And there are always new couples emerging from the dark corners of the gym.

I miss all the drama, as usual.

"Maya, what's wrong?" My mother eyes me with suspicion, as

always. I only wish I could muster up the courage to actually warrant any of her distrust.

"Nothing." I sigh.

"Then why do you look like you're going to a funeral instead of your friend's wedding?"

I widen my toothy fake smile. "Better?" Maybe I should give my mom what she wants tonight, the dutiful daughter who is thrilled to wear gold jewelry and high heels and wants to be a doctor. But the high heels alone are so uncomfortable I can only imagine how painful the rest of the act would be.

"I guess a little happiness is too much to ask of my only daughter."

Dad's chuckling, head down. At least someone is amused by my mother's melodrama.

We step through an arc of red carnations and orange-yellow marigolds to a blur of jewel-toned silk saris and sparkly fairy lights strung in lazy zigzags across the walls. The Bollywood-ized suburban wedding hall feels pretty cinematic, yet the thought of the awkward social situations to come makes me turn back and look longingly at the doors.

But there is no escape.

The tinkling of her silver-belled anklets signal the not-to-be-missed approach of Yasmeen, who addresses my mother with the honorific "auntie," the title accorded all mom-aged Indian women, relation or not. "*As-salaam-alaikum*, Sofia Auntie!"

Yasmeen is only two years older than me; in my mom's eyes, we should be BFFs. Our parents have known each other since their old Hyderabad days, and my mom has been trying to make a friendship happen since Yasmeen's family moved to the States several years ago. But in real life, we're a dud of a match. Also, she's an annoying kiss-ass.

But the girl's got style. Yasmeen is dressed to snare the attention of a suitable young gentleman. Preferably more than one, because a girl needs options. Her peacock-colored *lehanga* that sweeps the floor, her arms full of sparkling bangles, her emerald-and-pearl choker, and the killer *kajal* that lines her eyelids make her the perfect candy-colored Bollywood poster girl.

"Asif Uncle! How are you? Mummy will be so excited to see you both. Maya Aziz, look at you. You're adorable. That shade of pink really suits you. You should wear Indian clothes more often, you know?"

I don't even try to hide it when I roll my eyes. "You've seen me wear Indian clothes a million times."

"Come on, Ayesha is getting ready in the bridal room."

My mom winks her blessing at Yasmeen. "Take her, *beta*, and show her how to be at least a little Indian." So much for family solidarity.

Yasmeen wraps my wrist in a death grip and drags me through the lobby to the tune of *"Ek Ladki ko Dekha,"* an old Bollywood love song that inspired millions of tears.

Everyone seems happy to be here, except me.

It's not just that I hate weddings, which I do. But also because it's Ayesha. I've known her most of my life. She's five years older than me, and in middle school I was in awe of her. The arsenal of lipsticks in her purse and her ability to deploy them perfectly was the kind of social prowess I dreamed of. I never imagined her succumbing to an arranged marriage, especially not right out of college. Even if it was a modified arrangement that involved three months of clandestine dating.

Yasmeen leaves me at the door when she spots her mom summoning her to meet another auntie. And the auntie's son. Sweet relief.

When I step into the bridal prep room, I stop short.

Ayesha is the living embodiment of an old-school Hollywood halo filter. It's breathtaking. I take a moment to absorb the sight: my bejeweled friend in her intricate *ghagra choli*—a ball skirt and short blouse of cherry-colored silk embroidered with gold threads and encrusted with tiny beads and pearls.

"Ayesha, you're stunning."

"Thank you, love."

I've seen Ayesha smile a million times, but I've never seen her smile like this, like she invented the concept of joy.

"I-I have a surprise," I announce, stammering. I remove my camcorder from my bag and hold it up like a trophy. "I'm shooting a movie of your wedding . . ."

Before Ayesha can respond (or protest), the door swings open. Her mother, Shahnaz Auntie, triumphantly arrives with the bridal party in tow. They are ready to take their positions. And only an hour behind schedule, which is basically on time for an Indian wedding.

"See you out there," I murmur.

I blow Ayesha a kiss and walk backward, filming the pre-processional scramble. I take a tracking shot into the wedding hall, aglow with thousands of candles, red-and-orange bouquets bursting from the center of tables. I follow the gold organza that drapes the ceiling and trails the flower-strewn aisle leading to the *mandap*—the traditional wedding canopy under which the vows will take place.

My mother sees me. Too late for me to hide, even with my camera in hand. She beckons me over to her table, not with a subtle head tilt or single finger hook, but with a full arm wave, drawing the entire room's attention. She's chatting with another middle-aged, sari-clad woman. And a boy—I'm guessing her teenage son.

But my aunt Hina is also at our table. Salvation.

It's hard to believe she is my mother's sister. Hina is ten years younger than Mom, has short hair, a zillion funky pairs of eyeglasses, is this amazing graphic designer and cool in ways I can only aspire to. The weird thing is, you'd think my mom wouldn't get along with Hina, but they have this unbreakable bond.

My mom is still waving madly at me. I steel myself, lower my camera, and walk over.

"As-salaam-alaikum, everyone," I say and bend to kiss Hina on the cheek.

"Maya, this is Salma Auntie." My mom takes me by the elbow to draw me nearer, then raises her voice. "And this is her son, Kareem."

Did I mention that subtlety is not my mother's strong suit?

I glance over at my dad, deeply involved in a conversation with Kareem's dad—no doubt about the economy, lawn-mowing equipment, or the trend of teeth whitening at the dental practice he runs with my mom.

"Maya, Kareem is a sophomore at Princeton," my mother says, "studying engineering." I can practically see the cartoon light bulb over her head as she speaks.

"How's it going?" Kareem asks. He scans the room, disinterested. Not that I can totally blame him; no doubt he gets my mother's message loud and clear. He sports a goatee that I assume is meant to make his boyish face look older or tougher. It does neither. On the other hand, it succeeds at drawing my attention to his rather gorgeously full lips. He has a nice mouth in spite of whatever might come out of it.

My defenses are up. "It's going fine." I cross my arms. "Did you fly in for the wedding?"

"My mom asked me to come. I took a long weekend." Kareem's wandering eyes finally meet my own. His are brown, like mine, like most Indians', but so dark that the pupil almost completely fades into the iris. They're liquid and beckoning. And his lips. There is no denying that Violet would label them delish.

"Kareem, Maya will attend University of Chicago next year."

This from his mother, whom I've never met. But I understand her attempt to draw out the conversation.

"I got in, but I haven't decided yet," I correct.

Inside, I'm squirming. Nobody here but Hina knows my secret. I've applied to NYU and been accepted. NYU is my dream school. I'm not going to the University of Chicago if I can help it. The mere fact that I've pulled off this feat—under the radar, in spite of the ever-present gaze of my parents—represents a tiny victory, one that fills me with both hope and guilt. My stomach churns every time I get close to telling them. Especially my mother.

But I have to tell them. And soon. This secret has an expiration date. How, though? How can I tell my mother that I don't want to go to a great school—one that's an easy commute from home, but also from endless family obligations and her constant hovering?

"Decide? What's to decide?" my mom demands, as if reading my thoughts. "You've gotten into one of the best schools in the country. It's decided."

Sitar music fills the lapse in conversation.

"Maya, I saved you a chair next to me," Hina offers.

"Thanks," I whisper. I sit and squeeze her hand under the table.

"No problem." She leans close, lowering her voice. "Cute guy, by the way—"

"Shh." Now I'm full-on blushing, afraid Kareem, or worse, his mother, will overhear.

The sitar music fades into a remix of a forever classic, *"Chaiyya Chaiyya."* It booms from the speakers. I raise my camera. One thing I've learned: people love a camera, and when I'm filming, they see *it*, not me, so whenever I need to, I can quietly disappear behind my trusty shield.

Ten guys, the groom's friends and family, led by a man playing the *dhol*, an Indian drum, begin to dance their way to the *mandap*. The music slows while the groom walks down the aisle with his parents. Rose and jasmine garlands encircle the groom's neck.

Ayesha's cousins and friends follow in an array of colorful saris. Each one cups a glass lotus-shaped votive—their faces radiant above the candlelight. I zoom in to catch the dramatic effect. Finally, Ayesha and her parents appear at the door. The music slows, and a bright Urdu love song takes over from the sonorous *dhol*. The guests rise. As Ayesha enters the room, a wave of *aaahs* and camera flashes precede her down the aisle. She floats toward her groom. Shahnaz Auntie, the bride's mother, looks grim, probably worried about her daughter's reaction to the wedding night.

Note to Shahnaz Auntie: Ayesha is not going to be shocked.

The cleric begins with a prayer in Urdu, translating everything into English for the many non-Urdu speakers. I catch my parents looking at each other affectionately. I can't turn away fast enough.

The vows are simple, the same kind of pledges I've heard at weddings of every faith. Except at the end, there is no kiss. I close in for the money shot anyway, hoping for a moment of rebellion from Ayesha and Saleem. But no. No public kissing allowed. Full stop. The no kissing is anticlimactic, but some taboos cross oceans, packed tightly into the corners of immigrant baggage, tucked away with packets of masala and memories of home.

WHEN THE MUSIC COMES back on, waiters appear with appetizers and plate after heaping plate of mouthwatering food—*biryani* and kebabs and *tandoori* chicken and *samosas*. The room fills with happy chatter. I spy Ayesha and Saleem sneaking out, maybe hoping to steal that kiss in private.

"Maya, put the video camera down and eat, for God's sake," my mother says.

She gives me the Indian bobblehead waggle that can literally mean anything: *yes, no, why, what's up, maybe, carry on*. I want to keep filming the choreography of waiters moving seamlessly in and out the kitchen doors, hot plates in their hands and smiles on their faces, each doing a little half-turn as they walk through the door, pushing it open with their shoulders. In editing, I can slow down the waitstaff action and time it to "Pachelbel's Canon." It will be wedding-y, but irreverent, too. Resigned, I exchange my camera for a fork.

"Maya is the family documentarian," my father explains to Kareem's parents. As if my behavior necessitates explanation.

"She makes beautiful films. One day, she'll take Hollywood by storm," Hina says. My aunt always makes me believe I can fly.

Dad clears his throat. "Well, it's a good hobby, anyway." Translation: *don't get any ideas*.

I narrow my eyes at him. After all, it's his fault I fell in love with making movies in the first place.

A few years ago, in an uncharacteristic burst of after-school special inspiration, my father planned a daddy-daughter day for us that included mini-golf, McDonald's, and a documentary about a racecar driver. He was so proud of his movie choice because the director was Muslim. And Indian. Well, British. But Indian. I forced myself to smile throughout because I didn't want to crush him with my complaints. But I was rolling my eyes and har-rumphing on the inside until the first scene when a tousle-haired, smiling young man filled the screen. *Senna* grabbed me by the throat and heart and didn't let go.

My dad loves the agony and ecstasy component of sports

movies. But I saw a story about destiny and rivalry and tenacity. I saw a director, the Muslim-Indian director, capture the smoking, tragic charisma of Ayrton Senna. I couldn't stop thinking about it or talking about it.

So later that summer, when I was making my annoyance about having to attend my cousin's wedding in India well-known to anyone in range, my dad bought me an entry-level camcorder and suggested I put together a movie of the weeklong festivities. It was love at opening shot.

"There was a great Satyajit Ray retrospective at school last semester."

Kareem's voice catches me by surprise.

I smile and nod. "The Apu Trilogy is one of my favorites. I love his use of light, and did you know that François Truffaut stomped out of the first movie, *Pather Panchali*, at Cannes because he couldn't stand watching a movie about peasants eating with their hands? Total pretentious jerk."

Kareem doesn't answer. He seems to be studying me. You know how some people have smiling eyes? His eyes dance. I lose track of what I was saying. I bend down and pretend to fix my heel so he can't see the abject horror and embarrassment on my face. When I pop back up, I start shoveling food into my mouth.

"Slow down; there's more in the kitchen," Hina whispers.

I chew and swallow hard. "Thanks for saying that, by the way," I murmur to her. "About me making beautiful movies and all."

"I meant it." Hina bends close again, her mouth at my ear. "You need to tell them soon, you know."

I nod, careful to keep my voice low. "NYU wants the deposit in a few weeks. There's no way they'll let me go. But I have to go. So many amazing directors have gone there. I mean, James Franco teaches there."

Hina laughs. "You might not want to lead with that."

I laugh, too, in spite of myself.

"Maya, you won't know what your parents will say unless you ask," she adds. "Lose your courage now, and you'll regret it. And frankly, how many more Indian lawyers do we need?"

"You done eating?" Kareem asks suddenly.

Before I know it, Hina is in the midst of a conversation with my mother and Kareem's mom.

I look at my still half-full plate. "I'm waiting for dessert."

Kareem grins. "I don't think you're in danger of missing it. Want to take a walk?"

"A walk?" I echo.

"Maybe get more shots for your movie? I could be your key grip."

"Do you even know what a key grip does?"

The question flies from my mouth before I have a chance to regret it, but his eyes still dance.

"Well, not exactly. But obviously it's important, or else why would it be called *key* grip instead of average grip or not-so-critical grip?"

I smirk. "Well played. The grips deal with lighting. So fiddle with the light bulbs and see what you can do with that disco ball and all those random reflections." I point to the mirrored orb dangling in the center of the dance floor—if there were going to be dancing at this wedding.

Kareem pushes back his chair. "I'm up for the challenge."

I like how he accepts the supporting role and doesn't try to desimansplain things to me. He's willing to try new things even if he might fail or look like a dork. It's a different kind of confidence than I've seen in some of the guys at school, and it's really appealing.

"We're going to get more footage, Mom," I say as I stand up and grab my camera.

My mom looks at Kareem's mom, then raises an eyebrow at me. "Don't get lost, you two."

Kareem walks close to me. His arm grazes mine. Heat spreads through my body. Then he does it again. Clearly, it's not an accident. He towers over me. Which isn't hard considering I'm five-three. He looks ahead, but I sense him smiling.

"So I take it this isn't your first feature film starring an Indian wedding," he remarks dryly.

"I'm actually a highly sought after director on this circuit. I specialize in goat sacrifices and masterful film school angles of aunties with muffin tops."

"And how did that come to be your film style?"

"It's kind of a long story."

"We've got time. It's an Indian wedding. They do tend to drag on. Haven't you heard?" Kareem gives me a little nudge.

I grin. Probably for a little too long.

"Like three years ago, my parents dragged me to a family wedding in India which I did not want to be at, and my camera gave me an escape. I mean, I still had to endure ludicrous cheek pinching and itchy clothes and too-late dinners and too many questions, but the camera gave me distance and something to hide behind, literally. I ended up making this twenty-minute documentary capturing all these weirdly lit, unglamorous aunties-yelling, caterer-butchering-the-goat moments and even included a brief montage of crying babies right before the final shots of the unsmiling and garlanded bride and groom exchanging their vows under the *mandap*."

He nods gravely. "So we're talking Oscar material here."

"Shut up," I say, swatting at his arm.

"Seriously. It sounds amazing. I'd love a private screening sometime."

I come to an abrupt stop. I have to force myself to speak because suddenly my tongue is made of wood. "There's the cake. Let's get a shot before they cut it."

I train my camera on the four-tiered fondant behemoth. The sides of the base layer are decorated with Indian elephants connected nose to tail. Each of the other layers is trimmed in red-and-gold paisley. And there are flowers, real ones. Red and orange roses surround a tiny Indian bride and groom on the top layer.

"Check it out. The tiny bride is wearing a sari. We've so arrived." Kareem laughs. "I wonder what she's made of." He reaches toward the dolls.

"Stop," I warn him, but continue to film.

Kareem yanks his hand away in mock dismay. "I wasn't really going to touch it. I'm not a total idiot." I swing the camera to his face. "I thought I'd add a little drama to your movie. You know, 'after one too many cups of tea, the handsome Kareem fled with the bride. Chaos ensued. The bride's father swore vengeance on the guest who had stolen the bride's heart before the nuptials.'"

My face feels warm, but if I'm blushing, he can't see it. Through the lens I take in his broad shoulders and lean, muscular arms. I focus on his face as he continues his narration about the kidnapped plastic bride. The lens is drawn to his dark eyes, and so am I.

Kareem takes a step toward me. "So are you going to the after-party?"

I feel a flutter of nervousness as I lower the camera. "After-party?"

"At Empire, in the city. One of Saleem's friends put it together. So the young desis can throw down away from the prying eyes of our parents. It's a surprise for Ayesha."

"Not as if she didn't have other plans for her wedding night." The words spill out of my mouth before I can stop them, and I turn bright red.

Kareem laughs. "I'm sure they'll only put in a brief appearance. I can pretty much tell you there is only one thing on Saleem's mind right now, and it's not cutting that cake."

I sweep the back of my hand across my eyes, trying to wipe away my embarrassment.

"I've never met an Indian who blushes so much. Have you devised a method to defeat desi DNA?"

"You can't expect me to give up all my secrets that easily."

Kareem takes another step forward. "So you in or out for the after-party?"

"I could crash at my aunt's place in Chicago, but I don't have a change of clothes. And I don't have a car—"

"Come with me. I can drive you home tomorrow, too."

"The thing is, I work in the morning."

"I get it. You're the responsible Indian girl. Give me your phone."

I wince at Kareem's presumption, but essentially he's right. "Why do you need it?"

"Trust me."

I self-consciously hand him my bedazzled phone. Kareem dials a number. His phone rings. "Now I can live-text you from Empire and tell you how much fun you're missing."

"Let me guess, you give good text."

"When it counts," Kareem breathes into my ear and slips my phone into my palm.

As we step away from the cake, Kareem edges closer to me and puts his hand on the small of my back. The warmth of his handprint sinks into my skin through the thin silk of my clothes. There's a tingle along my collarbone. Part of me wants to run outdoors into the cool evening to get a handle on myself. Instead, I breathe in deeply and let this new sensation consume me.

The young man studies his face in the mirror. The scruff on his chin makes him look boyish, a kid dressing up as a grown-up for Halloween. Only the bruise-colored circles under his eyes betray his age. It's a step in the right direction.

His fingers vibrate with the soft buzz of the clippers. Waves of thick black hair fall into the rusty basin.

When finished, he moves his hand across the top of his stubbly head, pausing briefly at the scar halfway down the back of his scalp, a souvenir care of his father's belt buckle. The past, made visible.

His mother, who loves his hair, will be devastated. He scowls, curling back his lips to bare his teeth.

It doesn't matter.

She will never see him again.

CHAPTER 2

Kareem: The party wasn't the same once you left.

Me: Awww, you say that to all the documentarians, don't you?

Kareem: Only the cute, irreverent ones.

Rereading Kareem's flirty texts in bed, I still feel the touch of his hand on my skin. It's all a little cliché for my tastes—the words on the phone, the silly smile I can't get rid of—but so is being seventeen and unkissed.

Kareem: So are you a doc film purist?

Me: I love old classics and foreign films, too. And I can always find something to mock in a blockbuster.

Kareem: In other words, you're open to temptation.

Me: Totally depends on the tempter.

That dialogue! It's even unfolding like a screenplay. We had the meet-cute, so I allowed us the full rom-com text treatment this weekend. Now it's Monday morning and I'm second-guessing, right on schedule.

Staring up at Aishwarya Rai on the *Bride and Prejudice* poster above my bed—a typically well-meaning, completely misguided gift attempt from my mom—I hope I'm not getting ahead of myself. But maybe that's the message my mother meant to send with the poster. *"It's a desi* Pride and Prejudice*! You love that book. But it's better because there is singing and dancing!"* She left out the part about obedient daughters and no kissing. The all-important subtext. She literally clapped when I agreed to hang it on my wall.

I sigh. "You probably always know what to say to the cute boy, don't you, Aishwarya?" I whisper. "I mean you probably don't even need to speak; you just bat your beguiling eyes—"

eat some breakfast before school," my mom

er if she heard me.

eryone at the party was telling me you're so thin," she adds.
There is no acceptable in-between for Hyderabadi moms.
You're either too skinny or a little too chubby.

I scurry to get ready. I pull on a favorite blue V-neck sweater over a pair of skinny jeans. I search through my jewelry box and come up with an orange-and-blue beaded choker and a pair of silver crescent-moon earrings—from Hina. I dab a little mineral bronzer on my cheeks and run a reddish-brown gloss over my lips.

Before I walk out of my room, I wink at Aishwarya, perpetually cool and confident. "Maybe there's a kiss in my future after all, Aishwarya. Maybe lots of kissing."

I don't want to eat, but my mom hovers in the kitchen. She always hovers. I wolf down a little cereal for her benefit.

"Let me make you an omelet," she says. "You're skin and bones. Skin and bones."

"I'm not hungry, and Violet's going to be driving up any second."

She waves a wooden spoon in her hand. "Not hungry? How can you go to school on two bites of cereal? You need to take care of yourself, *beta*. I'm not going to be here forever, you know. Then what will you do with no one to look after you? You can't cook a thing."

"That's why God invented takeout."

My mother blinks, her face blank. She should be used to my snark by now. These days, honestly, she just seems bewildered by me. I'm an eternal stranger forced to reintroduce myself to her one bon mot at a time. Lucky for me, the silence is broken by three telltale honks from the driveway: Violet. My escape.

"I'll take an apple with me, okay? Don't forget I'm working after school. I'll need your car. *Khudafis.*" I'm halfway out the door.

"We need to put cooking on your biodata," my mom yells after me. "No suitable boy will marry you if you can't cook."

"Counting on it," I whisper to myself.

MUSIC PULSES FROM VIOLET'S vintage Karmann Ghia, a gift from her dad shortly after they moved to Batavia, Illinois, from New York City. The orange paint and vanilla interior remind me of a Creamsicle. Sometimes I have the urge to dart out my tongue and lick the hood and see if it tastes like summer.

Violet tosses her blonde hair over her shoulder and bats her eyelashes.

This is Violet. She will flirt with anyone. Even me.

"How was the dance?" I ask. It's a courtesy. I don't need to fish for juicy gossip; I know Violet's been chomping at the bit to tell me in person. "Did Mike fawn all over you?"

Violet rolls her eyes and backs out of the driveway. Mike's been crushing on Violet since she moved here freshman year. Clearly the guy's an optimist.

"You know you love the attention," I tell her.

"You're right, I do." With a laugh, she shifts into drive and heads toward school. "But it got a little wild." She's still smiling. "You missed the fight."

"The fight?" I repeat. My cinematic imagination immediately takes over. "As in droplets of blood bouncing off the well-buffed wood floor of the gym?"

She groans. "You should listen to yourself talk sometimes, Maya."

"I know how brilliant I sound," I shoot back dryly. "So what happened?"

"No blood, but plenty of drama." Violet glances at me. "It was Phil and Lisa."

My heart thumps a bit. "Phil?" I repeat, before realizing I neglected to add Lisa to my question.

Violet nods. "Apparently something is rotten in the state of super couplehood. I couldn't hear what they were saying, but Lisa made a huge scene of stomping out of the gym during a slow dance."

A flaw in the perfection of Phil and Lisa is like my parents allowing me to go to prom (even if I had a date)—impossible. I almost sit on my hands to prevent the ridiculous gesticulations I want to make. I am a whirling dervish of what-ifs.

"Maybe this means Phil will be available for prom." Violet raises her eyebrows at me. "For a certain hot, yet unassuming, and often exacting Indian chick."

"Whatever."

"Well, why not?" Violet prods. "I mean, you've had a thing for him forever. Like, literally, forever."

I shake my head. "I have not had a 'thing' for him for any amount of time. I may have said I thought he was hot once—"

"Revisionist," Violet interrupts. "Saying Phil is hot is not a confession; it's a profound grasp of the obvious. You like him, like him. Admit it."

Phil and I have known each other since kindergarten, but we've never been really close or even truly friends. Then in health class last semester, the teacher assigned us to be partners for a project on "Aging in America." We had to record oral histories from senior citizens in a retirement home. I braced myself to do all the work. But Phil showed up and charmed everyone. I remember looking over at him talking to one of the oldest residents at the home. He held her hand and listened to her so intently and smiled at her with this dimple in his cheek. He charmed me, too.

Since then, he occasionally sidles up to me for a lunch-line chat while he chomps on a basket of cafeteria fries. The conversations aren't deep or anything and only last five or six fries, but still, they leave me a little breathless and focusing a little too keenly on that dimple. I know better than to read into it. Phil is taken. Extremely. Or is he? Regardless, we inhabit separate planets.

I take AP classes and blast Florence + the Machine in my earbuds.

Phil is the quarterback and homecoming king. (Seriously. That's what he is.)

And at Batavia High School, never the twain shall meet.

"I plead the Fifth," I say finally. I look out the window. If I don't change the subject, Violet's enthusiasm will feed my tiny hopes, and I will implode from possibilities. And Phil is impossible. Beautiful and impossible. Through middle school he was this gawky and goofy kid with a cute smile. But every year since, he's grown into himself. And grown on me. Especially since our health class project first semester.

"So who was this wedding guy you texted me about? Any actual details?"

BY THE TIME WE reach school, I've shared all the flirty memories—about Kareem, not Phil—that I know will thrill Violet. Kareem's whispers and innuendo, his hand on my back, the PG-13 suggestive texts we exchanged after the wedding.

She jerks to an abrupt halt in the parking lot and turns to face me. "He's Indian, goes to Princeton, and took your number. And you're not jumping out of your seat why?"

"And he's Muslim," I add for full effect.

"He sounds like your parents' wet dream," Violet says. Noting my disgust, she adds, "It's a metaphor. All I'm saying is, he sounds perfect on paper. And he's older, which is hot."

I allow myself a smile. "Well, he's definitely more available," I admit. "And, suitable."

"Suitable?" She laughs. "You sound like your mom."

"I know. But all my iconoclastic eggs are in the NYU basket. I can't fight my mom on every front."

Violet shrugs and takes the keys out of the ignition. "One battle at a time. I get it."

After filing in with the other kids, we drop our bags at our lockers and grab our books for first period.

I pause to look in my locker mirror and run a comb through my long hair. I don't need to, since my hair is generally tangle free, but combing my hair has this calming effect on me. It's a morning ritual.

My locker is decorated with a postcard of Edward from *Twilight*, circa 2008, courtesy of Phil, actually. Last semester, he heard me tell a friend in health class that I refused to see *Twilight* even though she considered it a classic. Phil jumped into the conversation to give me a hard time about it—he claimed that *he* liked it, after all—and the next morning, I found this postcard taped to my locker. On the back he wrote, *Sparkly vampires rule*. He didn't sign his name, but when I looked around, he was at his locker watching, grinning.

It's embarrassing to keep a public display of affection for . . . Edward, but I can never bring myself to get rid of it. So my answer to this unwarranted Team Edward affiliation was to identify with

Team Kubrick. Specifically the famous, terrifying scene from *The Shining* where Jack Nicholson's demonic smile and bulging eyes appear through a splintered door. I positioned it so it looks like he is leering at Edward. Plausible deniability.

Below that is a Wilco concert poster. Of course, I've never been to a concert because I'm not allowed, but when I dream about going to a show, Jeff Tweedy is crooning, "I Am Trying to Break Your Heart."

"Hey, Maya."

I spy Phil's reflection in my mirror. Hair artfully disheveled, grin adorably rakish, dimple bared.

I try to embody Aishwarya, hoping her elegance and nonchalance will rub off. "Oh, hey, Phil." It works. I utter three perfect syllables. Total grace under pressure.

"Listen, uh, I, want to ask you a favor," Phil says while tapping a pencil against his left cheek. "I'm wondering if you might . . ."

I wonder if he's looking for Lisa, worried she'll see us talking.

"Lay on, Macduff," I say. I'm a bit terse. And I'm quoting Macbeth. I'm in high school. I have to stop quoting Shakespeare. At this rate, what will I have to look forward to in college?

"Can you help me with my independent study paper for Ms. Jensen's class? I have to read *The Namesake*, and I thought—"

"You thought I'd know everything about it because I'm Indian?" His request catches me by surprise. A good surprise. But also totally annoying.

"No. I mean, maybe? Sorry . . . I didn't mean . . . I know you like to read," Phil stammers. It's actually a little endearing to catch him off guard.

"I do love that book. The movie, too. But it's not only because I'm Indian, you know? Like, do you like every movie that's about football?"

"Every single one," he says, without missing a beat, back to form. "Including documentaries."

I start to laugh. "Okay."

Phil grins. The dimple appears. "As in, okay, you'll help me?"

I nod, looking down. I don't want to stare. On the other hand, he's staring at *me*.

"Hiya, Phil." Violet materializes at my elbow. Loudly.

"Hey, Violet."

"I'm walking Maya to first period. Unless, of course, you want to abscond with her?"

My head jerks back up. My mortification is complete.

"Sure," Phil says. But he stumbles to correct himself, "I mean, no. I gotta get to class, too."

I shut my locker, ready to escape. I turn to Violet. "Let's go. See ya, Phil." We start to walk away.

"So maybe tonight?" Phil calls after me.

I turn my head to look back at him. "I'm working at the bookstore until seven—"

"I'll swing by then."

A meet-cute with the suitable Indian boy. The hot football player at my locker. I feel queasy. I was joking with myself earlier, but now I'm wondering how it's possible that I've stepped into the most predictable teen rom-com ever. How is this my real life?

But I go with it. My mind plays a slow-motion close-up of Phil walking down the hall. An improbable gust of wind ruffles his just-long-enough, perfectly mussed chestnut hair. Low-key lighting casts intriguing shadows in the hall, and my filmic version of Phil turns to look at me, his twinkling green eyes catching mine.

Sure, it's all my imagination.

Except the last part.

He really did turn to look.

The sun rises over the motel parking lot.

He stands in the middle of the small, spare room in his underwear. Despite a recent shower, beads of sweat form above his lip and on his newly shaven head. He wipes his face with the threadbare motel towel and pulls on a pair of faded jeans and an army-green T-shirt. The shirt is loose on his wiry frame. A pair of black leather boots stand at attention by the side of the bed. The young man strides over to the dirty window and lifts it the full six inches it will rise. Bending down, he takes three quick breaths of the tar-infused air.

Outside, a garbage truck pulls into the lot. It groans and screeches with its task, mechanically swallowing the contents of a foul-smelling dumpster. Neither the sound nor the stench registers. For a moment he is only conscious of the trees in the distance, across the highway, their green tops swaying.

CHAPTER 3

Violet drops me off at my house. I run to my room to change and frantically reapply my makeup before heading off to the bookstore. I leave a note for my parents: *Back late, studying with Violet after work. Will grab dinner with her.*

It's a lie. And it's not my first one, either.

Twenty minutes later I'm parking my mom's conspicuous Mercedes in front of the Idle Hour.

For my parents, their matching Benzes signal the success of their practice or having made it in America. For me, the cars simply shout, "Hey, look at me." I don't want the attention, but I don't have a choice.

Not wanting attention is part of why I love working at the bookstore. That, and opening up boxes of new books, their pages crisp, spines unbroken. My parents insist it's unnecessary. They actually remind me that they provide me with whatever I want. What they don't say out loud, what they *mean*, is that time working can be time spent on other activities that *they* prefer, like homework and learning to cook.

I want to make my own money to spend or save as I wish. It's mostly spend, though, and honestly, mostly spent *here*. While I get a discount from the couple who owns the place, Richard and Anna, massive chunks of my paychecks still go toward the Idle Hour's books on cinematography and the history of old Hollywood and the studio system and biographies of famous directors and actors. At least the DVDs are free.

Granted, nobody wanted them in the first place, but I pleaded with Richard and Anna to spare their celluloid (well, digitized) lives. It was how we met. I convinced them to open a DVD library in the corner of the store, like a public service preserving our cinematic history. They not only agreed, they offered me a part-time job. Since then, basically, it's only been a public service to me because they let me borrow as many movies as I want.

The store is nearly empty tonight, so I can browse a bit before sitting at the register. Alone in the stacks, I run my fingers across gleaming paperbacks and matte hardcovers. I lose myself in the titles. It's meditative, and it clears my mind, although being at the register also allows me to check out a bit and let my imagination wander. Before I know it, I'm in the film section, naturally. My eyes settle on a book I'd spotted earlier: *Hoop Dreams*. I pull it off the shelf and start thumbing through it.

"Anything interesting?"

I look up. Phil is heading toward me. He has this walk that is somehow languid and confident at the same time. Like a slow-moving river that doesn't need to show its strength because it's a known fact.

When he gets closer, I notice the tiniest speck of shaving cream in the little nook where his jaw meets his ear. Then he smiles, and all I can see is that dimple again.

I'm cotton-mouthed, so I clear my throat. "It's a book about two high school athletes, actually. It was a documentary first, in the nineties. Then they expanded on it for the book." I give him a hopeful look but stare into a blank face. I snap the book shut and point at the title. *"Hoop Dreams?"*

"A basketball movie?"

"It's not just about basketball. It's about family relationships and survival. And the world crushing your dreams."

"So it's a comedy," Phil says.

I laugh. "It's really great. You should watch it sometime. If you can bring yourself to watch a movie about a lesser sport."

He shrugs. "I actually tried playing basketball in middle school. Loved it. Still do."

"Why'd you give it up?"

"I got no vertical. Like literally, the coach told me I'd be warming the bench a lot, but I had a good arm and was kinda fast, so he suggested football."

"And the rest is Batavia High School history."

Phil looks down at his shoes. "Something like that."

Crap. Did I say something wrong? I reach out to touch Phil's elbow, but a terse voice makes me drop my hand.

"Hey, man, what are you doing here?"

It's Brian, a football player in my French class.

I tense slightly as he comes toward us down the narrow aisle. He's not as tall as Phil, but he's more broad-shouldered. His eyes are sunken and hollow, fixed on Phil as if I'm not there. He sits behind me, so I never really get a good look at him during class. But right now, he looks like he hasn't slept in a week. He clearly hasn't shaved the last few days, either.

"Hey, man," Phil echoes. "Maya's helping me with the independent study project."

Phil and Brian bump forearms. All the athletes do this. It's like they have the swine flu and are trying to avoid germs.

"That's why I'm here, too." Brian holds up a book. "I'm reading *American Sniper*." He jerks his head toward me. "What's with the help?"

Phil's face darkens for an instant, and he takes a step closer to me. He laughs, sort of awkwardly—a boy who's never awkward—and I sense an attempt to diffuse some sort of sudden moment I have yet to read. "She has a name, dude. It's Maya. She goes to our school. She works here. But you know that."

"Whatever." Brian turns and walks away in the direction of the register. One hand clutches his book against his chest; the other is clenched in a fist at his side. "Say hi to Lisa!" he calls.

It's a dig. At me. And it stings. I ignore it, because I'm not eager to talk about the possibility of a still-existent girlfriend whom Phil has most likely recently kissed. But I can't ignore how despite my standing in front of him, despite us being in class together, Brian totally erased me. Also, he completely creeps me out—his face, his eyes, the simmering anger in his voice.

"Sorry about that," Phil says. "He's been weird this whole semester. Really since before the season ended . . ."

"Weird how?"

Phil stops himself. His unfinished thought lingers in the air for a moment. Then he shakes his head, smiles, and points to the café at the front of the store. "Shall we?"

I search for something to say, but I come up blank. We walk together silently to find a table.

Phil probably has a good ten inches on me, but unlike the other tall kids I know, he isn't gangly or clumsy. He carries himself with a certainty and ease that make him appear older. He's always had that air about him, even before his growth spurt. I envy how comfortable he is with himself.

As I settle into my seat, Phil walks to the coffee counter.

A minute later he returns, balancing two coffees and a piece of chocolate cake. "I thought we could share," he says.

"Thanks. I love cake." I want to slap the palm of my hand against my forehead. I sound like a sugar-obsessed three-year-old. I wonder if I'll ever not be bumbling and weird around Phil.

Probably best to just concentrate on the reason I agreed to meet him, instead of on his twinkly green eyes. "Do you have your essay?"

"Cake, then homework," he protests. "Unless . . . you're in a rush?"

"Not at all. Dessert definitely takes precedent over homework."

I want to high-five myself for managing to sound breezy and casual. Then I realize I'm smiling like an idiot, and my face warms with embarrassment.

Phil smiles back. Oh, God. My cheeks all-out burn. "You blush a lot," he says.

"It's a weird genetic anomaly. I call it the Maya Paradox. I'm a world-class visible blusher despite loads of melanin. I'm pretty much a scientific wonder." I have to eat. Now. That way words will stop falling out of my mouth.

We sit there, devouring cake, occasionally locking eyes until I look down at the disappearing slice between us. Phil and I reach for the last piece at the same time. He battles me for it before cutting it in half and nudging the bigger piece toward me.

I finally relax a little. "So you picked *The Namesake?*"

He nods, his dimple vanishing, his brow furrowing. "I missed a day of class, and so I got stuck with this book and the topic of 'forging identity.'"

"Then you got lucky. That's pretty much the theme of the whole book. What ideas do you have so far?"

"I have zero ideas." He pauses and meets my gaze. "Well, okay, there's that weird thing with Gogol's name. Like, why does he need two names? It's actually kind of confusing."

"It's confusing to him, too. Plus Gogol is not an Indian name, so he's like a total outsider, even in his own culture."

Phil pauses and leans back into his chair. "So that's why he intro-duces himself as Nikhil to the girl in the bar, even though she already knows him as Gogol?"

I nod. "Moushumi. That whole relationship was so sad."

"Not for her. She cheated on him," Phil responds.

"True. But they were all searching for belonging. She was, too. Not that it's an excuse to have possibly mind-blowing sex with a French dude . . ." My mouth clamps shut, but it's too late. I can feel my face heating up once more; it started the moment the word "sex" slipped from my lips.

Phil chuckles and raises his coffee cup. "To not having random sex with French dudes."

I lean in to touch the tip of my cup against his, then pull it away. "I feel like I should keep my options open," I blurt.

Phil laughs, nearly spilling his coffee. His laugh is round and deep and makes his shoulders shake. The dimple in his cheek is back. I think I was making a joke; I think I wanted this reaction, but part of me isn't sure.

It occurs to me that this is the longest time we've ever spent alone together in all the years we've known each other. Yet somehow I've stopped being nervous and started to have fun. I reach for Phil's book to find a quote on identity.

Our hands touch briefly.

His skin is warm, a heater for my icy fingers. I hold my breath and tug at the book; Phil teasingly pulls it back.

My phone buzzes.

Violet! I curse silently, snatching the phone off the table before turning it over and pulling it closer to my chest, expecting a shouty caps demand for details.

You're right. Senna is amazing. But I'd like your IRL color commentary. Next weekend?

It's not Violet. It's Kareem.

I run my thumb over the screen to wipe away an unexpected pang of guilt. I look at Phil and think of his fight with Lisa at the dance. I think of his sudden desire to be a good student. Overwhelmed, I seek refuge in *The Namesake* and turn to a dog-eared page—and a familiar line jumps out at me:

You are still young. Free . . . Do yourself a favor. Before it's too late, without thinking about it first, pack a pillow and a blanket and see as much of the world as you can.

He sits on the edge of the bed and pulls on his black boots, wrapping the long laces twice around the tops. Last night, he polished and buffed the leather, not that it's necessary. Not that it matters.

He doesn't like the way his fingers shake. It's weak, but he chalks it up to adrenaline. He takes a breath to steady his hands. Satisfied, he takes a sealed envelope from the black gym bag on the floor and lays it across the veneered pressboard desk, making sure it's straight. He surveys the sparsely furnished room.

Everything is in order. He steps to the door and wraps his clammy hand around the knob. Then pauses. The door still closed, he moves to the middle of the room. Looking out the eastern-facing windows, he falls to his knees, bows his head, and recites something like a prayer.

CHAPTER 4

"Hey," I say as I approach Phil's table for another evening of tutoring. He's been waiting for me for thirty minutes while I finished my shift at the Idle Hour.

Phil pushes a chair forward for me.

As I sit down, I see a slice of chocolate cake with two forks resting on the plate. I smile at Phil.

"Chocolate cake is like our tradition, so . . ." he starts.

"So two times officially equals tradition?"

"Well, football players are superstitious creatures of habit."

"I thought that was only for game days."

"It is," Phil says, dimple bared as he grins.

"Well, who am I to flout tradition?" I look away. "Plus, you know, cake is pretty much my favorite thing." I add, raising a forkful to my mouth.

"Cake, not *barfi*?" Phil asks.

I'm gobsmacked. I look up. My eyes widen. "The *barfi*? You remember that?"

"Of course. Though the name is kind of unfortunate."

I laugh. "Tell me about it. Like, every boy in the class started calling me 'barfy' or making barf jokes. But when you took one of the sweets and ate it. It, like, shut them up. I never forgot that."

I'm not lying when I say this. I was seven and made the colossal mistake of asking my mom to bring my favorite Indian dessert to school for my birthday. Phil eating the *barfi* might not seem like a big deal, but to a quiet girl who was shrinking into herself with every "barfy" shout-out, Phil walking up and taking one little square of almond paste and sugar and popping it into his mouth was a lifeline.

Phil looks at the floor for a second and then back at me. "I think I ate, like, eight of them. Total sweet tooth."

I smile. He smiles. There is smiling,

I know I shouldn't read into Phil's memory. The fact is, *barfi* is a pretty memorable word. Also, fact: two days ago, Violet and I spied Phil and Lisa kissing, and apparently making up, in an alcove by art class. I guess sometimes a *barfi* is just a *barfi*. Except when you have my imagination. Then it's . . . more.

"So you guys look busy today." Phil's voice snaps me back to the present.

"It's a Sunday night bookstore rager. Not like there's anything else to do in this town."

"You really don't like living here, do you?"

"There are things I love about it. My friends. This place. But I want to be in New York already. You know, a place where I can live and do what I want and not be *the* Indian girl or *the* Muslim girl. A place where I can just be me."

"Do you really feel that different here?"

"I am different. I mean, literally; we're the only Indian Muslim family in town."

Phil taps his pencil against his cheek. "I never thought of it that way. To me, you've always been the girl who knows the right answers."

"Funny, because I don't even know all the questions."

"Really? What don't you know?" Phil asks.

I hesitate, choose my words deliberately. "I guess I don't know how to live the life I want and still be a good daughter."

"Can't you do both?"

"I wish. I want to go to NYU. My parents want me to go to

school close to home. They want me to be a lawyer and learn to cook and marry a nice Indian doctor and—"

"You want to make movies. Like you did for class."

"What?"

"You did three movie projects for health class. Health class. A class that requires barely any work. Like for the whole *tobacco will kill you* unit? You made that movie with all those clips about the smoker from *The Breakfast Club* . . ."

"Judd Nelson," I name the actor for Phil. I'm in disbelief because Phil has *memories* of me. Plural. As in, more than one image encoded in his brain.

"I thought Mr. Chandler was going to die."

"Yeah. He called it 'highly unusual.' For some reason he gave me an 'A,' anyway."

"Of course he did. It was awesome." Phil pauses after he says this. He looks at me. "I actually downloaded *The Breakfast Club* after that. My mom loves that movie, so she watched it with me. She sang along to the credits. That was embarrassing."

I laugh. "Oh, my God. I can't imagine watching anything with my parents that mentions drugs or even has PG kissing. We mostly watch old Indian movies together. Ancient ones."

"There's no kissing in Indian movies?"

"Back in the day, it was totally banned. Not so much anymore, but there's still limits. I tried to talk to my mom about how there are all these contradictions in Indian culture. I mean, if you have a real hard-core arranged marriage, you basically have sex with an almost stranger, but modesty is this huge part of the culture, too . . ." And I've managed to bring up sex again.

Silence. An unbearably long silence. "So are you . . . I mean . . . do your parents have a guy picked out for you already?" he asks.

I burst out laughing and give him a little kick under the table. "No. I'm only in high school."

"Good." He seems to relax, which makes me light-headed.

"Besides, my parents had a love marriage—"

"A love marriage?"

"When you meet someone and fall in love and decide to get married. In India, it's called a love marriage."

Of course he's confused. What non-desi wouldn't be? Still, he continues gamely. "You mean dating, getting engaged—"

"In secret. It's a lot more common for Indian Muslims here, I guess. It's basically a don't ask, don't tell policy for dating."

Phil nods and looks down at the cake. "So, um, does that mean you can't date?" Somehow we've both managed to forget about eating.

"Don't ask, don't tell only applies to proper Indian Muslim boys. With limits." I take a deep breath.

Phil glances up. "But that's not how you want to do it?"

"No. I don't want to hide anything, and I don't want something . . . expected. I want to go to film school and be the first Indian American to win an Oscar, and then I can meet the One and fall in big, heart-bursting love, and we'll travel the world, my camera ready to capture our adventures." My cheeks flush; I know I'm blushing, but I can't bring myself to shut up. "Oh, my God. I want my future life to be a cheesy romantic comedy."

He shakes his head. "No," he says. "You want it to be an epic."

I nod. He stares back at me without blinking. And it's not creepy at all. It's perfect.

My phone rings. I jump from my seat. Suddenly our moment has a club-thumping Bollywood soundtrack. Maybe I should think about changing my ringtone.

I squirm, frantically checking the screen. It's my mom. Of

course it is. I let it go to voice mail and shoot her a quick text to give her my ETA.

When I turn back to Phil, he has picked up his own phone and is also furiously texting . . . someone. He doesn't make eye contact.

There's a charge in the space between us. Of course, the likeliest source of this electricity is my overactive imagination because right now he's probably texting Lisa, making plans to meet up after this, to which she will respond with a string of heart emojis. I keep forgetting that the reason everyone seems to like Phil is because when he talks to you, he makes it seem like you're the only person in the world even when it's only polite chitchat. And I can't even blame him, because it's not pretense; it's just being a nice guy.

I'm quiet while he finishes texting. He grins at his phone before putting it away. "What are you doing over spring break?"

The charge is gone. Like I thought, polite chitchat. I shrug. "Not much." I think of Kareem, the date I've agreed to go on. I wonder if Phil is thinking about Lisa even as he listens politely to me. "My parents can't shut down their office for vacation, so I'll be stuck in Batavia, editing film clips, inhaling copious amounts of ice cream. Violet wants me to go to Paris with her and then pop over to the south of Spain for a couple days to try and get some beach time. Of course, my parents would never let me go. Anyway, I'm not a beach person."

He blinks at me, as if this doesn't compute. "You don't like the beach?"

"I get antsy just lying around, and I can't really swim and—"

"You can't swim? Seriously?"

Why can't I keep my mouth shut? I'm always having to explain my life. I hate explaining, but out it comes. "When my mom was young and on holiday in Bombay, she saw this girl get swept out to sea by a huge wave. So when my dad tried to teach me, my mom was constantly hovering with a life preserver in hand. I couldn't deal with her anxiety, so I gave up . . . We don't take beach vacations, anyway . . ."

Phil sits back in his chair, disbelief written all over his face. I cross my arms in front of my chest, my standard defensive position.

"I'm going to teach you."

"No. No. I can't. You can't—"

"I can. Literally." He's not letting me off the hook. "You know, I lifeguard at the Y in summer, and swimming is a necessary life skill. I can teach you. I want to."

I nod along, but regret every word that has slipped out of my mouth. I don't even own a swimsuit, something Violet teases me about relentlessly.

"It'll be fun. I promise. I won't let a rogue wave take you." Phil smiles, giving rise to the irresistible dimple. Maybe I don't want him to let me off the hook.

"Stop smiling. Fine. I'll do it, but I'm not going to be happy about it."

"Great. The weather's actually supposed to be hot next week. We should take advantage of global warming while we can."

"Don't you have something better to do with your time than watching me potentially drown?" I'm hoping for one very specific answer, but then the image of him kissing Lisa in the art alcove pops to mind.

"I usually go to Michigan with Lisa's family, but not this time." Phil stares out the big plate-glass window. Then he turns back to me and says, "I guess I get to be the tutor now."

The late-morning sun makes him squint. He hates driving east on the freeway at this hour. He leans forward in the driver's seat, gripping the steering wheel with sweaty palms. There's hardly any traffic. Or maybe he just doesn't notice it. His heart beats loudly in his ears. Voices fill his head.

The repetitive, barely audible prayers of his mother.

The rasp of his father's demands to do something with his life.

The bark of the nasty woman, telling him he wasn't needed for a second interview, thank you very much.

The calm whisper of the instructor: relax your shoulders, drop your elbows.

The talking heads in the basement. Sweat-beaded faces, lips moving all at once.

And a lone voice of encouragement: the middle school teacher who gave him a gold star. He remembers the teacher's name. But he won't allow himself to say it out loud or allow it to linger in his memory. He forces the teacher from his mind.

No time for sentimentality.

He eyes himself in the rearview mirror.

There is no turning back.

CHAPTER 5

Hina meets me at the train station, a squat green glass behemoth that looks too big for a city block. My pocket camcorder raised to my eye, I film the Saturday afternoon crowd entering and leaving. I love how inconspicuous this camera is; it fits in the palm of my hand. As we exit, I turn my lens to the pink banners fluttering from the lampposts—ads for a fund-raising walk for breast cancer in a few weeks. I make sure to capture them on film.

Hina designed them. They're all over the city. I'm in awe of her again, as always.

I pan down the line of taxis, right up until Hina and I enter one. She squeezes my shoulder as I adjust my belt. "So glad you're going on a date and doing teenagery things. Try to get into at least a little bit of trouble, okay? And where is the young, dashing Kareem taking you?"

"A fondue place not far from your apartment."

"Geja's Café? He must want to wow you."

"Don't worry. He's not going to pop the question or anything," I reply coolly, though my pulse quickens.

"Well, my wry little niece, he's definitely trying to make an impression. And he asked your parents for permission to see you, right? A very suitable boy, indeed."

The driver pulls over in front of Hina's place. I love my aunt's condo—a two-flat walk-up in Chicago's Old Town neighborhood. To me, it is freedom.

"Go ahead and get settled in your room. I'll get lunch together." Hina steps into the kitchen while I head down the hall.

The comfy bed is piled high with Indian patchwork pillows in rich hues of chocolate, burgundy, and emerald embellished with tiny mirrors and gold tassels. The raw silk duvet cover is a deep bronze color. A wooden partition carved with intricate floral designs serves as the headboard. It belonged to my grandparents and smells like the sandalwood incense my *nani* used to burn day and night.

I unpack my dark skinny jeans, the slightly wrinkled black silk camisole I borrowed from Violet. I hang them in the closet. Then I fold my cherry-colored cashmere sweater and place it on a chair. After that, I kick off my beat-up, round-toed black flats and flop onto the bed, turning to stare at the ceiling. Kareem is picking me up at seven. That leaves five hours for nervous anticipation. I need to get all the blushing out of my system now.

It's been two weeks since we met at the wedding, and weirdly, it feels like a million years ago, but also yesterday. We've texted or messaged each other lots. But that also means my contact with Kareem has been virtual, and my contact with Phil has been real. But for years—literally *years*—Phil was neither real nor virtual; he was a faraway dream. Until now. Only now I'm about to go on a date with a guy who is actually available, infinitely more suitable, and definitely interested.

This is why they invented drugs for heartburn.

The guest room door is half open, but Hina knocks anyway before coming in. I sit up on the edge of the bed as she perches next to me. "How about we eat a quick lunch and go to a movie before your big date? Or we can on-demand something. Have you seen *Roman Holiday*? You know, about a princess who feels trapped in her life?"

I smile. "Yeah, that sounds about right."

"Trust me: Gregory Peck and Audrey Hepburn are pretty

much Saturday afternoon perfection," Hina says, giving my hand a squeeze.

My mom picks *Bride and Prejudice*. Hina picks *Roman Holiday*. Somehow their movie choices totally define my relationships with them. They both try. One misses the mark. The other nails it.

AFTER THE MOVIE, WE sit on the couch, sipping cups of creamy spiced chai.

"Did I ever tell you about Anand?" Hina asks out of the blue. She rarely talks about the guys she dates; it must be some tacit agreement she has with my mother. So I immediately perk up.

"Ummm, no. But I am all ears."

Hina smiles. "It was in India, before I left to study in England. He was such a beautiful boy. You know I went to the same Catholic girls' school as your mom, in Hyderabad? Well, there was a brother school run by priests. We shared the same athletic fields. That's how I met Anand. I was at field hockey practice, and he was playing cricket."

"Awww. And it was love at first sight?"

"Not exactly. Maybe? I don't know. I never really thought about it in those terms. Anand just started showing up to my field hockey practices and our games, and one day I finally asked him if he was going to talk to me."

"Bold move, Hina."

Hina chuckles. "My friends were so scandalized. But you know, I've always been a straight shooter."

It's one of the things I love best about my aunt.

"Well, he started bringing tiffins, and we would have little picnics of *samosas* and *chaat* and *pakoras* with mango juice in glass bottles."

"So he would cook for you? How adorable."

"Oh, no. He had his cook do it, and then his driver would bring it to the fields so it would still be warm after practice."

"Must be nice."

"It was. Of course, we could never really go anywhere, so the entire fleeting romance took place on school grounds."

"I'm guessing from his name he was Hindu?"

"Exactly. But honestly, we barely even talked about that. We both knew nothing more could come of it. So we spent that spring talking and eating and laughing, and then he went to Bombay to study architecture at university."

"That's it? That's the whole story? You never saw each other again?"

"We saw each other once more, when he came home for holiday. I went to see him at Nampally Railway Station just when he was leaving to go back to school."

"And . . ."

"And that was my first kiss. A little peck in a dark corner of a bustling train station."

"That is so cinematic," I say.

Hina laughs. "From you, that is high praise, indeed."

"So were you heartbroken? Did you regret it?"

"Heartbroken? A little. Regret? No. What was there to regret? I wasn't going to Bombay with him. We were both young and different religions, and I had no desire to elope and bring down the entire wrath of both our families on our heads. So now it's simply a sweet memory. That's all it was ever going to be."

I sit back and stare into my half-empty teacup.

"Something on your mind?" Hina asks. "First kisses, perhaps?"

"Yes. No. Maybe, but not necessarily with Kareem . . ."

Hina raises an eyebrow at me and gives me a warm smile and settles into the couch.

I hadn't planned to, but I end up telling her about Phil and the tutoring sessions and how my stomach roller-coasters every time I'm around him and about how he has a girlfriend. Then I talk to her about Kareem, who is the parental dream of suitability. But he's a lot more than just his biodata.

"The thing is," I say, after my breathless debrief, "the timing is all so bizarre, I mean why now? Why me?"

She stares at me as if I'm totally clueless. "Why *not* you?"

Even Hina can make me blush. It really is a disorder.

"What *is*, in fact, bizarre, my dear," she continues, "is that you don't see what a beautiful, brilliant young woman you are. You still think of yourself as that gawky, flat-chested seventh grader with braces and two braids."

I'm not sure how to respond. I wouldn't admit this to anyone, not even Hina; I can barely even think it when I'm alone, but there are moments when I catch a glimpse of myself in the mirror and I'm happily surprised at the reflection—it's me but not me. I can see the shiny black hair that falls below my shoulders, the woman's body that looks good in a fitted sweater and tight jeans. Plus I can see I've been upping my lipstick game.

Hina clearly wants more juicy details, wants to know which boy I prefer, but even getting near that thought makes my stomach lurch. I don't know who the Gregory Peck is to my Audrey Hepburn; I have no idea if *either* boy is or isn't. I check my watch. "Crap. Kareem will be here in an hour. I need to get ready."

I hear Hina chuckling to herself as I bolt off the couch and run into the guest room.

FORTY-FIVE MINUTES LATER, FRESHLY showered and changed into Violet-approved denim and silk, I slip into my black satin shoes. I put on a pair of dangly silver chandelier earrings and grab my sweater, then study my reflection. There is a lot of skin. My skin. I chew on my lip, hoping it's not too much. For my final task, I dab on a bit of bronzer and a claret lipstick like I promised my mom. My word is my bond—at least about lipstick. Finally, I decide to go big and add eyeliner and mascara.

The bell rings. He's five minutes early. How un-Indian of him.

Hina buzzes in Kareem and then disappears into her bedroom. I'm glad I'm not home. My parents would linger, inquire after Kareem's parents, demand that we stay and chat over a cup of chai while insisting that the restaurant would hold our reservation.

I open the door.

Kareem is taller than I remember. Maybe cuter, too? I try not to stare into those sparkly dark eyes. He's dressed in indigo jeans, a navy blazer, and a light blue collared shirt, the top two buttons unbuttoned.

"Hey." God, I hope I'm not trying too hard, because that's the exact opposite of cool. Eau de desperation.

He steps in and bends down. I think he's coming in for a hug, so I move forward. Our heads bump as he tries to give me a kiss on the cheek.

Awkward. I step back, cheeks already aflame.

Kareem laughs. "Ah, there's the blush. That took, what, fifteen seconds?"

"Ha, ha. Come on in." At least I've provided the icebreaker.

"You look amazing, by the way," Kareem adds casually. He steps forward and puts his hand on my forearm. If he's trying to keep me blushing, he's doing an excellent job.

"Uh, thanks . . ."

Thankfully Hina chooses this moment to appear from the back.

"*As-salaam-alaikum*, Auntie," Kareem says. His respectful nod oozes *tameez*, proper Hyderabadi-boy etiquette.

Hina laughs. "Please, Kareem, call me Hina. No need to stand on ceremony with me." Then she raises an eyebrow. "So, Geja's? Going for dark, romantic, and sophisticated, are we?"

I'm going to die.

"Uh, yeah," Kareem smiles. "I . . . we . . . uh . . . have a seven-thirty reservation, so we should probably get going." He turns to me. "Are you up for a stroll? Nice evening for a walk."

I nod and snatch my purse. I've already double-checked it for my mini-cam. I couldn't leave home without it—in case I want to record any part of the evening or, more likely, hide behind my lens if things go from awkward to painfully bad. "I'm set."

"*Khudafis*, Auntie—I mean, Hina. Thanks again for letting me pick up Maya here. Does she have a curfew?"

Hina shakes her head. "Not at my house. Have fun." She kisses me on the cheek and winks as she closes the door behind us.

"ONE OF US HAS to say something soon. Ideally a witty or brilliant observation," Kareem says. We've been walking silently for almost ten minutes. I keep trying to think of something to say, but apparently I've lost the connection between my brain and mouth.

And that's my cue. We haven't even made it to the restaurant yet, but it's time to draw on my trusty shield. I reach into my purse and pull out my tiny camcorder, switch it on, and focus on Kareem. Roll camera. I adopt my documentary voice-over tone. And action. "Kareem, where are you taking Maya tonight?"

"You're referring to yourself in the third person now?"

I pull back to meet his gaze. "I'm the director. Kareem and Maya are the subjects in the movie. Go with it."

"Fine."

We're both smiling and trying not to at the same time.

I pick up where I left off. "So what are your plans for tonight?"

Kareem straightens an imaginary tie. I love that he plays along; I also love that he can't see how delighted I am. "I want to show Maya a good time, and so I chose Geja's Café. It's terribly romantic, but I fear that it might also be terribly messy—all that melted cheese." He pauses with exaggerated drama and strikes a ridiculous pose. "I'm willing to take that risk because I'm the kind of guy that lives on the edge. You know, carpe diem. Suck the marrow out of life."

"So you're a Thoreau fan."

"Nah, just pretentious."

I stifle a laugh. "So besides tempting fate with melted cheese and literary airs of pretension, what else is in your risk-taking repertoire?"

"The usual: skydiving, Formula One, feeding sharks . . ." He pauses, either pretending to remember or remembering to pretend. "My mom does say I was an adventurous kid. A trouble-maker. Mainly I was curious. Oh, and I loved pirates. Anything on the high seas that involved danger and swashbuckling—you know, big swells, treasure, damsels in distress. My mom loved it, too. She provided the pirate booty. She would put her banged-up jewelry and broken bangles in a small box and bury the treasure chest. I'd have to find it and dig it up. It was pretty awesome, actually."

I envision a skinny, buck-toothed version of Kareem, running around with his mom, shrieking with laughter. "*Arrh*, matey!" they shout at each other. I'm smiling, but I feel a twinge of sadness. I don't have those Kodachrome images of my own childhood escapades. It's just not how I grew up.

"And now?" I ask, determined to bring us back to the present. "Do you still live a life of adventure?"

"My high-seas days are over, but I'd say tonight has the potential for excitement." He looks directly into the camera. "Don't you agree?"

"I'm documenting, I can't interfere—it's not my story." I'm blushing behind the camera. This time, I'm sure he notices.

And I'm right, because he approaches and gently pushes the camera away from my face. "This is totally your story."

I look into his brown eyes. Out here on the street, they're less dazzling but more gentle and warm and inviting. They embody him. We continue walking.

Suddenly he stops short. "This is it . . ."

Our arrival catches both of us by surprise.

Kareem pushes open the door, holding it for me. I step into a dark labyrinth of fluttering candles, shadowy nooks. A flamenco band plays somewhere. Wine bottles line the walls and create partitions between tables. I put my camera back in my purse and let myself breathe it all in; there's no point in trying to film because there isn't enough light. A host shows us to our table—a booth toward the back, partially hidden by velvet curtains that can be undone to shroud the space entirely. A waiter quickly arrives with menus, explains the three-course fondue meal, and leaves.

"I guess this place is kind of over the top, huh?" Kareem asks.

I smile back. "It's very film noir. All we need is a fog machine and a dame with a gun and checkered past."

Kareem laughs. "Wait. That's not you?"

"You never can tell."

His eyes narrow; he strokes his goatee. "So you're not actually this sweet girl who lives in the suburbs. You have a whole double life where you're carrying on in a nefarious way . . ."

I totally get into the act. I love that I feel comfortable enough to do it. "I'm not as simple as you might think."

Kareem shakes his head. "*Simple* is never a word I'd used to describe you." He smiles, then reaches across the table and takes my hand in his.

I'm frozen. But I don't want to move. I stare at the candle between us, feeling as if the flame has leapt inside me. I know I'm blushing, but I don't care about that, either. Kareem holds my hand tighter. I bite the inside of my lower lip.

When the waiter arrives to take our order, I reluctantly pull my hand away.

"Let's go for the works," Kareem suggests, leaning back.

"Sounds good."

Then Kareem asks me what I want to drink. "A glass of red, maybe? I'll have a glass of the house Bordeaux." He's talking about wine, studying the wine list as if this is something he always does. This is . . . unexpected. I've only tried a drop of alcohol once in my life at Violet's house, but the guilt left a bitter taste in my mouth that lasts to this day. Then I remember: he's twenty-one. He's *allowed* to do this. But that still leaves the question: *Why* is he doing it?

"I never . . . I don't . . . really drink," I sputter. "There was one time . . . Also, you may be twenty-one, but I'm not . . ."

Kareem smiles. "You're right. I shouldn't be corrupting you on our first date. Seriously, no worries. And no pressure. I enjoy a glass of wine with dinner once in a while, that's all."

I'm still at a loss. "But . . ."

"Why am I drinking in the first place?" Kareem raises his eyebrows.

I nod several times. "Does your mom know?"

"Of course. I had my first sip with my parents."

My mouth drops open. The stars are misaligned. This is not normal, not for a desi Muslim kid. "But aren't your parents . . . ? I mean, I heard your mom talking to my mom about going to the mosque and—"

His laugh stops me. "They're not sitting around getting wasted, denying the existence of God or anything. My dad considers himself a believer. But he also believes in enjoying a glass of wine now and again."

I'm too dumbstruck to think of anything else to say. My own parents aren't exactly the fire-and-brimstone types, but they've never had a drink. Of that I'm certain. Guilt plows into me. They always take me to the mosque on important holidays; they fast during Ramadan; they sometimes close their office to attend Friday afternoon prayers. I'm wracked with guilt as the waiter sets a wineglass in front of Kareem, then pours a small splash from the bottle.

Kareem lifts the glass by the stem, swirling the dark purplish-red liquid into a little tempest. He tilts the rim to his nose and inhales deeply, then puts the glass back down on the table.

"It needs to open up a bit," he says to the waiter, who seems to understand whatever this means. The waiter leaves us.

I am staring at him, not sure what to make of his expertise, but envious of it. I want to be worldly and sophisticated.

"Maya, relax. It's not like I eat pork."

We both crack up, because we know it's the one line even most lapsed Muslims won't cross.

The appetizer arrives—a steaming Crock-Pot of bubbling cheese fondue with three types of breads and apples with tiny dipping forks. I move the candles around on the table in hopes that the addition of the canned heat under the pot will maybe give me enough light to get a decent shot. I take my camera and film as

Kareem dips a piece of bread into the cheese, spinning the melted strands around the end of his fork. He plops it into his mouth. "H-h-h-o-o-t-t!" he yells.

"Water," I suggest, but continue to record Kareem's open-mouthed struggle with the piping hot cheese—total culinary drama.

He downs a full glass of water. "I can't believe you didn't stop filming. What if that cheese had burned off the roof of my mouth and it was the last morsel of food I would ever enjoy?"

"All the more reason to preserve the moment," I reply. "Priceless." I put the camera down because I don't need a shield anymore and because I'm hungry.

We dip and eat and talk about our parents and being Indian and the pressure to be a doctor and the Indian aunties who always think you are a little too skinny or a little too chubby and never perfect. We rate our favorite Indian foods and joke that how the first thing we both want when we fly back from India is an actual Big Mac.

"I wish getting a Big Mac was still my biggest concern when I pass through customs these days," Kareem mutters.

"What is it, fries?" I joke.

"More like hoping I don't get chosen for the special Secondary Security Screening lottery."

My smile fades. He's not joking.

"Crap. That's happened to you?" I sigh. Not sure why I am at all surprised.

"Twice, coming back home. The first time they took me into this back room. I waited for, like, two hours with all these other brown dudes before being called into a separate room and being asked these basic questions like is this really my name and what was I doing in India and do I have relatives in Pakistan. Whatever."

"That's horrible."

He flashes a bitter smirk. "Hey, at least I wasn't handcuffed to a wall, right?"

"Don't even joke about that."

"It's not a joke."

"I'm sorry," I say and lightly touch his arm.

He places his hand on mine. "Don't be. You have nothing to apologize for."

WHEN WE'RE A BLOCK away from Hina's apartment, I realize it's drizzling. Maybe it's been drizzling since we left the restaurant; I'm not even sure. Kareem clutches my hand, and we run to take cover under a crabapple tree. It's April, so everything is in bloom. Pink petals fall on us, clinging to our wet faces. I glance up through the branches, backlit by the streetlamps. I breathe in the sweet, delicate scent. It lasts only a few weeks each spring. If I'd dreamed up this mise-en-scène, I would've thought it a cliché. But in real life, it is perfect.

"What are you thinking?" Kareem whispers.

I look at him. "If this were one of my parents' retro-Bollywood faves, I'd run behind that tree right now and come out singing and in a different outfit."

Kareem gently hooks a finger under my chin and draws my face toward his. "But if this were an old Indian movie, I couldn't do this." He bends down and gently brushes his lips against mine. The earth stops moving. I am frozen in this spot of time.

Turns out, I'm fond of kissing. Extremely. I close my eyes, losing myself in the falling petals, the light rain, the strength of his arms, his breath on my lips. I revel in the moment, the echo of his skin against mine.

Kareem pauses, strokes my cheek with his finger. "Your lips are so soft."

I blush even as the rain cools my face. Kareem's lips taste of wine and chocolate. He puts his left hand around my waist and pulls me closer so that our bodies touch. Thunder rumbles in the distance.

I pull away because I feel myself being overtaken. "I should be getting inside. I'm soaking wet, and—"

"Okay, okay." Kareem nods. "You're a good Indian girl. I shouldn't move too fast."

I cringe a little, but he's speaking the truth. "No, I'm not . . . I mean, I am, but it's that, you know, we're in front of my aunt's place."

Kareem laughs. "Then please allow me to escort you to the door in a gentleman-like fashion. But first . . ." He grabs me and kisses me again, longer and harder. I let myself sink into the kiss—wild, reckless, until it's suddenly too intense. I pull away, breathless.

Kareem takes my hand and leads me to Hina's front door. He's not merely being polite; my feet are wobbly.

"I want to see you again, Maya," he says softly. "But next time, I'll make sure there are no Indian relatives around."

"Thanks for dinner," I gasp. "I had a great time. Have a safe trip back to school . . ."

Kareem sneaks in one last quick kiss. I gape at him as the rain falls harder. Then he slips into his car. I unlock the front door, turning to wave goodbye before he speeds off.

Once his engine fades to silence, I shut the door and take a deep breath. I'm dizzy as I walk up the stairs to my aunt's place. I can still feel the tickle of Kareem's goatee on my face. I walk into the apartment and see the clock on the microwave flashing 12:05 A.M. and laugh out loud. If this were my house, my parents would have called the police by now. And there wouldn't have been any kissing or hand-holding; I would've been too afraid of withering under their interrogation.

I slip out of my shoes, tiptoe quietly into the guest bathroom to strip off my wet clothes, and hang them over the shower rod. Wrapped in a fluffy white towel, I examine myself in the mirror. I run an index finger over my lips and notice a few flower petals in my hair. After brushing out the long, wet strands, I wash off what little makeup is left on my face.

I savor the memory of the moment under the trees.

But when I relive it in my mind, the lips I'm kissing are Phil's.

As she opens the door, the young teacher shields her eyes from the bright sun. It's been an unusually warm spring, especially for Springfield, she thinks. She's overdressed for a day spent with toddlers, maybe a bit too professional-looking in her pale yellow skirt and white cotton blouse, her thick, dark brown hair twisted into a low bun. But the day-care center, mostly for the children of employees, isn't what she wants to do permanently. She plans on getting certified to teach kindergarten by the next school year.

She dresses for the future.

And the springtime.

Good morning, she singsongs to a little boy in tears. It's his first day, and it has not started well. His mother is reluctant to leave him.

The young teacher has seen this a hundred times before.

She kneels down beside the boy and tenderly strokes the back of his head. It's going to be okay, she says. She takes his small hand in hers, a chubby star against her broad palm. I think we're going to have a lot of fun together. Do you like fire trucks?

CHAPTER 6

Sunday night. I'm uploading shots from the weekend onto my Instagram: the crabapple trees where I kissed Kareem (nearly stripped bare after the rain), a cat tucked behind a bush, Hina's collection of silk patchwork pillows. I check Violet's account and see she's taken France by storm: *religieuse* pastries, *macarons*, rainy cobblestone streets, angled Eiffel Tower shots, and a selfie with a mystery guy kissing her cheek. For once, I feel unfettered happiness for her without a touch of envy. There will be stories. But this time, I might have one or two of my own to add.

A chat bubble pops up on my screen. Phil.

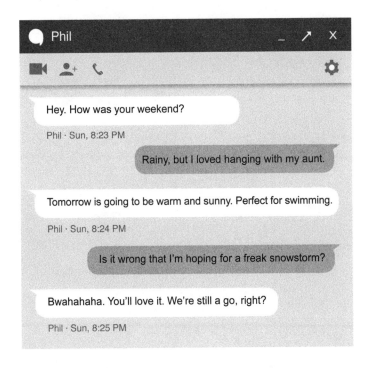

Phil

Hey. How was your weekend?

Phil · Sun, 8:23 PM

Rainy, but I loved hanging with my aunt.

Tomorrow is going to be warm and sunny. Perfect for swimming.

Phil · Sun, 8:24 PM

Is it wrong that I'm hoping for a freak snowstorm?

Bwahahaha. You'll love it. We're still a go, right?

Phil · Sun, 8:25 PM

Guilt washes away any excitement.

I gave my mom a G-rated report on my date with Kareem. I wonder what Hina told her. She has not stopped talking about Kareem and his proper Indian manners since I got home. To my relief—and at my insistence—he promised not to ask my parents' permission for any future dates. Best to take my mother out of the equation. But that's also the trouble: the Future. I committed to seeing Kareem again. And I do want to see him. But I also wonder if I'll be picturing Phil while Kareem kisses me. It's pretty crappy, especially for Kareem. Maybe not so much for me.

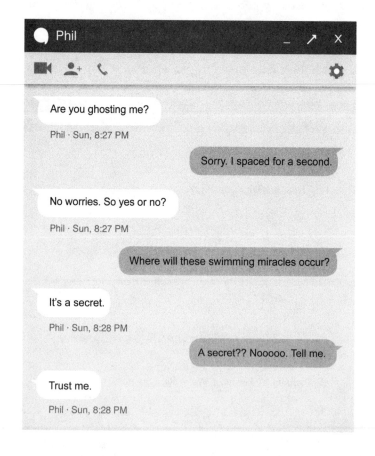

I pull my hands away from my keyboard. *Take the leap of faith, Maya. Suck the marrow out of life.*

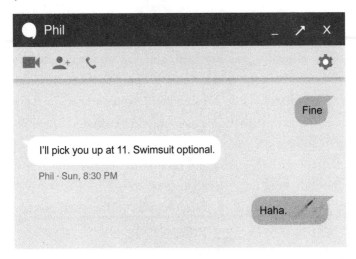

I should be thrilled, but I imagine I'll either sink like a stone or flail like a clown. In front of Phil. It's impossible to be cute or aloof while thrashing around in abject fear of drowning. But I don't need to be cute or aloof, do I? Phil still has a girlfriend. There is no doubt about this. I wanted there to be doubt; I admit it. But Violet and I literally ran into the depressing, irrefutable PG-rated evidence of Phil's and Lisa's still-kissing coupledom.

I can't imagine how Lisa will feel about these secret swimming lessons. Phil would be an idiot to tell her even if all *our* interactions are G-rated. Another wave of guilt crashes into me, but it doesn't knock me over.

I walk over to my dresser and dig out the red bikini Violet compelled me to buy. She sees these swimming lessons as my opportunity to nudge Lisa out of the way and assume my rightful place on Phil's arm. She also knows about Kareem, of course. She is thrilled at how romantically frazzled this situation makes me. She lives for this stuff.

Damn it. I need to wax. Fortunately, almost any household with an Indian woman is well stocked with depilation products.

Big surprise: My mom's never once spoken to me about sex. She's never even uttered the word, but she's covered all the bases regarding ablution, hair removal, and the power of *kajal*—the sooty black eyeliner favored by generations of South Asian women. During our first *kajal* demonstration, I poked myself in the eye. Mom heaved the dramatic sigh of a mother from an Indian movie whose daughter desires to marry a simple peasant instead of the rich, suitable suitor. You cannot mess with her *kajal*.

It's only 9 P.M., but I'm exhausted.

As I climb into bed, my mom knocks on the door. Naturally, she barges in before I can respond. "See, I knocked," she says.

"But you didn't wait for me to—"

"Why are you always making things difficult, Maya?" she interrupts. "I'm your mother. You don't have to hide anything from me."

The irony makes me squirm.

"What do you want, Mother?" I groan.

My mom isn't always the best at picking up on my subtleties, but she knows that "mother" equals annoyed. "Mom" is for regular days, and the Urdu "*ummi*" for increasingly rare moments of filial affection. She sits on the edge of my bed. "No need to be so upset, *beta*."

"I'm sorry. I can't stand when you and Dad treat me like a child."

"But you are our child." Her voice catches. "You always will be, even when you have children of your own."

My mom's eyes moisten; I quickly turn away. I'm never quite sure what to do in these uncomfortable moments, so usually I pretend they aren't happening.

"I knoooow, Mom, but can you please give me my privacy?"

She sniffs. "I just wanted to ask if Kareem called you today."

"Mom."

"Can't a mother ask a simple question?"

"Not if it's a nosy one. I already told you everything, anyway. Dinner was nice. He was nice."

"And?"

"That's it. End of story. We didn't secretly get engaged or anything."

My mom tilts her head to the ceiling and raises her hands to prayer position. This is her being sarcastic. But also totally serious. "I don't want you to end up alone."

"I'm in high school, Mom. In the twenty-first century. I don't have to get married by the time I'm twenty-two or risk becoming an old maid."

"*Arraaayy, beta.* Who is saying anything about marriage? We want you to finish your studies. But I was married when I was only a few years older than you."

Classic Mom again: *I'm not saying you should follow my precise example, but of course I really am.* I have to laugh. "And you had a love marriage that Dad's parents didn't exactly approve of, right?"

She gives me a sharp look. "Listen to you. We raised you with too much American independence. Talking back to your elders. And all this privacy business. Who needs privacy from their parents?"

The best way to get out of this conversation is to keep my mouth shut. I totally know this, yet apparently I prefer to bang my head against the wall over and over because I think arguing can change my mother's mind. Note to self: It can't. It never has.

"Please. All I'm asking is that you give me a little space. If Kareem and I decide to get married, I promise you'll be the first to know."

My mom stands and shakes her head. "We should have sent you to a boarding school in India. Then you would have learned to be a good daughter, not like these ungrateful girls here who can't cook and don't know how to show proper respect to their parents. Some even marry white American boys."

She means boys like Phil. Boys you secretly tutor and meet for surreptitious swimming lessons. Shiny-eyed, beautiful boys that can pull you in the wrong direction.

I fake a huge yawn. "Can you continue your marriage pep talk another day? I swear I won't run off and marry a heathen tonight."

She heads toward the door. "What are you doing tomorrow?"

My pulse quickens as I make up an alibi. "Sleep in. Then maybe go to a movie or the mall if any of my friends are around. When is your last appointment?"

"Your dad scheduled a root canal at five P.M., so we won't be home until later."

"Okay. *Khudafis.* Have a good day at work in case I don't see you in the morning."

"*Khudafis, beta.*" My mom tosses me a final wan smile—*I love you, but I remain disappointed*—and shuts the door. I settle beneath the covers. If I ever direct a retro-Bollywood melodrama, my mother will be the star.

The guard straightens the back of his navy blue baseball cap with his left hand, curving the bill with his right. Stitched in bold white letters on the front is SECURITY, but the cap's newness screams ROOKIE.

He is younger than most of the other men on the crew. Eager to prove his seriousness, he rarely betrays any emotion. He chomps rhythmically on his gum. But this morning the new teacher at the day care smiles at him, and he smiles back.

Security. Safety. She feels safe here, thanks to him.

The sun shines like it's summer.

It is a good day.

CHAPTER 7

The sun screams through my blinds. I wake up, but make sure to stay in bed until I hear my parents' car back out of the driveway.

My mom left me a note.

Eat something. Love, your mom.

She's hovering, in absentia. I scarf down the bowl of oatmeal she left for me on the kitchen table along with a banana, hoping doing at least one thing my mom asks will soothe my conscience.

It doesn't.

But my feelings of guilt rarely compel me to change my plans, either.

I still have an hour and half before Phil's supposed to pick me up. I'm not sure if breakfast was a good idea, given the way my stomach is churning. I focus on what to wear over my bikini, troublesome even without the buyer's remorse. The temperature is going to hit a ridiculously high eighty degrees for April. It's already a bit muggy. I reach for a crimson cotton sleeveless dress, tie-dyed Indian *bandini* style. The association with the method is unfortunate, because unlike the large psychedelic Deadhead patterns and colors, *bandini* tie-dyes are delicate and intricate. But before putting it on, I hesitate.

First I need a look at myself in just the bikini.

In front of the mirror, I wince. My breasts are held back from total exposure by a few inches of string. I double-knot the halter at my neck—insurance against accidental breast spillage—then reach for the dress. I step back.

This is actually okay. Good, even. With flip-flops, I'm swimming-lesson ready. My clothes are, anyway.

My phone buzzes. It's Violet. Eight hours later . . . so it's late afternoon in Paris. I imagine her texting from some café at sunset, some French boy hanging over her shoulder, jealous of me on the receiving end.

Violet: ARE YOU WEARING THE BIKINI?

Me: Why are you yelling?

Violet: Because that's what I'm going to be doing if you're not in it.

Me: I exchanged it for a granny one piece with a ruffle. Mistake?

Violet: / / Did you wax?

Me: OMG 🙄

Violet: There better be mascara on those rolling eyes. Waterproof.

Me: Yes. Happy?

Violet: Me? You're the one kissing two different guys over spring break.

Me: One.

Violet: I'm aspirationally texting.

Me: I'm aspirationally kicking your ass.

Violet: Haha. Gotta run. Meeting Jean-Paul. Who I will definitely be kissing. IRL.

Me: I would be disappointed to hear anything else.

Violet: Bisous. 💜

When the doorbell rings, I take a last look in the mirror, then take a deep breath before walking down the stairs.

I stop short. I spy Phil through the slightly frosted glass panels in our door. He's checking himself out. He runs his fingers through his hair, structuring it just so. I knew that tousle was too perfect to be disinterested bedhead. Then he breathes into his cupped hand. I bite my lips so I don't laugh and give myself away before he's done primping. Pausing a beat, I open the door and step out into the warm sun.

"Don't worry," Phil says as we walk to his car, "I won't let anything happen to you. Besides, the water's not very deep."

"What do you mean? Where would this not-so-deep water be?"

"You'll see."

"Is it the Y? The Waubonsee pool?"

Phil smiles across the car at me. "I thought you wanted to go someplace without witnesses present."

After taking a right turn into the Fabyan Forest Preserve, Phil follows a side road that runs parallel to the river for nearly half a mile and then parks by the old Japanese Garden, which has been closed for over ten years. The park district didn't have the funds to restore it. The garden is overrun with weeds, the koi pond dried up. Phil parks next to a sign that clearly reads, NO TRESPASSING.

"We're here," he says.

I grab my bag and get out of the car, though I have no real idea what "here" exactly is. "The Japanese Garden?"

Phil takes a plaid blanket and cooler out of the trunk. "Not exactly. Remember what I said? Trust me."

He leads the way down the dirt path, through the trees that create a perimeter around the garden. "You know, the entire forest preserve used to be Fabyan land. Old man Fabyan died without any heirs, so he gave it all to the town. The Visitors Center on the other side of the river used to be his main house. He actually built the Japanese Garden because he fell in love with the culture when he visited. He wanted to bring a bit of it back home. See the little cottage?" Phil pauses, pointing to a small stone structure in a little clearing. "That was his summer retreat. I guess he would ride his horse out here and chill. Basically, it's the original man cave."

I follow his arm, and shake my head. "How do you know all this stuff? I had no idea this cottage was even here."

He laughs. "Another school report. Eighth grade. Ever since then, I come here when I want to get away."

As we come upon the single-story cottage, I see that there is no glass left in the windowpanes. Gnarled old vines cover half the façade of the house, and the yellowish stones are smoothed from rain. I imagine the cottage feels haunted at night, but surrounded by trees in the spring sunlight, it is beautiful.

"So gothic romance isn't exactly my thing, but if I ever direct one, this is so going to be the spot. I'm thinking, *Dracula* meets *Wuthering Heights*, but, like, contemporary where Heathcliff is a vampire, because that would explain why he is such a jerk." I've been taking in the surroundings, sort of forgetting Phil for a moment while I imagine how to capture the light around the cottage. I pause and look at him.

He's just standing there, grinning. "I have no idea what any of that means, except for vampires."

"What I'm trying to say is, it's amazing." I peer inside. The wood slats on the floor are weathered and worn. A beat-up recliner rests in the corner. There's a fireplace at one end of the main room with a flashlight on the mantle; the inside is blackened with ash and the charred remnants of logs, as if just used.

"Do people hang out here?" I ask.

"That's me. I didn't clean out the fireplace last time." He shrugs. "Like I said, I come here sometimes."

"But you didn't tell me that you had taken up residence." A vivid image of Phil and Lisa sharing a romantic evening in front of a fire springs to mind.

He laughs again, quietly. "Sometimes I *wish* I lived here."

"So should we get started with, you know, the lesson?" I stumble over my words, wondering if he meant to add he wished he lived here with *her*. "The sooner we get started, the sooner it's over."

"Okaaayy." Phil scrunches his eyebrows together

He leads the way to a larger clearing. As we emerge from the narrow path between the trees, a perfectly round, still pond magically appears. The sun glistens off the water. The truly enchanting part is that there's a small carpet of sand and a folded lawn chair.

"Don't tell me. This is your beach."

"I'm pretty proud of it. I lugged a few wheelbarrows of sand here from that playground they're building off of Maiden Lane."

"You stole sand from little kids."

"For a good cause."

"Meaning you," I tease.

"Well, yeah, but also teaching *you* how to swim." Phil walks over to the beach and lofts the plaid blanket in the air; it billows out as he brings it to rest on the sand. I kick off my shoes and settle on my back. The sun warms my skin.

He stands over me and takes off his shirt, momentarily blocking my sun. I stare up at him, happy to be wearing sunglasses so he can't see my eyes grow wide.

"Is it . . . the water . . . clean?" I ask, not moving. I'm still covered up. I don't know how I can face him in a bikini.

"It's spring fed, so it's relatively clean. I wouldn't drink it, but it's not all gross and leech infested . . . at least I don't think it is." He smirks and runs into the pond with a splash, diving forward and swimming to the middle until the water is up to his chin. Then he raises his hands to show he's standing. "See, this is deep as it gets."

"That's still over my head."

"C'mon. The water's pretty nice, actually."

I stand up. Phil's hands fall beneath the surface. He treads water, staring at me.

"Can you turn around? I'm self-conscious."

Phil does as I ask, but before he turns his face away, I catch a glimpse of that dimple emerging from his smirk.

I drop my dress on the blanket, and every inch of my exposed skin blazes red. I sprint into the water for relief.

"It's freezing." I'm in three and a half feet of cold water, goose-bumps popping up all over my skin. "I thought you said it was nice in here."

Phil swims up alongside me. "You'll get used to it. You need to dunk your entire body in. You'll see."

"As in, put my head under? As in, get my hair wet?"

"Getting wet is pretty much a requirement if you're going to learn to swim. I forgot I have something for you." Phil swims back to the beach. Thin rivulets of water stream down his back and arms. He plucks the mystery gift from his backpack and wades back toward me. I hope it's an inhaler because I can't quite breathe.

"Goggles," he says, handing them to me. "You wear contacts, right? I thought this would make it easier for you."

I put on the goggles. I probably look ridiculous, but I'm impressed at Phil's attention to detail. "Thanks," I whisper.

"No problem. Now hold your nose and dunk your head—for a second."

I bob up and down a little and then splash into the water. I come up. My eyes are squeezed shut, despite the goggles. "Much better. Now I'm only mildly hypothermic." I speak through chattering teeth.

Phil laughs. "Can you do the dead man's float?"

"That's the name? That's terrible marketing."

"It's called that because that's how corpses float. You have to float before you can swim."

"So on my stomach . . . pretending I'm dead."

Phil nods, businesslike. "I won't let you die. Now take a deep breath and relax your body into the water, extend your arms in front of you, and keep your head down. When you need a breath, come up."

Then he demonstrates. His voice is calm and patient. He shows me exactly how to do everything—flawlessly, athletically. I try to copy him, but how can I? My muscles tense in the water. My jaw tightens, and I pop up after only a few seconds, blowing out the air from my lungs.

"Good," he says. "Let's do it one more time, except when you need air, raise your head for a breath and then go back into the float." He demonstrates again. "You'll drift forward a bit, but don't panic. You can always stand up."

I bite my lip. I can always stand up.

I repeat Phil's words as I try again. I manage to float for three pop-up breath lengths before inadvertently getting water up my nose. I stand up gagging and sputtering.

Phil gently takes my arm. "It's okay. I'm right here. Try to relax and enjoy the water. Don't overthink it. You won't drown."

"How do you know?"

"You have built-in flotation devices." Phil eyes my cleavage.

My mouth drops open. I immediately cover my chest with my arms. "Oh, my God. I can't believe you said that."

He shrugs with an impish grin. "I'm just stating a fact. As your instructor."

Despite myself, I grin back. I quickly put my face back in the water to hide my reddening cheeks and practice the float for a while longer until I realize I'm not going to drown. I'm actually floating. In the water. By myself.

When I come up for air again, Phil places his hand on my

shoulder. "Now I want you to float on your back. It's the same idea as the dead man's float, but you don't have to hold your breath, and you can keep your eyes open. See?" Phil lies down on the water like it's a feather bed. "You can kick a little if you want to propel yourself."

I imitate Phil's movements. And it sort of works.

"Great. Tilt your head all the way back until the water covers your ears. Relax your neck."

I kick my legs and find myself moving softly through the water. Before I know it, I'm parallel with Phil in the middle of the pond.

"Isn't this nice?" Phil asks as he gazes up at the few cumulus clouds in the sky. "I could float for hours. It's so relaxing."

I open my eyes to a sky the color of blue cornflowers and tree-tops swaying in the light breeze. It's quiet all around except for the sound of our movements in the water. I turn my head and shoulders to look at Phil. My body begins to slip into the pond. Water fills my open mouth. I'm caught by surprise and splash wildly.

Phil grabs me, one arm under my legs and the other behind my back, forming a sort of chair for me in his arms.

"I got you. Are you okay?" He furrows his brow, and when he looks at me, his green eyes tighten with worry. He draws me a little closer into him.

I cough, partly out of embarrassment. "Y-y-y-e-e-s-s. I'm fine." My lungs burn. "I hope you were right when you said the water was clean."

"You can probably skip the tetanus shot. But I'm sorry. I should have told you to keep your body as horizontal as possible."

"I bet you say that to all the girls."

"Pretty ballsy talk for someone who can't swim." Phil loosens his grip on my back as if he might let me fall into the water.

"Don't," I yell and wrap both my arms around his neck.

Goosebumps rise up on every millimeter of my body. My chest smashes up against Phil. He averts his eyes, but tightens his grip around my back. I'm suddenly very aware that my skin is a living organ because it registers the slight temperature change as his hand edges from cool to warm. I can feel the wrinkles of his pruney finger-tips embedding their whorls into my body. The world slows down. My breathing, the journey of the drips of water that trail from his skin onto mine, the rise and fall of his chest, the blink of his eyelids.

In the movies, you can achieve slow motion in two ways, first, by overcranking, basically capturing each frame at a much faster rate with your camera than it will be played back on a projector. Then there's time stretching, where you insert new frames in post-production between the ones already filmed but linger longer on each one. That's what this feels like, but where each of the new frames I add is just a blank screen of longing.

"I can make it from here, thanks," I whisper as I slip out of his arms back into the water.

In a movie, this would be The Moment for the couple. But right now, I'm the only one in this moment. And anyway, you can't have The Moment when your feelings are buried so deep you're afraid they'll burn up if they see the light.

We wade back to shore.

Phil collapses onto the blanket, faceup in the afternoon sun. He closes his eyes.

I wind my towel tightly around myself and sit down. I pull out my ponytail and comb my fingers through my hair. It falls loose across the width of my back, the wet strands sticking to my body. The sun warms my skin as I tuck my knees up under my chin. Phil's eyes are still closed, and I watch his chest rise and fall with his breaths. Droplets of water on his skin slowly dissolve into the heat. Phil's arm is bent under his head, the muscle in his biceps taut and smooth. I twirl a small section of dripping hair around my index finger and try and force myself to look away and out across the water. It's hopeless.

Phil touches the small of my back, startling me. "Are you hungry?" he asks, sitting up. He reaches for the cooler and pulls out sandwiches, a bag of potato chips, and a couple of pops. "Turkey and Swiss. No pork. I remembered."

"Thanks," I say as Phil hands me the sandwich. "It's sweet of you." Violet is the only one of my friends who ever thinks about my dietary restrictions.

"Swimming always makes me hungry, so I figured I'd bring provisions."

"I wasn't exactly swimming." I take a bite, realizing how hungry I am, too.

"You'll get there."

I chew for a while, pretending to focus on my food, but really focusing on him. "You're a good teacher. You have way more patience than me."

"When's our next lesson?" Phil asks.

It's the question I've been hoping for all afternoon. On the other hand, it means flailing around in the water again. "After the pond hits ninety degrees?"

He laughs. "That will be . . . never. How about tomorrow? I'm not working until the afternoon. Same time?"

I hesitate. I should hesitate. But I can't help myself. "I have to be at work at three."

"Perfect. I'll pick you up at eleven."

I'll probably regret it, but for now, for a minute, I allow myself to be the character in the romantic movie. The adorable girl who gets the guy. Because this definitely doesn't feel like real life, not mine, anyway.

His training has prepared him. He's ready.

Every day for the last week, he scouted the route, noting when the mail arrived, by what hour the parking lot filled, when the guards went on break and took lunch. From across the street, he watched the cars drive by the manned security gate—a simple red-and-white metal arm, operated by one guard in a wooden kiosk.

Easy.

Today, four blocks from the building, he eyes a slow-moving police car in his rearview mirror. He pulls up to the curb and lets the cop pass, holding his breath, waiting to see if the car circles the block.

It doesn't.

CHAPTER 8

It's Wednesday and freakishly warm, and it's my third swimming lesson. I walk out of my room, rubbing the sleep from my eyes, and bump into my mother. Literally.

"*As-salaam-alaikum, ummi.*" I sound too chipper.

"You are in a fine mood, *beta*," my mom replies. Of course, a wave of suspicion passes over her face. "What are you up to?"

"Can't I just be in a good mood?"

"That's more like it," my mom says, a rare twinkle in her eye. It strikes me as weird that she's not pushing me on this, but then I realize she must think my "fine mood" is because of Kareem. I wonder if she talked to Kareem's mom and if they are planning something. Crap. And I can't ask her. Now I'm obsessing. And guilty. She has this uncanny gift of delivering guilt tied up in a bow, and without fail, I accept it.

My dad honks from the driveway. My mom kisses me on the cheek. "Your dad is always rushing me."

"*Khudafis*, Mom."

"*Khudafis*, *beta*. And don't forget—"

"I know, I know. I'll eat something."

The front door closes as I step into the bathroom and look at myself in the mirror. Definitely tanner. One more day of sun and Mom will notice. I'll have to lie again to explain how I could possibly get this tan at the bookstore or at the mall. I don't have a choice. The lies make life easier for everyone. It's not even that I'm interested in someone other than Kareem. That's tiny compared to the big, fat NYU lie of omission.

The response deadline is May first, only days away. I'm still fantasizing that a deus ex machina will descend from the heavens to resolve the situation. Greek tragedies with their revenge, suffering, and extreme sorrow are roughly equivalent to dealing with my mother, so an intervention from Zeus or Athena seems a fair ask.

Of course, I hate when that happens in movies. Because it is one hundred percent the opposite of real life. Like if *Lord of the Rings* were a documentary, Frodo and Sam would've totally died in the fires of Mount Doom, but instead giant eagles fly into the end of all things *after* a fade to black to rescue them. So why didn't Gandalf give the ring to the giant eagles in the first place? This has always bugged me. Whatever, though. Violet and I just watched the trilogy for twelve hours of Aragorn. No regrets.

I step into the shower, hoping to wash away my anxiety. It doesn't work. If I don't make NYU happen, I might doom myself to the stay-close-to-home-become-a-lawyer-and-marry-a-suitable-boy life that my parents dream of.

I grab a towel as I step out of the shower. "I have to tell them," I say out loud, hoping to convince myself. Hoping to work up the courage.

I take a peek at my phone. Three missed texts. All from Kareem.

Kareem: Morning, sunshine.

Kareem: Sleeping in?

Kareem: I have a surprise for you.

My spirits sink a little lower. He's trying too hard. Death knell. Of course, it's not like I've been discouraging him. I mean, I text-flirt and wink my virtual lashes at him. I desire his interest. Basically, I'm leading him on. Now I feel like garbage.

At least the texts, while not exactly a deus ex machina, reveal a stark truth: Kareem isn't the one. He hasn't actually done anything wrong, except not be Phil. I know I have to break it off, but it's never been totally on, I guess.

We did kiss, though. And it was a good kiss. Better than good. It was romantic. *He* is romantic. And it's still not enough. I have to tell Kareem the truth about Phil, or I'll be halfway to engaged by next summer. My mom already has visions of a big Indian wedding dancing in her head; I could see it in her eyes when she said goodbye.

I fall back on my bed, pulling my knees into the towel knot. A montage of the kiss plays in my brain. The flower petals. The rain. The closeness of Kareem's skin to mine. I close my eyes for a moment, take a deep breath, then another. I trace my collarbone with my index finger. He might not be *the* one, but so far at least, he's been the *only*.

When I turn to the clock, it's 10:50. Phil will be here in ten minutes.

Whirling around the room, I throw on my clothes, pull my hair tight into a low ponytail, and snag my bag and camera. Hearing Phil's car in the driveway, I look in the mirror and frown, then slather on lip gloss. It'll have to do, because the doorbell is ringing.

MY CAMERA ROLLS AS Phil and I walk toward the garden. He pushes open the hip-high, rusty iron gate. I zoom in on the metal curlicues and then pan up from the gravel path to Phil's face. He gazes directly into the camera, reveals the dimple, and begins his smooth narration. "We're in the Fabyan Forest Preserve."

He talks and walks, and he's not self-conscious at all.

The camera loves him. He's an easy subject to follow. He points out the sun-bleached wooden moon bridge, slats missing, that arches across the dried-up pool. When he points, I train my camera on the knotty dead trunks of Japanese maples and the cherry and ginkgo trees—gnarled limbs reaching toward blue sky. The buds on a weeping spruce cascade over a small embankment—a little hint of life beneath the desiccated vines and leaves. He knows all their names.

When we reach the foot of the bridge, Phil pauses, sweeping his hand over the vista as he talks about the vision of Taro Otsuka, Fabyan's private gardener who designed this place. I walk up a gentle slope that leads to the bridge to get a long shot of Phil with the garden around him. I lose myself in his voice, imagining the garden in full bloom—pink cherry blossoms, burgundy leaves of the maple tree, yellow forsythia, red azaleas . . .

I'm not paying any attention to where my feet are. My flip-flop slips on some loose earth, and all at once I'm skidding downhill.

"Careful," Phil says. He's at my side in a flash. "Are you okay?"

"I'm fine. I was still rolling, so it'll be a good action sequence."

Phil laughs. "Is that all you think about?"

"Not all," I manage to whisper. I bite my tongue and look away. I don't trust myself not to blurt something ridiculous.

"You're bleeding . . . your knee."

A drop of blood trickles down my leg. "Crap. I don't suppose you have a tissue?"

Phil rifles through his backpack, pulls out a napkin, and holds it to my knee. For a moment I forget about the sting of the cut and the embarrassment of my awkward nerd-crash. Phil's hand is on my knee. Separated by a questionably clean napkin, but still. "I have a first-aid kit in the cabin," he says, blotting and squinting at the wound. "Are you okay to walk?"

I almost laugh. "I think I can make it," I say dryly.

He helps me up and wraps his arm around my waist. The gesture is completely unnecessary, but I pretend my little injury is maybe worse than I thought. I luxuriate in the warmth of Phil's arm holding me. When we arrive at the stone cottage, he directs me to the recliner and disappears into the small back room—a simple kitchenette—and emerges with the first-aid kit.

"You're such a Boy Scout."

"Always prepared." Phil uses alcohol-dipped swabs to clean the small gash on my leg.

"Ouch."

"Sorry. I want to make sure it won't get infected. It's not too deep." Phil slathers bacitracin on the cut and covers it with a couple bandages, then uses his water bottle to rinse away the dry blood from my leg. "We shouldn't go into the water today. The pond is pretty clean, but there's still random stuff floating around in there, and those bandages aren't waterproof."

"Okay, doc. Should I take two aspirin and call you in the morning?"

"Aspirin is a blood thinner. If it hurts, take ibuprofen."

"You really know your first aid."

"Hope so. I want to study to be an EMT. I have ever since middle school."

I'm taken aback. There is so much I don't know about Phil. So much more I want to know. "Really? I had no idea."

Phil walks toward one of the paneless windows. "My dad had a heart attack when I was in seventh grade."

"What? Oh, my God. So glad it all turned out okay."

"Yeah. Me, too. It's totally because of these two EMTs. He wouldn't have made it without them. The two of us were at home, shooting hoops in the driveway, and suddenly my dad starts clutching his arm and having these chest pains. I totally froze. But my dad told me to call 911. I did. And when they got here, they basically diagnosed it, stabilized him, and ten minutes later, they were wheeling him into the surgery."

"That must've been terrifying."

"It was. I don't think I've ever felt so scared and helpless in my life. And I never want to feel that way again. All I could think was, I didn't want my dad to die . . . I didn't know what it was called then, but the EMTs basically performed an ECG—an electrocardiogram—right there, transmitted the data to the hospital, and an interventional cardiologist was waiting for us when they wheeled him in. They got a balloon to open his blocked artery in less than sixty minutes from when I called. That's what saved his life. I'll never forget how calm and together and fast the EMTs were. After they got my dad secured in the ambulance, the EMT who rode in the back with me made sure I was okay and explained everything to me. She didn't talk down to me like I was some dumb kid, which is what I basically felt like. She was so kind and understanding and answered all my questions and stayed with me until my mom and brother got to the hospital."

"She sounds amazing."

"She was. After that, I wanted to learn everything about what happened to my dad, so I researched everything I could, and I, like, put myself in charge of his rehab at home and was on him all the time about his eating habits."

"So that's your origin story," I say, brushing my hand against his shoulder.

"I guess it is," he says, a shy smile emerging on his face, which had turned serious when talking about his dad.

"So if we're not going swimming, do you want to head back?" I pray the answer is no.

"Not unless you want to. I'm not working till later," he says.

"Me, neither."

"Cool. I left our lunch cooler in the car. I'll be right back."

The door shuts behind him. The spare room is shadowy even

with the sunlight filtering through the small windows. I notice a rolled-up sleeping bag in a corner along with an inflatable camping pillow. I get up to explore and step into the little kitchen. Cans of food line a built-in wooden shelf. There are a couple gallons of water, a thermos, and a large plastic cup filled with plastic forks and knives. *The ultimate rustic bachelor pad*, I think. I wonder how much time Phil spends here alone versus with Lisa.

Lisa.

She probably wouldn't be happy knowing I'm here now. Best not to dwell on it. I take a blanket and walk outside, spreading it over a grassy patch in front of the cottage. I lie back. Passing clouds cast shadows across my face. I shut my eyes.

"MAYA?"

My eyelids flutter open. Phil's face floats over mine.

"I thought for a second you'd fallen asleep." He settles in next to me and hands me a sandwich. We eat quietly for a moment.

I catch him eyeing my cut, making sure the bandage is in place. "Can I ask you a question?"

He looks up at me. "Sure."

"Why haven't you told anyone you want to be an EMT? I'm sure your parents must be thrilled."

"They say they're cool with it, but I think they secretly wish I would go to school but then come back home and run our family gas station with my brother. And pretty much everyone else assumes that, too. I mean, some of my friends, they're already making plans to come back to Batavia after college . . . That's just not what I want."

And by friends, I'm assuming he means Lisa.

"So the old expectation thing? Believe me, I totally understand."

Phil nods. "It's not that my parents are upset. They're actually pretty happy that I'm interested in something other than playing college football. But they wish I wasn't going so far away. My mom has been researching all these Midwestern places where I could get certified."

"Where are you going?" I feel like I should know this, but realize I never bothered to ask.

"Green Mountain College in Vermont."

"Sounds all outdoorsy and autumnal."

The tone in Phil's voice lifts. "It's awesome. But, you know, in the wilderness. I'll major in Adventure Recreation and take classes in emergency medical services, so when I graduate, I can be a paramedic or work with programs like Outward Bound."

"Adventure Recreation?"

"I know, ridiculous name, right? My mom asked me why I couldn't have adventure and recreation closer to home and someplace cheaper. But it's one of the best programs out there that teaches survival skills—"

"Like surviving a bear attack?"

"When I find out how, I'll let you know."

"I can't wait." I place my hand on his arm. He doesn't flinch. "But I still don't get why you won't tell any of your friends."

"There's no football team."

This comes as almost more of a surprise than anything else Phil has told me because he's literally the poster boy for Batavia High School football. "But don't you want to play football? I mean, at all?"

"I was recruited to play football at a couple smaller Division One schools. Eastern has a really good coach. That could've meant a partial scholarship, but I honestly don't care if I don't play football at school. Like I told you, it wasn't even my first choice of sport. It sort of just . . . happened. I love it, but now everyone expects me to play, but I'm ready to move on—try something different."

"If your parents are okay with it, then you're set, right? Does Lisa know?" I don't know why I say Lisa's name. This time, this space between me and Phil, it's like this perfect, intricate diorama, and when I say her name, it reminds me that we're just paper figures taped inside a shoe box.

He shakes his head and lowers his eyes, twirling a few blades of grass between his fingers. "No. You're the first person I've told outside my family."

A tiny flicker of hope lights up inside me. If Lisa doesn't know about his college plans, she and Phil can't be that serious anymore. Right? This could mean . . . something. On the other hand, I am certain they haven't broken up. Violet is definitely certain, and I rely on her to determine the truth regarding all *affaires de coeur*, especially long distance from Paris. Maybe I'm just another one of Phil's secrets.

He lies back and stares into the sky. "It's complicated."

"How?"

"She's going to Eastern. She thinks I'm going with her. I know I need to tell her. I just can't bring myself . . . I've been avoiding it."

"Tell her what you told me. She'll understand." I clamp my mouth shut, but too late; the words are already out. Not only am I giving him relationship advice, but it's totally hypocritical because it's advice I'm dishing out but totally not able to take. From myself. I'm hiding from my parents. And, to be honest, from Kareem, too. Phil's hiding from Lisa. We both have truths that we're hiding from practically everyone else, except each other.

"Doubt it. She is not into the outdoors, at all. I mean, maybe an outdoor mall . . ."

I see a chance to ask Phil the question that's been gnawing at me for three days. I've been holding back, because I know I shouldn't fish in none-of-my-business waters. Now I cast my line. "Lisa must love this place, though. It pretty much defines outdoorsy."

Phil is silent for a moment. "I've never brought her here," he says finally.

My heart thumps against my rib cage like it has wings. My brain floods with words, but I don't blurt them out. I hold onto the stillness of this moment, waiting for what he will say next.

"I've never brought anyone here. Except you. You're the only person I can talk to about this stuff. Tom won't get me not wanting to play football. You know Tom, right? He's going to Eastern, too, along with Megan. All of them—Tom, Megan, Lisa—especially Lisa, have this idea that we'll be together there and after college be back here . . ." Phil's voice trails off.

I shake my head. I do know Tom, but in my mind, he's pretty much indistinguishable from the rest of Phil's teammates. "They're your friends; they'll get it."

"Maybe." Phil turns his attention away from the clouds and focuses on me. "Remember the other day when we were at the café and you were saying how you wanted to be in New York and were sick of being so different here? I got that."

My heart is still beating fast. "You get wanting to go to New York and being the only Muslim girl in school?" I make a joke, but I'm keenly aware that Phil understands me more than anyone else because he's keeping a secret, too. Maybe more than one.

Phil laughs and sits up. "Exactly. It's cool that my whole family stayed in Batavia, but I want to see what else is out there. I want to take some time to *explore*. On my own. Out in the wild. I'll carry everything I need to live in my backpack."

My talk with Kareem springs to mind. But I don't see him;

I don't even hear his voice. I see only Phil in front of me. "You want to go to the woods to live deliberately. You want to suck the marrow out of life."

He blinks at me. "That sucking marrow part went over my head, but yeah, that's the gist of it."

"I'm quoting Thoreau."

"That explains it." Phil laughs again and fishes out a worn piece of paper from his wallet. "I want to show you something. A couple seasons ago, Coach Roberts had this sports psychologist come and talk to us, and he did this exercise where he told us to write down three goals on a piece of paper and then fold it up and put it away. We weren't supposed to show it to anyone. Of course we did, anyway. Turned out that we all wrote pretty much the same thing. We wanted to win homecoming or bench-press more weight or set the school rushing record . . ."

"Is that what you wrote?"

He shrugs. "More or less. Because I knew what would happen. But it felt phony. Laughing with all my friends later, I almost felt sort of sick inside, and I've never felt that way before around them. You know, fake. So that night at home, I wrote another list and put it in my wallet. It's been there ever since." Phil slowly unfolds the piece of paper and hands it to me. "Here . . ."

I take the crinkled treasure from his hands and read his chicken-scratch writing.

1. *Hike along the Knife Edge Trail to the top of Mount Katahdin.*
2. *Swim in the Pacific Ocean.*
3. *Kayak the Colorado River.*

A tiny lump wells in my throat. I'm quiet.

"It's stupid, right?"

I shake my head. Is Phil taking my silence as judgment?

"Not at all," I say in a rush. "It's nice. No. That's not the right . . . I mean, it's—it's beautiful." I stumble for words. I can imagine how difficult it must've been for him to show me this hallowed piece of paper. "I hope you get to do it all and much more." I place the paper back in his hand, letting my fingers linger across his palm.

He smiles. "Number four was 'teach Maya to swim.'"

"Liar." I laugh.

"Okay, maybe I just added that one. But I'm going to do it." His eyes meet mine. "You believe me, don't you?"

I nod. I don't trust myself to speak.

"I like that I can be myself around you." Phil rolls up a towel and places it on the ground, snug against my thigh. Then he puts the top of his head on my leg, his neck supported by the towel roll. He closes his eyes. "Do you mind?"

"Not at all," I manage to whisper. I bite my lip. I'm thankful he can't see my face, that his eyes are closed, because I am flushed. Every muscle in my body seems to be screaming, but I am as still as the woods. I watch the rise and fall of his T-shirt. I breathe evenly to relax, to match it.

Without a word Phil reaches out, grazes my fingers, and pulls my hand gently toward his chest. I'm not sure how much time passes. No one else exists. Only us. We sit, hands clasped, until it is time to leave.

She wakes before dawn to say her first prayer.

She's always loved the ritual: starting off the day with a devotion to God. Sitting on the prayer rug with her legs curled beneath her, as the thread of dawn appears against the horizon.

This is the moment when she feels most at peace, before she makes breakfast for her husband, before they drive together to their small grocery store, before the shop fills with the cacophony of women searching for fava beans, cumin, apricots, dried lentils, rose water, pistachios, cardamom, pickled eggplants in vinegar.

Even after many years in this country, some still try to haggle as if they are in the bazaar back home.

She pushes the complaints from her mind.

In a few days, she will be the one preparing the feast. Kamal comes home, and there will be reason to celebrate. He will drive the entire way, seven hours, from Springfield to Dearborn. She worries the drive will be too tiring for him, that he will eat too much fast food on the way and not be hungry for dinner.

Ma, I am always hungry for your cooking, he assures her.

More and more he sounds like an American. But at least he knows how to show his mother proper respect.

CHAPTER 9

Friday. The last day of break. My last day with Phil before school starts again on Monday—when we return to the respective corners of our social cliques. Soon enough, these lovely last days of swimming in cool water under a bright blue sky will fade from our memories like a pastel drawing left in the sun.

But today is perfect.

Phil runs into the pond ahead of me. I step forward, my usual hesitation giving way to a tiny spark of confidence. I secure my goggles, check the waterproof bandage on my leg, and swim six remarkably even strokes to reach Phil. Swimming. Me. In water. I'm not exactly giving Katie Ledecky a run for her money. Still, I did a thing I was scared to do. But there's no way I could've done it without Phil.

"You're swimming. For real." He's standing in the water, arms crossed, beaming at me as I come up from the water.

"It was only a few strokes."

"In the next couple hours, you'll be swimming laps."

"Thanks to you."

"It's the only thing I could teach you—you're better than me at everything else."

"You're forgetting wilderness first aid and avoiding bear attacks . . ." I almost add *and football* but decide against it. "Both are way more practical than dissecting literary symbolism."

"Probably not in New York City." Phil turns to swim the length of the pond.

I follow him in and try to remember to move my arms and legs in harmony with my breath. Slow but steady. I swallow a few mouthfuls of water and lose count of my strokes and mess up my breathing. But I don't panic. I right myself.

When I start shivering, I step out of the water, grab my towel, and sit on our beach so I can warm up in the sun. I film Phil as he swims, capturing his grace, how his smooth strokes barely ripple the surface. I need to cinematize this, all of this. I'll want proof later. I'll need to know this isn't all the land of make-believe.

"So what exactly are you going to do with all this stuff you're filming? I'm asking because if you're putting it on the Internet, I want to make sure the clip goes viral." Phil joins me on the blanket.

I grin. "Nothing like that. It's the documentary of my life, with an audience of one—me. One day when I'm old and gray, my Mac hard drive will be my memory. Along with my dozens of backups."

"Worried your computer's gonna crash?"

"Afraid I'll forget how I see the world."

"What do you mean?"

"Filming is the way I see things. Really see them. I can capture what is important to me at a particular moment. That way, I keep it forever."

"Nothing lasts forever."

I shrug. "Movies can remind us of who we are or were, show us what we can be. What would the Lumière brothers think if they could walk into a theater today?"

"The what brothers?" he asks with a smile.

"Lumière. These French guys who basically invented movies—they made the camera and showed the first film—a bunch of people exiting a train station . . ." My voice trails off. He's staring at me. "What?"

"Your face lights up when you talk about the movies."

He's right about that—literally—because I sense the blushing coming on, of course. I avoid his gaze, looking down at the camera at my side. "Movies are the only real magic that I can make," I say.

He catches my eye. He opens his mouth to say something, then pauses. Clears his throat. "So I guess you will be telling your folks about NYU."

I chuckle miserably. "This weekend. As long as I don't lose my nerve. I asked my aunt to come and be moral support or rescue me in case my parents try to ship me to India and marry me off to a distant cousin."

"Why are they so against you going away for school, anyway?"

"I guess they're nervous to send me away because they can't keep an eye on me. In India, plenty of women live at home until they get married, but things are changing there, too. But my parents are frozen in the past, in the India of their youth."

He nods. "My parents are frozen in the past, too, in a way. Batavia's past."

I get it. Batavia is so small. I wonder if we will ever be alone like this again. Phil and I have known each other since we were five years old, but I've never *truly* known him beyond the obvious, beyond what the world knows. That he plays football, dates Lisa, and works for his dad at the station. And that he's good-looking. Really good-looking. Perhaps beyond this pond we'll go back to the way we were, unknowable to each other. We can only exist together here in our little mise-en-scène at the end of the path— the setting of our own documentary short.

Phil interrupts my thoughts. "I know what you should call it."

"Call what?" I ask.

"The movie that you're going to make about your swimming lessons—*Hidden Beach*," he says, but I wrinkle my nose. "No? How about . . . *Stolen Beach* . . . *Stolen Water* . . . no, wait . . . *Stolen Spring? Stolen Spring.* Get it?"

I shrug and give Phil a little grin, waiting for him to explain.

"Well, it's spring right now, and we've, like, stolen this place for ourselves." Phil is on a roll. "I can imagine the trailer now." He tries the cadence of a movie voice-over: "It's senior year. She's a beautiful budding filmmaker. He can swim and fix cars. They don't know where the path beyond the stone cottage will lead."

I blink. "You think . . . I . . . I'm . . ." My voice is a whisper. I can't say the word. I'm afraid to.

"What?"

"Uh . . . Nothing. Your trailer sounds like it could be a horror movie or maybe . . . you're not going to get all sparkly in the sunlight and confess to being a vampire, are you?" There's a hint of teasing in my voice.

Phil smirks. "We don't know how it's going to end yet, do we?"

He stares into my eyes as my chest rises and falls. He leans toward me. My heartbeat echoes through the trees. His face inches closer. I will our lips to meet. I want to wrap my arms around him and press my mouth to his, but my body hesitates.

Phil plucks a little leaf from my wet hair and shows it to me. "It was stuck," he says. His arms slacken. He rises awkwardly and reaches for his T-shirt. The spell is broken. "I gotta get going. If I'm late for work, my brother will kick my ass."

Suddenly there's a dark storm inside me. I snatch my things. I'm not sure what happened right now. It felt . . . natural, like the moment in a movie when the guy and girl who've been kept apart finally kiss, under the moonlight or in an airport, or on a crowded street—or by a secret pond. Maybe I imagined it all because the difference is the guy and the girl in *that* Hollywood movie have fate on their side. In the bleak indie movies, they don't get the happy ending; they get a tragedy. They get *Romeo and Juliet*.

And the Muslim? The Indian? That girl, she doesn't even get

the *dream* of the football captain. She gets a lifetime of being stopped by the FAA for random bag searches every time she flies. She gets the nice boy, the sensible boy, the one her parents approve of and who she will grow to love over years and children and necessity.

We walk down the path to the car. I glance back to steal a final look at our little beach and the pond and then hurry through the trees and beyond the cottage. I don't say a word. Leaves and twigs crunch underfoot. I wish I were home already or at the bookstore rearranging the shelves, anywhere but here, next to Phil and this painful reminder of everything that I can't have.

When we pass the Japanese garden, Phil finally speaks. "Sorry we had to pack up early today. I promised—"

"No problem." My voice is clipped. I walk faster, moving past Phil, to try and save myself from the humiliation that builds with each second we're together.

I climb into the passenger seat and slam the door. I sit with my arms crossed over my chest, my lips a tight line. This moment is so cruel. For a second I forget myself. All I want is to be the normal girl, with parents who let her date and a house that smells of seasonally appropriate candles and not fried onions. I slink back in the car seat. I know I can wish for life to be different. I can click my heels and hope I'm somewhere else. But in the end, I'm here. I'm me.

WE'RE STILL A COUPLE blocks from my house when Phil pulls the car over. He turns off the ignition. On any other day, my hands would get clammy, and my heart would pound. Right now I just feel sick.

"Do you want me to get out here?" I ask, a raw edge in my voice.

"Tell me what's wrong."

"Nothing." I stare out the windshield.

"You're not a very good liar."

"I'm better than you know."

"Why won't you talk to me?"

I sigh. Loudly. "Phil, please take me home." My eyes burn. I blink rapidly. I'm on the verge of tears. I need to get out of his car.

"Maya?" Phil whispers my name and takes my limp left hand in his. It might as well be a phantom limb. I'm a shadow. "I'm sorry."

I turn away. I have to; otherwise, I will burst into ugly sobs. I bite the inside of my cheek. "You don't have to apologize. Please. I want to go home." A few tears roll down my face. I brush them away with the back of my free hand. My shoulders droop. The air in the car is too heavy to breathe.

"I'm sorry. Please don't cry."

I try to clear away the lump in my throat, to compose myself. "No worries. You're going to be late for work if you don't get going."

"It's only . . . the timing of all this . . . I shouldn't have."

He clenches the steering wheel; his veins pop up against his skin. He opens his mouth as if he wants to form words but has forgotten how. I want to put him out of his misery, so I touch his forearm, barely graze it, and steady my voice. "It's okay. I understand." I open the door. "Look, I'm going to walk the two blocks home."

He takes my forearm and draws me back. "You don't understand."

"Trust me, I do. I know who I am and I know who you are. Thanks for the swimming lessons. We're even. See you Monday."

Phil won't let go. "Look. I want you to know that I meant what

I said back at the pond. You are . . . I think . . ." He can't say it. He can't bring himself to say anything, really.

So why am I still here? I pull my arm away and slam the car door. I hurry down the block while my held-back torrent of tears splashes down my face. I'm glad Phil can't see me. I race home, hoping no one notices the bawling brown girl with a tangled mess of wet hair. I rush inside and run to my room. Thankfully, I'm alone.

I throw myself onto the bed and cry into my pillow. Huge, heaving sobs.

The camera in my brain lets me run all the scenes of my life in slow motion. I freeze-frame every time Phil touched me. The perfect afternoon when he held my hand. The impossible instant when his face hovered inches above mine. He could have kissed me, but didn't. He couldn't even bring himself to say any words, express a single emotion.

And there's Lisa.

How I envy her. I'm angry with Lisa even though none of this is her fault. She's out of town with her family, blissfully unaware of all the time Phil and I have spent together. Completely ignorant to the split second when time froze, when I was sure we were going to kiss. I try to squeeze Lisa's face out of my mind, but it's impossible. On Monday, Lisa and Phil will be holding hands, walking down senior hall, the inevitable king and queen of prom. And I'll be spending prom night watching old movies with my aunt. I'm an idiot for believing my fantasy could be real. I should know better; I'm a documentarian. It's not a John Hughes movie. It's my so-called life.

Officer Evans drives his squad car up Sixth Street and takes a left turn on Adams.

His partner called in sick, so he's out solo today. His patrol started at 5 A.M. The morning was quiet. He got an early lunch, stayed a bit longer than usual at the counter of Kelly's Diner. A cheeseburger, medium well with the works, a side of fries, and a cup of black coffee. Same thing every time.

It was a ritual (one of the few) he was going to miss in retirement.

Six more months. Kelly jokes she might have to make his usual the Creature-of-Habit special and send it to him long distance. Because in six months and one day, he and Anne will head to a Florida fifty-five-plus retirement community for their "active adult years." Their two-bedroom condo is all picked out, halfway between Orlando and Tampa, perfect for a visit from the grandkids. But the best part will be the end of Illinois winters.

When he was a younger man, the freezing temperatures and piles of snow hadn't bothered him so much, but last winter was too brutal. He decided it was the last winter they would spend in Springfield. Cruising down Adams, he reminds himself to circle around the old state capitol.

He wants to check on a white truck that was parked at Fifth Street in a thirty-minute zone.

CHAPTER 10

Can't wait to see you, babe.

I sit on the edge of my bed and stare at Kareem's text. I want to crawl back under the covers; I'm about to break it off with a sweet, romantic guy I've kissed because I'm stitching my heart back together over a taken guy who has no desire to kiss me. Maybe this will become the pattern of my life: every story ends before it has a chance to begin. Not exactly riveting material for a documentary.

My mom yells up from the kitchen, crashing my self-pity party. "Maya, Kareem and his parents will be here in half an hour. Get up."

"Down in a minute." At least the day won't be a total loss because I can smell the *parathas* that my mother is making for Indian brunch. The layered, flaky flatbread is my absolute favorite. I love plucking them from the *tawa*, the cast-iron pan my mom reserves for this specialty, with a little pat of butter. Total food heaven. Making them also takes effort, so I know she's trying to impress Kareem's family, even though I overheard her assuring Salma Auntie that she was only preparing a "simple home meal."

I smell onions caramelizing, too.

"Mom, are you making *kheema parathas*?" I call down, hungry. My mouth waters for *parathas* stuffed with spicy ground beef. This is one of the great ironies of my life. I love Indian food, but not the days-old lingering smell of onions and garlic on my clothes. But when you love something, you have to be prepared to make sacrifices.

"If you get up, you can see for yourself," my mom calls.

With a groan, I pull myself off the bed. I shower and

change, swipe on a little blush and mascara. I take care to dress appropriately. Modest, but with a little flair. Skinny jeans and an emerald-green silk Indian tunic that hangs, untucked, covering my ass, with simple yellow embroidery around the neckline. Small gold hoops in my ears and a thin chain with a delicate gold *hamsa*—the hand of Fatima—resting in the notch above my collarbone. This outfit so wins the Indian-mom seal of approval.

"You look so pretty, *beta*," Mom proclaims as I walk into the kitchen. She's standing at the stove making *kheema parathas* as I'd hoped. The table is covered with steaming bowls of food. "Look, Asif—she's wearing makeup, too."

"Oho. Smashing." My dad nods in approval.

"You're supposed to say I don't need makeup."

"*Aaray*, can't I simply compliment my daughter without it becoming a federal case?" My mom turns to my dad and nods toward the cabinets—her silent way of asking him to set the dining table with the good china.

"I thought this was supposed to be no big deal," I say.

"Who's saying it's a big deal?" my mother asks with a shrug.

"Umm, you're wearing one of your favorite *shalwar kameez* and the necklace you wore to Ayesha's wedding."

"Don't be ridiculous. I would never repeat necklaces so close together—that one had the rubies in it. This one just has a few emeralds."

"Of course. Because emeralds totally scream casual brunch."

"Maya, *beta*, remember when you invite someone, as the host you must make them feel welcome and appreciated. In India, a guest is like a god in the house. You need to treat them with proper *tameez*." It's all part of the show, of course. She wants to prove that I'm a nice Indian girl from a good family. As if we should have to prove that. But more, she wants the day to be perfect. For a second, I'm sorry it won't be. For her.

"The house looks good. The food is ready. I'm going to make a few more *parathas*. And let me start the tea. I want to steep it a good, long time."

She's right. The house does look good. From the outside looking in, everything is as it should be. Too bad that façade is destined to crumble.

THE DOORBELL RINGS AT exactly ten-thirty.

"They're not on Indian Standard Time, I guess," my dad jokes as he walks to the door.

I muster a smile. "Yeah, somehow they've adapted to the strange American custom of arriving when asked." I follow him to the door. My mom trails behind. My mouth is dry. I realize I actually want to see Kareem. I thought I was going to totally dread this moment—breaking things off. But he's impossible not to like. I do like him. Just not enough, or in the right way.

"*As-salaam-alaikum.* Come in. Come in. Welcome. Welcome."

Kareem hands my mom flowers. I mouth the words "ass kisser" at him from behind my mom's back. He smirks but keeps his eyes on my mother. My mom thanks him effusively, going on and on about how he shouldn't have and congratulating his parents on raising such a wonderful son. In spite of all the food I can't wait to eat, I suddenly have no appetite. All this gushing adds to the myth of Kareem in my mother's matrimonial fancy—the suitable boy, the boy with *tameez*, the one boy to rule them all. But I'm also being as unfair to him as I'm being to her. He thinks we're something that we're not.

Kareem and his parents slip off their shoes in the foyer. His mom is also wearing a *shalwar kameez* with beautiful floral embroidery accented with gold jewelry. She's not as decked out as my mom, but then, she's the guy's mom, and it's always the girl's mom who is more invested, has more to lose. Because desi guys, especially ones as eligible as Kareem, always seem to have more options.

My mom guides Kareem's parents into the living room, her voice brighter and more singsong than usual. "The food is nearly ready. It's nothing much, home cooking, you know."

"Maybe we should put those flowers in water?" my dad suggests, louder and with more emphasis on the "we" than necessary.

"Yes, yes. Salma, can you please help me select the vase?" My mom flashes my dad an eye-smile.

"Of course." Salma Auntie plays along. "And I must see what you've cooked; it smells heavenly."

"Sajid, let me show you a few recent improvements I've made to the cabinets." My dad gestures to the kitchen. All four adults vanish.

And scene. Kareem and I are alone.

I turn to Kareem, hoping my cheeks aren't pink. "Not obvious at all."

"They're so smooth, aren't they?" Kareem laughs and steps closer to me. I scratch a nonexistent itch on my forehead; I am hyperaware of my own breathing. But my hand doesn't pose enough of an obstacle. He moves it gently aside and bends down to kiss me.

I hop back, shaking free. "Have you lost it?" I loud-whisper.

My parents are hidden behind the kitchen wall, voices chattering, dishes clattering. But I'm pretty certain my mom has x-ray vision.

He gives me a puzzled smile. "We're alone. They *want* us to be alone."

"Not alone. They're fifteen feet away. Believe me, my parents would not be cool with kissing under their roof, or anywhere else for that matter, even if you are Muslim and Indian and an engineering major and bursting with *tameez*."

Kareem shrugs. "Well then, I'll just have to figure out a way to get you alone—really alone."

I look into Kareem's dark, flirtatious eyes and remember why I liked him in the first place. I wish this day were already over. I wish my feelings were different. But they aren't.

Our mothers appear with two heaping plates of food and two mango *lassis*. My mom smiles a little too brightly as she hands a plate and glass off to me. Salma Auntie hands hers to Kareem. "Maya, it's such a beautiful day. Why don't you show Kareem outside?"

"Excellent idea," Salma Auntie says before I can answer. "I think I saw a picnic table out there." She winks at my mom as if neither Kareem nor I are present.

The day *is* beautiful, so there's no point in protesting. I lead Kareem out through the screen door into the yard, past my old wooden swing set (my parents insist on keeping it for posterity), to the weathered red picnic table underneath the weeping willow in the corner. On the plus side, the wide trunk and drooping branches completely shield us from the prying eyes of our parents.

"Alone at last," Kareem says as we sit across from each other. He reaches over the table to stroke my arm.

"My dad painted the shed so it would look like a little barn. It's the symbol of his American dream. Every lawn-cutting, hedge-trimming, barbecuing, suburban-dad device is in that shed. He's totally obsessed with Home Depot." I speak a mile a minute. My words are garbled; they bang and smash into each other.

Kareem smiles at me. I catch my breath for a second.

"He loves gadgets. He probably has gadgets that are supposed to make ice cream while they reseed the lawn. You should eat your food before it gets cold. My mom makes the best *kheema parathas*. Seriously."

I tear off a section of the buttery warm bread, dip it in the chutney, and stuff my mouth while gesturing for Kareem to do the same. I want to make sure my mouth is full in case Kareem tries to ask me any questions.

Kareem sits back in his chair and smiles. "So . . . tomorrow is the big NYU reveal. I think it's awesome. You're carpe-ing your diem."

I look up from my plate. I try to smile, but I'm afraid it comes off like a grimace. "Yup. I'll be sucking the marrow out of life. Probably sucking hard." I'm not surprised he brings it up; we've already talked about how I was dreading today. Of course, he doesn't realize I have more than one truth to tell this weekend.

Kareem laughs. "Is this the appropriate time for a *nihari* joke?"

"Ugh. It's never an appropriate time for a *nihari* joke. I had nightmares about sucking out the marrow from those bones."

"What? Are you not a real Hyderabadi? *Nihari* is delicious."

"Of course you loved it. That's why you're such a Thoreau pusher. You are what you eat."

"You'll be fine. Tell them straight up."

"I was considering using the stomp-my-feet-and-hold-my-breath technique. It proved highly effective when I was little."

"By any means necessary?"

"Whatever gets me to New York."

"Do you want me to put in a good word for you?" Kareem offers between bites of *paratha*. "I mean, I'm going to school in New Jersey, and I haven't turned into my parents' worst nightmare or anything."

When I look at Kareem's bright eyes, my hard candy coating gives way to my gooey inside. But it isn't attraction; it's because I feel sorry for what I'm about to do. I know Kareem is sincere and in this moment. I wish my heart would pound for him like it does for Phil. Life would be so much easier. I know that he's a lot more than the suitable boy trifecta—Indian, Muslim, and from a good family. But I can't fake it.

My mind time-travels to a future that will never happen, an alternate universe where I'm in love with Kareem. There are afternoons on the couch watching old Satyajit Ray movies, stuffing our faces with *samosas*. We share an unspoken understanding, two people from similar backgrounds raised in similar ways in America. I will never have to explain so many basic things to him. Explain why every adult is called *auntie* or *uncle* despite familial link (a sign of respect), why we always take off our shoes at the vestibule (we pray in the house, so the home is holy), or why the major Muslim holidays are on different days every year (Islam follows a lunar calendar). There will be a big wedding where Kareem rides in on a white horse and I will be garlanded in gold and roses and jasmine.

It's beautiful and perfect, but I can't fool myself. I don't want it. My heart belongs to Phil, even if his heart belongs to Lisa.

"Still there?" Kareem interrupts my Walter Mitty moment.

I take a deep breath. Firmly seize one end of the imaginary bandage. Carpe diem. "Kareem. We need to talk."

He straightens in his seat. His smile falters. "This can't be good."

I look down at the table and then up, past Kareem. My voice breaks. "I'm sorry. I don't know how to tell you this without sounding horrible. I don't like you the way you like me. It's not because of anything you—"

"Do not say, 'It's not you; it's me,'" he interrupts, but his tone is gentle. "That is too much of a cliché."

"But it's true. You've been so nice, and I enjoy talking to you, and I don't want to hurt you . . ." The words catch in my throat, and tears well in my eyes. "I'm sorry. I know I should like you, but it's that—"

Kareem half-laughs. "Maya, you can't force yourself to be into someone. And we've only been on one date, so I get it. It's not working for you. Plus, you know, I'd like to be adored for who I am."

Why does he have to be so kind? Can't he see that he's just making it harder on me? I swallow hard. "Of . . . of course. I'm sorry. I didn't mean that . . . I was forcing myself. God. I'm doing a terrible job at this. I want to explain. I . . ." I want to run away. But there is no place to go where I won't find myself.

Kareem stands up and walks over to my side of the table. He sits and puts his arm around me and draws me close to him. I sob into his chest. He caresses my hair and kisses the top of my head. I don't deserve this kind of understanding, but I am grateful for it.

"I'm sorry," I whisper.

"It's okay, Maya. As big as my ego is, this actually does seem to be about you and not me."

I wipe away the salt and tears and mascara that ran down my face. "Oh, my God. I must look awesome right now."

"You totally rock the raccoon eyes. Now what's bothering you?"

I sigh deeply. I want to tell him. Still, it is infinitely strange to talk to a guy you've made out with about a guy you *want* to make out with. But right now, at this picnic table with his arm still protectively around me, Kareem doesn't feel like the former. He is the big brother who'd fight off the schoolyard bully for me.

So it comes tumbling out, the whole Phil story—the tutoring

sessions and the pond and the cottage and almost kissing and Lisa and the anger. I tell him what I took forever to admit to myself, that Phil was my first real crush. That we've known each other forever. And it's only now that I've realized that maybe, just maybe, Phil has been noticing me, too. Phil and I are totally different, but at the core, we share something that made the pond our little self-contained universe. And it was almost enough.

I take a deep breath. "It's all such a mess. I don't know how I let myself fall for Phil."

"You can't help who you love," Kareem says, totally matter-of-fact.

I stiffen at the mention of the L-word. "Love?"

"Hate to break it to you, but that's kinda what it sounds like."

"I was afraid that's what it was."

"It's not outside of you. It's a part of who you are, not an object you can film and capture in different kinds of light. It's love. If it wasn't real, it wouldn't hurt."

"But I don't want this. I don't want to be . . . to be in love with him. I mean, we can never be together, and I'll end up—"

"Brokenhearted? You'll get over it." He laughs softly. "Believe it or not, Maya, there are a few people who once felt exactly like you do right now."

"Like their bodies are ripping apart?"

"Like the world is crumbling and their souls are being crushed."

"Looking forward to the soul crushing." I manage a grin.

"It isn't a consolation, but I'd put the number at around a billion. And that's just today. I'm not counting all of human history. Plenty of other people have survived heartbreak. Believe me, I know. And that's why I know you'll be fine. You're graduating from high school; there are going to be plenty of other guys out there waiting—"

"To rip my heart out?"

He pulls back and tilts my chin up, so we're face-to-face. "No. Waiting for a girl like you. And from what you've told me, I'd say you're wrong about Phil. He seems into you."

I'm at a loss. "You think so?"

Kareem lets my chin go and takes my left hand in his. "Let me give you the guy's version of the situation. Phil likes you. He could've spent spring break having sex with his girlfriend, but instead he spent a week with you, where the main action was five minutes of G-rated handholding. Obviously, he's got to break up with her, but he's scared. You might have heard this before, but guys aren't always the best communicators."

"You're pretty good at it."

"Yes," Kareem says, then leans back with both hands behind his head. "I am rather great, aren't I?"

We burst out laughing. Then Kareem gets serious for a second. "It gets better, Maya. Even if the world seems to be crashing all around you right now."

I sniff and nod. "Cue Bollywood dance number."

He nods back, matching my smile. "At any moment dancers will unfurl from the tops of the willow's boughs, lip-synching a reminder that the sun will shine again."

I start to shake my head no. But the thing about what Kareem says is, right now, the sun is, in fact, shining. I'm not trapped. I'm still living in the world of the possible, and I actually have the power to make the possible real.

"So what are we going to tell our parents? I'm pretty sure my mom already has the wedding invitations picked out." I ask because my mom's disappointment isn't merely possible; it's assured.

"Really?" Kareem says dryly. "I hadn't detected that enthusiasm behind her effusive welcome. Simple is best and most believable. We want to be friends. Boom. Done."

"Wow. I'm . . . speechless."

He winks at me. "Great communicators like me have that effect on most women."

I have to laugh again. "Thank you for being so—so *you*. You're amazing at it." I dab at my eyes with a napkin. "Do I look all blubbery?"

"You look beautiful. Now shall we?"

Kareem stands up and stacks the cups and plates to carry inside. I find myself floating off again to another possible future, where Kareem is getting married but I am not the bride. I think of how that mystery woman will have Kareem's caring arms around her and how he will gently kiss her lips and stroke her hair. For a moment I'm jealous of a future that another girl will have with the guy I rejected.

I sigh.

Apparently getting what you want still comes at a price.

The car idles. He runs his fingers rhythmically over the indentation on the back of his head. Buckle and scar.

His body sways gently, almost imperceptibly. Back and forth. Buckle and scar.

His mind slips to last fall and a writing course at the local community college.

He was filled with something vaguely resembling hope when he walked in and spotted a pretty, brown-haired girl in the third row with an empty seat next to her. He took a few hesitant steps toward her. When he reached down to pull back the empty seat, a hand grasped his shoulder from behind and pushed him aside.

Don't even think about it, loser.

For the rest of the class, he sat in the back row, staring at the smiling couple. Seething.

CHAPTER 11

Phil's smiling face fills my computer screen, but all I see is his luscious dimple. I've been rough-cutting shots all morning to create a montage of the time Phil and I spent together. One image of Phil fades into another—the ambient light in the shots shifts and casts shadows across his brow, his cheekbones, his lips. I'm trying to convince myself that I'm searching for the best shots, empirically speaking, but I'm not. I'm searching for his smile. Not just any one. The smile I'm sure is meant only for me. The smile that will prove Kareem was right about Phil liking me for real.

"This is pathetic," I say out loud, pushing back from my computer.

When I walk into the kitchen, my aunt is at the table sipping chai, and my mom is at the stove cooking.

"I didn't hear you come in," I say, happy to see Hina. Inviting her over as moral support was probably the best decision I've made in weeks. My resolve is bolstered just by her presence.

"Your *ummi* said you were working on a movie, so I didn't want to interrupt. But I'm dying to hear about the brunch with Kareem and his parents."

My mom starts aggressively stirring the pot in front of her. She doesn't acknowledge Hina's question, but she heard it. I slink into the chair across from Hina, who gives me a little shrug.

I sigh. "Well, I . . . we . . . Kareem and I are just going to be friends. I mean, he really considers me a little sister. It's sweet." I'm trying to sound as chipper as possible. My mom still isn't looking at us, so I open my eyes wide and gesture at Hina to go along. When she gives me a silent "ah" and nods, I know she gets me.

"Hhhhmmph. Little sister," my mom mutters under her breath and keeps stirring.

"Well, that's good, no?" Hina asks, trying to sound upbeat. "I mean, it's always good to have family, and since he's in college, I'm sure he's going to be a great source of advice."

"Exactly," I say. "I'm sure—"

My mom whips around, waving the wooden spoon in her hand like she's preparing for battle. "You're not sure of anything. That's why you're throwing poor Kareem on some ash heap before he even had a chance."

"I'm not throwing anyone anywhere. Seriously, Mom. It's not like I'm breaking off an engagement."

It's absurd. The thing is, Mom hasn't even reached peak melodrama yet.

"You should be so lucky as to get engaged," she says.

She's getting there.

"What? I can't believe—"

Hina steps in. "Come on now, *aapa*." I'm pretty sure she can see that I'm about to erupt. "You didn't really expect Maya to get engaged. She's not even eighteen yet. She has to focus on her studies."

My mom takes a breath and lowers the spoon. "Of course. We want Maya to finish school before getting married, but you know, it can't hurt to have someone in mind."

I open my mouth to say something, but Hina nudges me under the table, so I bite my lip and keep my sarcastic remarks to myself. This is not today's battle.

"Don't worry, *aapa*. Maya is quite the catch. I'm sure she will have no problem finding eligible suitors when the time comes."

"Of course she's a catch. She's my daughter, isn't she?" My mom turns back to the stove, pleased with her retort. I see her shoulders relax. The Hina effect.

My dad enters the kitchen, which is good. If he even sniffs a discussion about something emotional or feminine, he hightails it out of there. "*Aaray*, I'm getting hungry." He sidles up to my mom and puts an arm around her shoulders. I sit on my hands. I shift in my seat. Even this G-rated eyeful of parental affection makes me uncomfortable.

Hina swoops in to the rescue. "Maya and I will take these dishes into the dining room, and you can bring the rest when you're done, okay, *aapa*?"

"Two more minutes," my mom says and gestures to my dad to get water glasses from the cupboard.

Hina and I take out the *daal*, kebabs, and rice and sit at the table. I take a few breaths, savoring the calm. We just sidestepped one argument so we could dive into an even bigger one.

"So you have a plan, right?" Hina asks in a whisper.

"Yes. You tell them I got into NYU while I cower in a corner."

Hina laughs. "God, I'm not that brave. Be firm and let them know it's what you want. Tag me in as necessary."

"I'm going to carpe this diem," I say, and for an instant I imagine Kareem nodding his approval.

My parents join us in the dining room, carrying in the remaining dishes. They take a seat, and my mom fills our plates.

"Oh, I forgot the *naan*," she says, slapping her palm to her forehead. "Let me go heat—"

"*Jaan*, it's okay." My dad takes my mom's wrist, gently pulling her back to the table and her seat. "Let's all sit down and have a nice, peaceful family lunch."

I catch Hina's eyes. No time like the present. "Dad?" I ask, inflection rising. "This might not be the peaceful family lunch you hoped for."

"Why?" my mom asks, panic tingeing her voice. "What happened? What's wrong?"

"*Aapa*, there's nothing wrong. Let Maya explain," Hina says.

I gulp. This is happening. Right now. "Mom. Dad. You know how I love making movies?"

"It's a very nice hobby," my father says. His tone is firm. "We are all looking forward to the movie of Ayesha's wedding."

"It's more than a hobby." My voice falters. I look from my dad to my mom. I take a deep breath. I straighten my shoulders and sit up in my seat. If I don't sound convincing to myself, they definitely aren't going to buy anything I have to say. I clear my throat.

"I want to make movies. Forever. As a career. I want to study film, in school." My parents stare at me like they are looking into an abyss, searching for light.

"You know how I got into Northwestern and U of C?"

"Two excellent schools where you can study to become a lawyer." My dad's voice is firmer now. Flatter, too.

"Umm. Well . . . I sort of also applied to NYU and got in."

Dad drops his silverware. "Sort of?"

"Not sort of. I applied to NYU. I was accepted."

"NYU," my mom repeats.

"Uh-huh. Yes. NYU. New York University."

"But that's in—" She turns to my dad.

"Yes, Mom. It's in New York. That's why it's called New York University." Wrong moment for sarcasm.

"Maya." My dad's tone is sharp. "Watch how you talk to your mother. So what you're telling us is that you applied to this school behind our backs, and you got in, and now you expect us to let you go there?"

My mom shakes her head. Her expression is both less angry and more puzzled than his. "Maya, you're not going to NYU. The answer is simple. No. It's too far. We agreed that you would be staying close to home."

I feel a little prickle of anger. "No, Mom. You and Dad agreed. Not me. I want to go to NYU. It's one of the best film schools in the country. They say my films show a lot of promise, and they have amazing professors, and it's only two hours by plane. And I know it's more expensive than U of C, but I promise I'll work extra hours at the Idle to save money and even get a job in New York to make up some of the difference."

My parents start talking to each other in Urdu, the primary and personal language they share. Anytime the topic veers toward something serious or emotional, especially anger, they revert to Urdu. I get it. It's familiar, the language they grew up with and met each other in. I can keep up because I understand it, but they know I can't respond, not really. People in India always say Urdu is this sweet language of poetry, but to me, Urdu just sounds like my parents.

"She can't go. She has to stay close to home. This is your fault, you know. You're the one who got her that dumb camera. Always encouraging her." My mom is in free fall. "I knew we gave her too much freedom. Always letting her do whatever she wants, never taking her to the mosque—"

"*Jaan, jaan,* calm down." My dad tries to pacify my mother, but the bulging vein in his forehead tells me he is far from relaxed. "Let her explain. Maybe this is a phase." He turns toward me; the English language and I reappear in the conversation. "I don't understand how you simply . . . lied . . . so easily . . . and applied to NYU and now expect us to say, 'Okay, go ahead'? This isn't just a matter of money, Maya. You know that."

"Dad, I'm sorry. I should've told you. But I made a spur-of-the-moment decision to apply. I didn't dream I'd get in. And you're so adamantly against it . . . I did tell Hina, and—" The blurter emerges; it's a mistake to implicate my aunt.

Now my mom looks upset. She turns her fiery gaze on Hina. "You encouraged her? My sister and my daughter lying to me. What did I do to deserve this?" my mom yells as her eyes grow shiny with tears.

"It's not Hina's fault. I—"

"It's okay." Hina puts her hand on my arm and interjects, "I did support her decision. I do. Maya has a talent. You don't want her to waste a gift from God, now do you?"

"Oh, don't you start, as if you are so pious," Mom snaps. "Maya got this defiance from *you.* You've set a terrible example."

Hina lets the words wash right over her. She is serene. "*Aapa,* do you pray five times a day—regularly?"

"I . . . I . . . Well, you know each night I pray for Maya. Obviously I have not been doing a good job."

I throw up my hands. "What does praying have to do with going to NYU, anyway? I'm not modern or whatever because of Hina. I'm the way I am because I live now. In the twenty-first century. In America. And I want to make movies." My eyes are wide. I'm rebelling. I'm going to be a desi movie-making rebel. Just like Deepa Mehta. Of course, I could never mention her name as a role model, because even though *Water* was tragic and beautiful and amazing and got an Oscar nomination, it caused riots in India, and she got death threats. Not the image I want my parents to associate with me being a director.

Mom's expression grows bitter. "I really should have sent you to boarding school in India."

"Everyone, calm down," my dad urges. "Sofia, you're going to raise your blood pressure. And Maya, you need to listen . . ."

"Why can't you trust me?" I ask him, point-blank.

"*Beta.*" My dad tempers his voice. "It's not that we don't trust *you*. Your *ummi* worries what will happen to you if you go far away from home."

"That's right." Mom sniffs and dabs her eyes with her napkin. "You know, we're always hearing stories of our girls who live far from their parents and go with these boys and . . . get . . . into . . . trouble. Some of them even eat pork."

I stifle a laugh. Laughing would definitely not be appropriate right now, but I'm not sure how the apparently cardinal sin of eating pork equates with the kind of trouble you can get into with boys (say, premarital sex), but in my mom's logic, it does. "Mom, you know I'm not like that. I never go wild and eat pepperoni pizza. I don't even break curfew."

"But what if something happens to you?" my father asks. "We don't have any relatives in New York. Who will help you?"

"I guess I'll need to help myself," I say and then quickly add, "Plus Kareem is only a couple hours away at Princeton. I know I can call him for anything—he told me so."

My mother perks up at the sound of Kareem's name. Matchmaking hope springs eternal in the desi Muslim mom's imagination. "But how will it look if we send you away by your-self, a girl—"

"Look to who?" I ask.

"The community," my mom says. "You know how people talk."

"What people?" Hina jumps in. "Your friends? Your family? *Aapa*, this isn't back home. And it's not the same as it was twenty, thirty years ago, even in India." She offers a sly smile. "Look at me, the heathen. I live on my own, and you haven't disowned me yet."

My mother allows herself a smile, but then adds, "You're my sister. I love you . . . but . . . you're not . . . not . . ."

"I'm not married? You don't want Maya to be too independent like me? Well, I'm happy, if that matters to you. I have a great life and great friends, and I love being a graphic designer. I designed a banner that's hanging from every lamppost in downtown Chicago to raise money and awareness for breast cancer. And I'm proud of that. I hope Maya can have all the things that make her happy and more. And if she wants to get married, that should be her choice."

I squeeze my aunt's hand. It's escaped me how truly rebellious Hina's life really is, as far as desi-Muslim standards go—even by American Born Confused Desi-Muslim standards. Hina is forty-something, single, childless, and lives by herself. She's not just a rebel; she's a pioneer—what a lonely road it must have been for her to travel.

"Of course, Hina," my dad says softly, attempting again to soothe the flaring tempers. "We want Maya to be happy in her life, and you are a wonderful aunt. But we made our wishes very clear to Maya. She should have voiced her objections then, not after the fact."

"Yes, *bhai jaan*," Hina addresses him with the very respectful "brother dear" in Urdu. "You are her parents, and I understand your wishes, but remember how your own parents felt when you were coming to America? They didn't want you to go, but you wanted to do what was best for your family and your future. And Maya wants—"

"I remember very well how heartbroken our *ummi* was at the airport," my mom interrupts. "But I was much older than Maya."

"You were actually only a little older than Maya is now, my dear sister," Hina points out. "And Hyderabad is a lot farther from

Illinois than Illinois is from New York. And don't forget, you waited a long time to have a kid despite our *ummi's* pressure."

My mom narrows her eyes at Hina. "That was a decision between husband and wife. Why are you bringing up this ancient history?"

"Because it's important. Because a marriage certificate doesn't bestow maturity. And even you have to admit that Maya is much savvier than you were at her age. Let her find her new world, too, as you did all those years ago."

I'm in awe of my aunt's alchemy with words. It truly is magic. As Hina speaks, my parents' faces relax, grow wistful, as they remember when they were young and full of dreams.

I hesitate, but I take a chance and break the moment of calm. "I'm asking for the chance to follow my passion. If I don't take it now, I'm afraid I'll regret it one day. And I promise, if I hate it or don't have the talent they seem to think I might, I'll switch majors to a more practical one." I reach across the table and place my hand on my mother's. "But not premed. You know I can't stand blood."

This makes them laugh. I'm winning my case, but if I'm going to suck all the marrow out of this bone, I need to hear them say the words. "And I promise if you let me go, I'll call home all the time, and I won't turn into an ungrateful, pork-eating, miniskirt-wearing . . ." Hina puts her hand on my knee to stop my compulsive talking. It's too bad I won't be able to take her with me if this works out.

"*Beta*, you know we want what is best for you." My dad looks at my mom as he says this. He's caving. I can see it in his face. Finally he turns to me. "What is the timeline for deciding?"

"May first."

"That is . . . that is this Thursday," my mom yelps. "Maya—"

"I'm sorry. I know I should have told you earlier, but I wasn't sure how. I thought you'd be so mad you'd hate me."

"I am mad. But how can I hate you? You're my daughter. Your dad is right. We want what is best for you. We want you to be happy." My mom and dad look at each other, then at me. Something passes between them in that look. Some kind of silent communication married people share. And Hina's right: maybe I'll be able to share that sort of glance with my own husband one day, but on my terms.

My mom stands up from the table. "The food has gone cold now. Let me reheat it." She sighs. "I guess you are your father's daughter—always wanting to see new things."

THE MORNING LIGHT STREAMS into the kitchen. I don't think any one of us slept. It's clear in our bleary eyes and sluggish movements and hesitant syllables. All of yesterday's dishes are still in the sink.

"Maya, you left food on that plate. You have to rinse it properly before putting it in the dishwasher," my mom reminds me.

After Hina left, my parents didn't say another word to me about NYU. They didn't say another word to me, period. Mostly they were huddled in their room, presumably talking about me, but there weren't any raised voices, so I took that as a hopeful sign.

"Sorry, Mom." I'm not going to argue that our new dishwasher is connected to the garbage disposal so we don't have to be all old school about loading the dishes.

There were little cracks in the parental college resolve last night and I know what Hina would advise, so I try to channel her patience and understanding of my parents' anxieties.

My dad is at the table drinking chai. Out of the corner of my eye, I spy my parents steal another one of those silent, meaningful looks at each other. My dad gives my mom a wan smile.

"If you're going to be on your own, you can't eat off dirty plates. God help you." My mom shakes her head.

"On my own? You mean—" I turn to look at my mom who just shrugs. "Dad? Does that . . . I can go . . . to NYU?"

My dad nods once.

I'll remember this nod forever.

I turn from the sink, wipe my hands on my jeans, and wrap my arms around his neck and whisper a thank-you. I look at my feet. They are still on the floor. I don't know how this is possible.

My dad strokes my hair. It's been a long time since I've allowed that to happen. It grounds me. I am here; this is happening.

I walk back to the sink to hug my mom.

My dad clears his throat. "Your mom is right. Just because you're going to be far away doesn't mean you can eat off filthy dishes and what not."

I have a feeling we are not talking about clean dishes anymore, but I add extra dish soap to the sponge to get every speck of food off the plates, just in case. I nod and let my dad continue.

"When you're in the dorm, you will treat it just like you are in this house. All the same rules apply. Do you understand?"

"Yes, Dad." I smile, nod, and continue loading the dishes.

"That means you are going there to study, and that's it."

"We want you to make friends, too," my mom adds. "Nice ones. Girls. And maybe you can join the Muslim Students Association. You know, Yasmeen told me all about the one at her college. She organized their Eid party. It sounds perfect for you. You could film all the events."

I bite my tongue. Literally, I bite down on the tip of my tongue to stop the words that are about to roll off it. My muscles tense, but I keep a smile on my face. "That's a great idea, Mom."

My mom turns to my dad and nods, clearly pleased with herself.

"Maya, your mom and I are giving you permission to go to NYU, but don't think this means you can go behind our backs again. No more surprises." My dad pauses and gives my mom that silent look again that tells her to continue while he leaves the kitchen. Just before he walks out, he kisses me on the top of the head. Approval.

"You understand what your dad is saying, right? You're growing up. You need to be careful, especially when you're on your own. Especially with . . . boys. You see what I'm saying?"

"Yes, Mom. I promise. I'll focus on my studies. No surprises. I'll make you proud."

I don't know what else to say because of course I'm going to go out, and I hope there will be boys or a boy at least. Maybe even one here. But my assurances appease my mom, even if they feel false to me. I will study. I do hope I make them proud. But this is my first taste of adventure, and as Kareem might say, I'm going to carpe the hell out of every diem. Maya Aziz, beyond Batavia. I can't wait to tell Kareem I did it. And Phil. I want to tell him, too.

But I'll think about that awkwardness later. For now, I want to revel in the happiness that fizzes inside me. New York. New life. My parents' change of heart has to be a sign of good things to come—maybe Phil's not in my future, but my other dreams can be. They already are.

I tell my mom I can finish up in the kitchen. But she doesn't move. When I turn to look at her, she's gazing at me with tears welling in her eyes.

"Mom, what's wrong?"

"Nothing, *beta*. You're growing up. Hina was right. You are a wonderful young woman. May God grant you a long life and every happiness."

I step over to her and hug her, my soapy hands dripping on the floor.

She steps back. "I have to take the *nazar* off you."

"Mom, it's okay. No one gave me the evil eye. I'm good." My whole life, any time I had any sort of school achievement, or even when I get what my mom refers to as "compliments of envy," or especially when I would suddenly get sick, my mom would take the *nazar* off. Sometimes preemptively.

Don't fight her on her superstitions, I say to myself. WWHD? What would Hina do? Hina would quietly give my mom this little victory to assuage her concerns. I walk over to the fridge, take out an egg, and hand it to my mom.

She carefully takes it in her right hand and sweeps it over my head while she recites a quiet prayer asking God to remove the evil eye and keep me under his protection. The whole ritual takes barely takes two minutes, and it gives her peace of mind.

She smiles and hands me the egg. "Now go put it outside in the pot with the jasmine plant. I'll bury it later. Be careful—"

"I got it, Mom. Don't worry."

My mom goes to join my dad in the living room.

I start for the back door, but I lose my footing and slip on the sudsy water I dripped all over the floor when I hugged my mom. I throw my arms out to balance myself so I don't fall on my ass. I'm impressed with my catlike recovery, but sticky egg white and yolk drip down my fingers because in my effort not to fall, I've crushed the egg in my hand. I can imagine my mom's freak-out if she'd witnessed this sacrilege, so I quickly wash off in the sink and sweep up any remaining eggshell and dump it into the sink. I turn the water on and run the garbage disposal. My mom got the calm that came with the ritual, so I'm not going to tell her about this. What she doesn't know can't hurt her.

Cautiously he slides out of his parking spot.

The moment before, just before. He panics.

She makes him hesitate.

A small, dark-haired girl holding her mother's hand, looking up at her, a smile like sunshine, her dress red as a poppy bursting against green grass.

Collateral damage.

Sweat drips off the hook of his nose.

He bites his cheek. Hard. Blood fills his mouth.

At least now, they will know his name.

His right foot bears down hard on the accelerator.

CHAPTER 12

Violet fills the ride to school with spring break tales of kissing Parisian boys and exploring the villages of the Côte d'Azur. I nibble on the rose-scented macarons she brought me from Paris. But for once, I share stories, too. Good ones. Great ones. Life-altering ones. The stuff origin stories are made of. I devour the last macaron as we turn down senior hall.

That's when I see Amber and Kelsey, two of Lisa's best friends, leaning against my locker, arms crossed in front of their chests. Scowling. They both wear their matching cinnamon-brown manes in perfect, shiny ponytails that would make my mom weep with joy. We've been in school together since sixth grade, and in that entire time, I've probably exchanged fifteen words with both of them combined. If that. You can usually find them huddled with Lisa every morning, laughing or gossiping until Lisa breaks away to walk to class with Phil. When they see me, their scowls only deepen; they both straighten up.

My laughter comes to an abrupt halt.

Amber steps forward with one hand on her jutting right hip as Violet and I approach my locker. She stares down at me. "You know what I think?" she begins.

"That your parents shouldn't have given you a stripper name?" Violet responds.

I stifle an anxious chuckle because Violet always has my back. But sometimes she escalates before I even know if the situation calls for escalation.

Amber's mouth opens to a perfect "O" of surprise.

I put my hand on Violet's elbow and pull her back a couple

inches. "What do you guys want?" I ask. I notice we are drawing the attention of a few people in the hall. Luckily it's still a bit early, so senior hall isn't at full capacity.

Amber clears her throat and tries again, face sour, jaw tight. "Maya, don't even think about going to prom with Phil."

I laugh out loud. I expected them to hurl home-wrecker insults at me, so this is actually a relief. "That's why you came over here. All shirty?"

"What's 'shirty'?" Kelsey asks, disgusted.

Violet speaks up before I can respond. "It's none of your damn business who Maya goes to prom with."

"Wait. Why are you even bringing this up? Isn't Phil taking Lisa to prom?" I ask. My heart starts beating faster.

Amber and Kelsey look at each other nervously. Amber shrugs and lowers her voice. "They broke up."

The news strikes me like an anvil. Truly, I'm not sure if I should be thrilled or ready myself for a shit storm. Maybe both. Violet doesn't immediately respond, either, so I know she's in at least as much shock as me.

Kelsey fills the silence. "Phil promised Lisa he wouldn't go to prom with anyone else. So Maya can't go with him." She pauses, straightens her shoulders, and adds, "We came to warn you."

My brain is still spinning. Violet steps into Kelsey's personal space; Kelsey stumbles back a step. Violet is at least a couple inches taller than Kelsey and far scarier.

Now everyone is watching. I feel like I've crossed into some surreal world that I can't wrap my mind around. But right now my only job is to make sure this absurd scene doesn't turn into some ridiculous faux girl-gang turf war, so I pull Violet away and step in front of her.

"I have no idea why you felt this strange compulsion to tell me this, but whatever, you did. Now can you get out of the way? I have to get to class."

"You can't go with him," Amber says. "Final word."

Violet's eyes blaze. "Leave Maya out of your psychodrama, freaks."

We watch them turn and walk away, vanishing around the corner.

Other students turn back to their lockers, and the hall fills again with post-vacation catch-up chatter.

I quickly scan the hall—no sign of either Phil or Lisa, thankfully.

Violet and I look at each other, eyes wide. I mouth the words, *Oh, my God.*

She gives me this huge grin and a classic eye twinkle. She leans in and whispers, "It's so on."

"BONJOUR. ÇA VA?" MADAME DuPont greets us at the door. Her lilting accent never fails to capture the music of the language.

"*Bonjour*, Madame," Violet and I reply. My own accent is always a little too chirpily American.

The rest of the students file in and take their seats. Madame DuPont walks to the front of the class. *"Cette semaine, j'ai une petite surprise pour vous: nous allons regarder un film,"* she says, taking a DVD off her desk and popping it in the player. Turning back to the class, she smiles and continues, *"Et il y aura un test jeudi."* The class groans. *"Je vous presente: Paris, Je T'aime."*

I check to make sure my phone is turned off. I hate when people forget to turn their phones off during the movies. Nothing pulls you out of your suspension of disbelief faster than a stupid ringtone.

I've missed a text. From Phil. Actually, three of them.

Phil: I'm sorry about Amber and Kelsey.

Phil: I should've told you.

Phil: Can we talk?

Is it possible to be happy and angry at the same time about the same thing?

I tap Violet on the shoulder and show her my screen, but before I can say anything, the teacher gives me the stink eye. "Mademoiselle Aziz, *s'il vous plaît*," she says in a clipped tone as she motions for me to put my phone away. Phil will have to wait. Good.

Madame DuPont turns off the lights. The movie begins. The soft bluish glow of the television soothes me. I've already seen the movie—it's an anthology, a little collection of vignettes about life in Paris, each taking place in a different quarter of the city. My favorite is the one set in the Fourteenth Arrondissement.

It's a short film that follows a middle-aged postal worker on her first trip to Paris. But the conceit of the film is that it feels like a documentary, even though it isn't. It makes the character's story so much more poignant. She narrates the whole piece like it's an essay for a French class. And what I really love about it is the mood. She just feels so alone, like she's lived her whole life in "quiet desperation" as Thoreau would say, instead of sucking the marrow out of life. And it should be super depressing. It is, kind of. But there's this little moment, where she feels joy and sadness at the same time, and what she realizes is that you can find life even when you think it eludes you—

"Lockdown."

It's the principal's voice, barking over the intercom.

"All students are to remain in their classes. Teachers, begin lockdown procedures. This is not a drill. The all clear will sound when lockdown is over."

Madame DuPont rises from her desk. She hurries to lock the classroom door so it can't be opened from the outside. We all straighten up from our comfortable movie-watching positions, looking around the room wild-eyed. I am among the "we," but I am also just me, detached. Everyone speaks at once. Or some of us. I am silent.

Madame DuPont doesn't immediately shush us. She runs her hand over her face, trying to conceal her worry as she stands at the door looking out the slim glass window. I sneak a peek around her. A couple security guards rush through the hallways, walkie-talkies in hand.

Madame DuPont turns off the DVD. The lights stay off.

"What's going on?" someone shouts.

"You know as much as I do." She switches to English, her voice calm and commanding. "You heard the principal. Now I need all of you to move your desks to the left. It's going to be close quarters for a while. I want to make sure that no one can see you from the window in the door."

Metal desk legs screech against the floor, students bump into one another, backpacks fall with the thud of heavy textbooks. Madame DuPont cuts copy paper in half lengthwise and proceeds to paper over the skinny glass window in the door. She leaves a small flap untaped so she can check out the window if necessary.

"Why are you doing that?" Brian yells from the back row. He's usually quiet in class, especially lately. I don't turn to look. To be honest, I've been completely avoiding looking in his direction since that weirdness at the bookstore.

"So no one can see in to shoot us, duh," Jessica yells at him from the front row.

"Ssshh," Madame DuPont says. "There's not going to be any shooting. It's a precaution. Now we're going to stay in here until we get the all clear. No one leaves and no one comes in, understand?"

We all nod.

"We don't have the facts, so let's not speculate. The best thing for us to do is stay calm. I'm going to turn the movie back on, and you'll have more information as soon as I will—when the principal announces it."

Madame DuPont hits play on the remote, and the movie resumes.

I ALMOST LOSE MYSELF in the dreamy soundtrack until the cacophony of discordant ringtones starts. All at once, everyone has their phones in their faces.

The uproar is loud and immediate.

"There's been a terrorist attack," one student yells out.

"It's in Springfield," adds another.

Madame DuPont turns to her computer. A handful of students gather around her desk, searching for more information. One student tries to get reception on the cableless television. The information and misinformation comes in fits and starts. A bomb exploded at the Federal Building in Springfield. Homeland Security has issued a red alert for the entire state of Illinois. There's a shooter. No, it's a suicide bomber. A plane is missing. There are dozens of victims. Wrong. Hundreds are dead. It's a truck bomb. It's poison gas. The building was leveled. The National Guard is being called up. The army has been deployed. The president has moved to an undisclosed location. All schools and government buildings are on lockdown. No one is allowed in or out. Parents are at the school doors demanding to get their kids. Police are stationed at the entrances of the high school.

There's a steady flow of news and innuendo, and it's hard to discern the truth.

I'm frozen. My fingers curl tightly around my phone.

The entire room is in chaos, but I see the action as if through the blades of a whirring fan. Disjointed and surreal. My stomach lurches.

A terrorist attack. Another tragedy. Is there no end? Is this how life will always be? I want to know more, but there is one piece of information I absolutely hope I don't hear. I whisper a prayer to the universe. "Please, please let everyone be okay. Please don't let it be a Muslim."

I know I'm not the only one hoping for this. I know millions of American Muslims—both religious and secular—are echoing these very same words at this very same moment. I know I'm not a very good Muslim, but I hope my prayers are heard. Prayers for the dead and wounded. Prayers for ourselves. Prayers for peace, hoping that no more lives are lost to hate.

I'm scared. I'm not just scared that somehow I'll be next; it's a quieter fear and more insidious. I'm scared of the next Muslim ban. I'm scared of my dad getting pulled into Secondary Security Screening at the airport for "random" questioning. I'm scared some of the hijabi girls I know will get their scarves pulled off while they're walking down a sidewalk—or worse. I'm scared of being the object of fear and loathing and suspicion again. Always.

I remember my parents telling me about how devastating 9/11 was, how those burning buildings and all the posters of missing people are seared in their memories forever. Hina thinks that was the tipping point, when the Islamophobia went mainstream and became fodder for campaign slogans. It left American Muslims to fight for their Americanness and their beliefs. I know what Hina says about all of it, about not giving in to fear. I'm trying to hold onto that.

Violet touches my shoulder. "Are you okay?"

I jerk upright. "Yeah. I . . . I'm worried. I can't believe—"

"I'm sure we're fine," she interrupts in a rush. "They're probably going crazy overboard with security. I doubt Batavia is high on the terrorist target list."

"There is Fermilab."

Violet stares at me, her eyes wide. "Oh. My. God. I didn't even think of that. But they don't store weapons. It's physics research."

"It's a government facility. I'm guessing terrorists don't sweat the details."

"I'm calling my dad," she says.

As I watch Violet dial, I'm painfully aware that I haven't thought of calling my own parents. I look at my phone and see several missed calls from all their numbers. Worst-case scenarios no doubt colonize my mom's head. I call the office. No answer. I call home. Mom picks up. She speaks before I can even say hello.

"We've been calling and calling you."

"Sorry, Mom. My phone was on silent. The school is on lockdown."

"Yes, *beta*, we know. We called the front office. They say they will probably let you out soon. They want to make sure that everything is okay before releasing students from school."

"Can you believe this? It's horrible. What are they saying on the news?"

"They still don't know what happened or who is responsible. But it seems that a suicide bomber blew himself up inside the Federal Building in Springfield. They don't know much more. It's terrible. They are still trying to get people out of the building."

"Do they know if the bomber is . . . if he was . . . ?" I don't want to say it out loud.

"No. Nothing, yet." My mom doesn't want to say it out loud, either. "Those poor, poor people who died. I'm going to go pray for them. Your dad is coming to get you."

"No. It's okay. He doesn't need to. They still haven't said when they're letting us out, and I can get a ride with Violet."

"Okay. Call us if you want. The school secretary said the lock-down is a precaution. Don't be scared."

"I'm not scared." I lie because my mother's concern annoys me. I know it shouldn't. She's a parent. She's *my* parent; worry and love are part of the package. But to me, it feels smothering.

"Okay. We'll see you soon, then? Let us know when they let you go."

"Okay. *Khudafis.*"

"*Khudafis.*"

Violet puts down her phone at the same time. "My dad says they evacuated all the buildings at Fermi. There's police at all the entrances, and apparently there is going to be the Army or the National Guard, too. He's at home already."

"My parents are home, too."

After a few more interminable minutes, there's a loud knock at the door. The room falls silent, and we all instinctively scoot as far from the door as possible. Madame DuPont walks to the door and asks who it is, carefully lifting a free corner of the paper taped over the slim window.

She opens the door to a security guard. He hands her a piece of paper and asks her to keep the door locked with everyone in the room until there is an announcement. The classroom is completely silent. Madame DuPont's black heels click against the floor as she walks to the front of the classroom, paper in hand.

"It looks like the information we were getting on the Internet was correct in part. There was a bombing at the Federal Building in Springfield. At this time, they think a suicide bomber drove a vehicle past the security gates and straight through the front doors of the building. There is no word on the number of people killed. They are still sorting through the rubble."

We stare at Madame DuPont. The class is completely quiet. A couple students cry. Someone finally asks, "Are we under attack?"

"That's all the information we have so far," Madame DuPont says.

"It's a Muslim terrorist," Brian yells. "They hate America."

I turn to look at Brian. He stares right back. His glare is icy and unnerving, and he mutters something under his breath.

"I need you all to stay calm," Madame DuPont snaps. "Like I said, it doesn't help to speculate."

I turn to face forward. Madame DuPont raises an eyebrow. "Understand? All of you? I'm sure the authorities will release information when they have it. Now as far as lockdown, there should be an announcement soon to dismiss everyone. They are going to let you out by class—the freshman will be first, the sophomores next. If you take a bus home, all the buses will be lined up at the front of the building, waiting for you. If you drive, please go to your cars and leave the back parking lot immediately. No loitering."

IT TAKES ALMOST THIRTY minutes to get to us. We all hurry to senior hall, rushing by the grim faces of the school staff that line the corridors. Police and school security roam the halls.

Senior hall hums, the air thick with anxiety. We gather up our books and follow the stream of seniors exiting the hallway. I see Lisa at Phil's locker, sobbing, her head buried in his chest. Phil has one arm against her upper back and his other stiff at his side. Our eyes meet. He holds my gaze.

A vise clamps its jaws around my heart. The scene is a perfect metaphor. Phil stands at the edge of the frame in the film of my life, slightly out of focus. There's a girl in his foreground, but it's not me. The distance between us ever widening.

I hook my arm through Violet's.

As we walk down the hall, I have the distinct sense that we're leaving a tiny, crumbling world behind us. We step outside into the brash light of another world I can't possibly understand.

The Special Agent in charge, the man in a dark blue windbreaker with FBI emblazoned along the sleeve and back of the jacket, steps up to the podium. Now I'll take any questions.

Q: Do you have any more information on the white truck that was at the scene before the bombing?

A: We have a partial on the license plate from a security camera across the street. It appears that the truck drove through the security gate at 13:10 hours and directly into the building before exploding.

Q: Can you confirm that an Egyptian passport was found at the scene?

A: Yes, it appears to belong to one Kamal Aziz.

Q: Is he a suspect?

A: He is currently under investigation as a person of interest. We are working to positively ID his body and determine if he was indeed the driver of the vehicle.

Q: Has any terrorist group taken credit for the bombing?

A: At this time, there are no claims of responsibility. We are still looking into any possible ties between Aziz and known terrorist organizations or splinter groups. We are also working to determine any accomplices or known associates who may still be at large. We urge the public to contact us at the investigation hotline with any relevant tips or information.

Finally, let me assure the public that we will leave no stone unturned in our search for those who committed this heinous act.

CHAPTER 13

Carnage leaps, bleeding, from the television screen. Over and over on the news, it's the same image: the massive neoclassical building that used to take up an entire city block. One-third of it has been sheared off by the strength of the bomb. It looks like a giant meteor crashed through the roof, obliterating stone into dust. Bent steel beams and the pulpy ends of impossibly twisted floors are all that remain.

I sit on the edge of the sofa, my fingers digging into the fabric. Waves of nausea prevent me from eating anything but saltines and ginger ale. Death is everywhere. And the pit in my stomach grows and grows.

The ten o'clock nightly news confirms my quiet worry. The FBI holds a press conference at the site, corroborating hearsay that a passport found at the crater belonged to Kamal Aziz, an Egyptian national. They believe he is the suicide bomber.

It's selfish and horrible, but in this terrible moment, all I want is to be a plain old American teenager. Who can simply mourn without fear. Who doesn't share last names with a suicide bomber. Who goes to dances and can talk to her parents about anything and can walk around without always being anxious. And who isn't a presumed terrorist first and an American second.

I SLEEP DEEPLY, WITHOUT dreams, but when I wake up, I feel like I haven't rested at all. There is a dull ache in the marrow of my bones.

I trudge down the stairs for breakfast, trying to stomp out the self-hate and the doubt. I do not want to go to school.

"I made pancakes," my mom says, lifting a lid from a plate on the table. "They're still warm." Her face shows her hope that food will snap me out my mood. But it's not a mood. It's my life.

"Oh. Uh . . . I'm not hungry," I say, trying to sound as diplomatic as possible.

"But you have to eat," she pleads.

She looks so crushed, I plop down in the chair and consent to eat one pancake.

"Are you okay, *beta*?" my mom asks, never able to provide silence when I need it.

"I'm fine, why?" Even my syllables sound worn out.

"Your face looks so . . . tired."

"I apologize for offending your aesthetic sensibilities. Maybe I should've put makeup on before coming down to breakfast."

"No reason to take it that way, Maya." My father's voice edges into impatience. "We're worried about you."

"Sorry I'm not Miss Mary Sunshine, but a so-called Muslim sociopath attacked us. Again. If these jerks hate America so much, why don't they stay in their own countries? He killed little kids." My voice breaks. "I don't understand that kind of hate."

"It's a terrible tragedy. It's a sin. You know the Quran says that whoever takes a life of an innocent, it's as if he has killed all of mankind—"

"And if anyone saves a life, it's as if he's saved all of mankind. I know. But how is that supposed to change anything? How are we supposed to change anything?" My hands shake.

My father picks up where my mother leaves off. "These terrorists are the antithesis of Islam. They're not Muslim. Violence has no place in religion, and the terrorists are responsible for their own crimes, not the religion and not us."

"Then why is there so much fighting in the Middle East, and why are so many suicide bombers Muslim?"

"Terrorism has no religion. Think about Dylann Roof and that church in Charleston or the attack at the Sikh *gurdwara* in Wisconsin. Terrorists have their own ideology. Who knows what hatred compels them? They're desperate and unthinking and ignorant followers—"

I interrupt my mother. "Too bad none of that matters. We all get painted like we're un-American and terrorist sympathizers, no matter how loudly we condemn terrorism and say it's un-Islamic. It's guilt by association."

"Yes, *beta*. But our friends, the community, they know we are good people." My father explains what I already know, but in my rage against the bomber, I can't hold onto the truth of what he says.

"There is going to be a prayer at the mosque tonight for the victims of the bombing. We'll also be doing a fund-raiser. We want you to come," my mom says. "We will leave at seven."

"You barely make me go to the mosque, except for religious holidays or weddings."

My father's face falls as he looks at my mom. "Maybe we should have been going more as a family and teaching you more."

"Oh, please. Don't get all regretful because of this. I can't deal with it." I hear my own voice oozing sarcasm and anger. Shame and guilt pummel me, but my anger is real, too. I rise from my seat. "I have to get ready. Violet's going to be here any second."

"Maya." The earlier tender tone in my mom's voice dissipates. "Enough of these sarcastic remarks. You can go to the mosque and pray for the poor people who lost their lives. You will go. That's final."

"Fine. I'll play the devout daughter for you."

"Maya," my father yells, but I ignore him. If I don't leave now,

I'll say things much worse than I already have. I take the stairs two at a time to get to my room.

My bedroom door bangs shut. I grab the lamp from my desk and pull back my arm, ready to slam it into my reflection in the mirror so they can both shatter into a million pieces.

I stop myself. Like everything else in my life right now, the act is pointless.

THE PARKING LOT PULSES with students who mill around, catching up. I'm sure they're talking about the terrorist. The Muslim terrorist.

As I step out of Violet's car, I see Phil. He's at his car, talking to his friend Tom—the one who's pushing for the perfect post–high school future at Eastern with Megan and Lisa—and a couple other teammates. Phil's in profile and half-hidden by one of his friends, but I see Tom laughing.

Then Tom sees me.

I wonder what it feels like to be so unaffected that you can laugh even when horrible things are happening. Tom points his chin in my direction and mutters to Phil, who turns his head and waves. I hold up my hand in half-hearted response. I don't know why I bother. My lips pull down at the corners. Those three texts I got in French class were the last I've heard from Phil.

Lisa and Megan bounce up to Phil and Tom. Lisa puts her arm through Phil's. Apparently, the rumors of their breakup were greatly exaggerated. I want to turn away. I should. Evidently, I'm a glutton for punishment.

"Let's go," Violet says to me as she frowns at Phil.

We move through the parking lot and begin walking up the ramp to the school doors. From the corner of my eye, I see Brian. He's jogging toward us. I get a queasy feeling in my stomach.

Instinctively, I speed up.

When he's within earshot, he yells, "Is that terrorist your uncle?"

He sounds gleeful and disgusted at the same time. There's a viscous, dreamlike quality to all of this. I turn to him. For a split second, I think maybe he didn't say what I thought he said. Maybe he's not talking to me. But who else could he be talking to? My mouth is wide open. My mind races to find a retort, but it's muddled. I've heard the words before. The taunts. I should know to expect them now. But the words still cut.

"Shut up, Brian," is all I manage to get out.

Brilliant. I wish I were better under fire with scalding barbs. Not my strong suit. There is so much more to say. So much more I want to scream. I want to get in his face, to tower over him. But I'm a foot too short for that.

"Go to hell, Brian," Violet yells. "You fucking jerk."

"Oooh, so touchy. Well, the terrorist has the same last name as Maya, doesn't he?"

"Yeah, and he's a sick asshole," Violet responds. "That's a thing *you* have in common."

He grins. I can see how our words are like fuel that incites him further. "Why don't you people leave America if you hate it so much?"

I wince, remembering the conversation I had with my parents. My own words spat back at me. "I was born here, you racist! And that guy was Egyptian. My family's Indian." My temples throb. Why am I even explaining? I shouldn't need to explain, and it shouldn't matter where my family is from. But I do. And it does.

A small crowd gathers around us, watching.

"Let's go, Maya. Ignore him." Violet takes my elbow. But the anger courses through me; my feet are cemented in place.

"Egyptian? Indian? What's the difference? You're both rag-heads." Spit comes out of Brian's mouth as he yells.

I want to slap him. I want him to hurt.

A smile spreads across his lips as he turns away.

For the first time, I'm aware of the tension in my body, a rubber band stretched to its limit. I let my shoulders relax from my ears. I blink back tears. I won't let myself cry. Not over this.

Violet moves in to hug me. "I'm so sorry," she breathes.

"Please, you don't need to be sorry."

"You're right. Enough of the Hallmark moment," she says, taking my elbow. She knows I want to move on. "Let's get to class. I doubt Brian will bother you again."

THE FIRST HALF OF the school day passes routinely. I don't see Brian anywhere, but clearly, word's gotten around. That's one of the things I hate most about a small high school. Everyone knows everything immediately. There's not even a semblance of ano-nymity. Or privacy.

At lunch, I want to grab a salad and keep my head down, but Phil walks up to me at the salad bar. It's the first time we've been in any sort of proximity since the painfully awkward crying moment in his car.

"I heard about what Brian said to you," he says, staring down at his tray. "I'm sorry. He's an ass. I'm going to talk to him. I should've said something to him before . . ." His voice trails off, like his mind has wandered away.

I give Phil a quizzical look. "Don't worry about it. It's no one else's fault. Besides, I'm over it. You kinda have to have a thick skin if you happen to be Muslim and live in America."

I want to talk to Phil. I want to snare his attention. But not for this. And I definitely don't want to open myself up to being hurt. Again.

"So . . . ummm . . . whatever happened with NYU?" he asks.

"I'm going. My parents gave in."

He finally looks up, his face bright. "That's amazing. Congratulations. I'm really happy for you."

I look into Phil's smiling eyes. For a second, my defenses come down. My heart leaps from my chest. I smile in thanks.

"Listen, Maya, I've been meaning to talk to you." Phil takes a hesitant half-step closer to me. "I'm sorry. Things got complicated."

"You mean with Lisa?" And the defenses are up again. Fully reinforced.

His mouth opens, but his words take their time coming out. "Well . . . no . . . I mean . . . I guess . . . but why—?"

"Maya."

I jump.

Dean Anderson has said my name. His voice is impossible to miss, the one no student ever wants to hear in the cafeteria, or anywhere else, really: grizzly, smoked too much over the years, always a few decibels louder than necessary.

Only this time, a police officer, who looks barely older than me, stands a couple feet behind him. The entire cafeteria tunes into the show. My chest tightens.

"Yes?" I ask and rub my forehead.

"I need to speak with you. Do you mind if we step outside?"

My gaze turns to Phil for a second, searching, but I'm not sure for what.

Dean Anderson adds, "Why don't you head to your table, Phil?"

Phil touches my arm. It's a small gesture, protective. But I shouldn't read into it. I know better now.

THE HALLWAY IS EMPTY. And silent. Except for my melon-colored Chuck Taylors, squeaking against the linoleum.

"Maya, this is Officer Jameson," Dean Anderson says.

Officer Jameson holds out his hand. "Nice to meet you, Maya." He takes off his glasses and tucks them in his shirt so I can see my distorted reflection in the mirrored lenses.

I bite my lip. I rub my clammy hands against my jeans. "You, too, Officer. What's going on?"

"Maya, there's been an incident at your parents' clinic," the dean begins. "They're okay. Neither was seriously hurt."

"Wh-a . . . wha-a-t happened?" My lip quivers, and my voice shakes.

Officer Jameson continues. "Someone threw a brick through the window."

I cup my hand to my mouth to hold in a scream.

"Your dad got a gash on the forehead," he continues in the same monotone. "A couple people in the waiting area have minor cuts from broken glass. Your mom was in a back exam room, so she's unharmed."

"My dad . . . did they catch who did it? I mean, why would . . ."

I look to Dean Anderson, who in turn looks back to Officer Jameson for a response. Dean Anderson can't even look me in the eye.

"It appears to be a hate crime," the officer says. "There was a note wrapped around the brick. Apparently, the bombing in Springfield angered the perpetrator. The brick through the window was a kind of warning."

"A warning? It's because our last name is the same as the terrorist's, isn't it?"

"We can't speculate right now," Officer Jameson explains.

Confusion, anger, and terror churn in my stomach. Thoughts fly through my brain at warp speed. First, Brian and the altercation this morning. And now this at my parents' office. What if they attack us at home? A message? What if this is only the first?

"Are we . . . I mean . . . are my parents going to be safe?"

"Maya, I assure you the Batavia police department is taking this very seriously. We will find the perpetrator," Officer Jameson says. I can see that he is trying to sound reassuring, but he might as well be telling me fairy godmothers are real, because nothing he says right now will make this okay.

"Can I go see my parents?"

"Of course," Dean Anderson says. "Officer Jameson will take you—"

Violet bursts out of the lunchroom doors and into the hall, silencing him. It probably took all her patience to wait this long. "What's going on?" she demands.

Dean Anderson frowns. "Young lady, I believe Officer Jameson and I were having a private discussion with Maya."

Violet stares at him like he's speaking an alien language, then turns to me.

"Someone threw a brick through my parents' office window." I repeat the officer's words, not really believing them. "My dad got cut and a couple patients, too. It's possibly revenge for the bombing."

"What? No way. That's horrible." Violet turns to Officer Jameson. "I assume this qualifies as a hate crime and that the police will be pursuing every lead with all their formidable resources?"

Officer Jameson's mouth betrays a slight smile. "Yes, miss. I was assuring your friend that once we catch the perpetrator, we will be throwing the book at him."

"Good. Maya, did you tell them about this morning?"

I shake my head, swallowing.

"This would be a good time, don't you think?" Violet says.

I don't want to have this discussion.

Dean Anderson raises an eyebrow at us. "What happened this morning?"

"They need to know," Violet presses me.

I hesitate, nervous what this conversation will lead to. I honestly can't deal with any more drama at school. "Brian Jennings . . ."

"Bullied her. Because she's Muslim. And there were witnesses."

"Why didn't you report this to me immediately?" Dean Anderson demands.

I don't know how to answer. I just want this interrogation to be over.

"Maya," Officer Jameson asks, "have there been any other incidents of this kind? Anything else off school property?"

"No. Nothing."

"I want to make it clear that you need to report any other events of this type to the school immediately. If you're threatened, and you're not at school, call 911." Officer Jameson reaches into his right front breast pocket and pulls out business cards. "You can also call me anytime, day or night. My cell phone number is on the card."

Violet eagerly takes his card. "Thank you, Officer Jameson. We will all rest easier knowing you're looking out for us." Her tone changes from terse and direct to something softer, and I look up to see that she's standing right in front of him, smiling. I almost laugh. Neither time nor circumstance will stop Violet's flirting. I resist the urge to cry or hug her or both.

Officer Jameson clears his throat and adjusts his collar. "Are you ready, Miss Aziz?"

Violet steps closer to me. "Dean Anderson, I'd like to go with Maya." She doesn't ask. It's not a matter of permission. She's going whether he approves or not.

After a moment, he nods. "Okay. You're responsible for any assignments you'll miss. And I'll call Brian in about this morning's incident. Gather your things. We'll wait here."

Violet takes my arm and whisks me down the hall. "I love that we're getting a police escort," she says in my ear.

"Yeah," I whisper and dissolve into tears.

Three men in dark suits knock on the door of a modest house in Dearborn, Michigan. Tarnished gold letters spell out AZIZ on the black mailbox.

It is dinnertime.

A woman in black pants and a loose-fitting white shirt answers the door and then calls for her husband. One of the men talks for a long time at incredibly slow speed. Though both the husband and wife speak English fluently, they look at the man as if he speaks in tongues.

They turn to each other briefly, silently.

Then the woman shrieks and runs wailing up the stairs into her bedroom. The husband steadies himself against the doorjamb before inviting the men to enter his home.

CHAPTER 14

Dozens of flashing lights blaze outside my parents' clinic. As Violet drives up, the world decelerates, and tiny details come into sharp focus. The surreal slowness of an empty swing moving back and forth, blades of grass seem to ripple individually, and brilliant sunlight sparkles off the jagged edges of what was once a plate-glass window that named my parents' practice: DR. AND DR. AZIZ, DDS.

I see my parents shaking hands with the mayor in the vestibule. Mayor Graham, Batavia's one local celebrity. If by "celebrity," you mean the guy who tosses candy from the back of a red convertible that leads Batavia's annual Flag Day parade. Truthfully, that parade is really popular. He knows what the job of small-town mayor is—he shows up at every football game and makes sure the garbage gets picked up and the streets get plowed when it snows. He's a good guy. My parents voted for him. Everyone did. He ran unopposed.

The action lurches back to full speed. My brain is speed-ramping life—from slow motion back to real time. This is not normal. None of this is normal.

I run from the car. I yank open the door, shove past the mayor, and hug my mom and dad at the same time. My whole body shakes. I step back. My dad brushes his index finger across my cheek. A tidy row of Steri-Strips marks a spot above his left eye. Brownish-red drops of blood stand out against the white of his lab coat.

"Dad, are you okay? I . . . I can't believe . . ."

"Maya, can't you see that Mayor Graham was so nice to stop

by," he says, ever aware of decorum. I'm relieved, honestly—relieved that he's himself and talking to me in the patient but admonishing tone people use to tell a five-year-old they've done something wrong. My mom, though, is pale and disheveled. She takes pride in her perfectly neat buns, but now strands of hair are carelessly tucked behind her ears, out of place. If I act according to Dad's wishes, maybe Mom will feel better, too.

"Hi, Mayor Graham," I say. "Thank you for checking in on my parents."

"No need to thank me, Maya," he says. He pauses, waiting until I return his gaze; maybe he wants to know that I'm reassured by his presence, that I know he takes this seriously. What he doesn't understand is that right now, nothing can reassure me.

He turns to my parents. "Asif, Sofia, I'll be in touch. You're in good hands with the Batavia PD." With that, he heads out. There are no cameras, no press. Nothing but policemen and an aide—I'm guessing? The aide leaves with him.

I might not feel calmed by the mayor's presence, but I can tell by the way my dad's shoulders have relaxed that the mayor's promises have eased at least a little of his worry. And for now, that's enough. I know I complained to Phil that Batavia is too provincial, but I think sometimes I take the positives—the people—for granted.

Violet bursts in and throws her arms around my mom. "Sofia, Asif, we were so scared. Asif, does your head hurt? When they find who did this, there will be a line of people who will want to kick his ass."

My father has always vaguely disapproved of Violet's casual way of calling him by his first name—not to mention her profanity—ever since we became friends. Today it brings a gentle smile to his face.

"I'm okay. Thank you, Violet. Only a cut."

"Thank you for bringing Maya here," my mom finally manages. Her words are slow, deliberate. Her voice is hoarse.

"Dad," I ask, "what exactly happened?"

"Your mom was in the back, and I was chatting with a couple patients in the waiting room, and a brick came flying through the window. Glass shattered everywhere. Patients started screaming. I felt a sharp pain, then felt blood on my forehead. At first we thought it was a bomb. I yelled at everyone to get out, and we ran out the back entrance to the parking lot. I called 911, and they told us to stay away from the building. The police came quickly with a special squad from the county in case it was an explosive. But when they went in, they saw it was a brick with a paper wrapped around it with rubber bands, not a bomb."

"What did it say?" I ask. My dad hesitates. He opens and closes his mouth, but no words come out.

"'You're dead—you fucking terrorists,'" my mom quotes. "And it had our home address written on the bottom." Her face is grim and her voice barely audible as she says what my dad won't. Or can't.

I cover my mouth with my hand. I've never heard my mom drop the F-bomb before. My stomach churns. I taste the bile rising in my throat.

My dad gently squeezes my mom's elbow. She looks away, not interested in reassurance or affection.

"We should stay somewhere else, in a hotel or with my sister," she says. "At least until they catch whoever did this. It's too dangerous to stay at home."

I shake my head instinctively. I get it. She's frightened. She's a mom worried for her kid's safety. But nowhere is safe. The logistics don't even work.

"But they might never catch the guy. And how am I supposed to go to school if we're at Hina's?" I'm trying to keep the panic out of my voice.

"Maya can stay with me," Violet offers. "I know my dad will be cool with it, and I drive her to school, anyway."

My mom shakes her head no.

Violet doesn't give up. "If you're worried, we can always ask the police to beef up the patrol around my house. And we have an alarm system since my dad is totally anxious about how quiet it is here."

"It will be safer for everyone if Maya stays with family."

"Will you please stop talking like I'm not here?" I demand. "I can decide for my—"

"No. No," my father interrupts. "No one is going anywhere. We're going to stay at home and go to work, and Maya will go to school like everything is normal."

"But it's not normal. Look at what happened today. After so many years in this town with no trouble. I'm taking Maya to Hina's. You can stay here if you want." My mother mutters the last words under her breath.

He takes her hand. "*Jaan*, you are right. It is not normal."

"It's a death threat!" My mom's voice turns from fearful to frantic as she begins arguing with my dad in Urdu.

I sigh. It was only a matter of time until they took to their personal language. Of course they do. It cloaks them in the feeling of home, but it leaves me on the outside looking in.

Violet and I walk out, leaving my parents to their quarrel. They don't even notice I'm gone. When I turn back to look at them through the glass door, I see my mom gesticulating wildly. My dad catches my eye and then nods at my mom to stop. They walk out to join us.

The chief of police approaches. He walks with purpose. Wide, confident steps. Eyes forward, shoulders back. I haven't done anything, but I still feel like I'm about to get busted. The fact that he carries a gun seems utterly redundant.

He stretches out his hand and removes his silver-rimmed glasses with the other. "Miss Aziz, I'm Chief Wickham. Batavia PD." He remembers to add a smile when he shakes my hand, like someone told him he's less intimidating that way.

"Hi. Officer . . . uh . . . Chief . . . Sir—"

"Officer Jameson tells me you reported trouble at school. A student named Brian Jennings harassed you?"

Crap. I did not want to bring up the Brian incident. Not now. Especially not with my mom in emotional overload. I catch Violet's eye. She gives me a sympathetic grin.

My parents take positions flanking me. They heard it all.

"What happened at school? Did you get hurt?" My mom's distress kicks into hyperdrive. "See, I'm right; it's too dangerous here."

"Mom, relax," I say, despite knowing that relaxing is not in her wheelhouse. I turn to the police chief. "Name-calling, that's all. No big deal." This is another situation best handled by a little white lie about my feelings.

The chief nods. "Has anything like this happened before? With Brian or anyone else?"

I shake my head. There was that weird incident at the Idle Hour when Brian saw me with Phil, but I don't think being a jerk qualifies as a reportable offense.

The chief turns to my parents. Clearly, they've already been acquainted. "Dr. and Dr. Aziz, I'll send Officers Jameson and Olson home with your family." He gestures to the two cops standing at their squad car. "I'll put them on first watch at your place."

"Can they check around our house in . . . for . . . in case—?" My mother raises a trembling hand to her mouth.

"Of course. And when we're finished here, I will personally escort your husband home."

"I can drive Maya and Sofia, and they can wait with me in the car until the officers give us the all clear," Violet offers.

"Thank you, Violet," my dad says. His voice is level. It's his response to my mom's frenzy. The more she freaks out, the calmer he sounds.

My dad nods to the chief, who turns and walks with long strides to Officer Jameson's car. "Don't worry, *jaan*," he says to my mom.

She walks away from us without saying a word. She's in tears by the time she reaches Violet's car.

I PAUSE OUTSIDE OUR front door, bracing myself. My mom has already rushed into the house. Violet hugged me extra long before driving off. I take a deep breath. Then another. I look down our street. It's quiet. The late-afternoon sun dances off the tops of the maple trees that are planted all along the parkway.

In autumn, the street is ablaze in the reds and oranges of the leaves. When I was a kid, I would gather the brightest reds of the fallen leaves and tie them with scraps of ribbon into little bouquets for my mom. She would always feign surprise and delight and place the leaves in a vase in the middle of the table. Maybe the delight was genuine? All I know is how happy it made my seven-year-old self. I would add water to the vase to make the leaves last longer. Even knowing that no matter my efforts, the leaves would eventually dry and curl in on themselves.

I wave to Officer Jameson as he steps back in the car after taking a look-see around the property. He's here to protect us. I clench my jaw, realizing we might actually need the protection. The vandal has our address. He knows where we live. I don't know if my mom will ever sleep well again. I don't know if I'll ever sleep again, either.

I sigh.

Alone in the house with my mom is the last place I want to be. I fold my hands across my body, grip my twisting stomach, and scan my memory for a moment of reprieve. My mind's eye comes to rest on Phil and us floating together in the pond under the warm sun and the delicious graze of his fingertips on my skin as he helped me relax in the water.

Inside the house, my mom stands at the kitchen counter. She winces while she stirs her tea, as if holding the spoon pains her. I shrink into myself. In a single afternoon my mom has aged. She seems grayer, her movements older and labored.

She opens her mouth. It takes a few seconds for the words to come out. "It's too dangerous—"

"The police are outside. We're safe."

She talks past me. "It's too dangerous for you to be far away. You can't go to New York. You need to stay close to us. It's decided."

She betrays no emotion as she says this. She turns her back to me and continues stirring her tea.

Tears flow down my face. My mom sits down at the kitchen table and takes a sip from her cup. I'm a ghost in the room.

I run up the stairs and slam my bedroom door. I don't even make it to my bed. Instead I collapse to the floor, sobbing for Phil, for New York, for the dead, for everything we've lost. And for what I've learned: that hope is just a million shards of broken glass.

At a church a few blocks from the site of the bombing, the residents of Springfield create a makeshift memorial. Pictures of those lost, flowers, teddy bears, candles flickering in the quiet night. People stand, some huddled in small groups, others alone, softly crying.

The mayor of Springfield, gray-faced and somber, speaks to the group from the church steps.

Springfield, Illinois, is a small city and a great one. As we mourn, America mourns with us. We will give aid and comfort to those who have been injured and to those who have lost loved ones in this tragedy. We will find our strength in our faith and in one another. We will emerge stronger. We will rebuild. We will dedicate ourselves to the unfinished work of those who have perished here. And through us, through our memories, their spirits will live.

He pauses, clears his throat. God bless Springfield. God bless Illinois. God bless America.

CHAPTER 15

I try to keep my head down at school, but the vandalism at my parents' office, combined with my friendly police escort, make me an attention magnet. And by attention, I mean openmouthed *you're a freak* stares or puppy-dog eyes and shoulder pats. I want to disappear, blend into the throng of students scurrying to class. But you can't blend in when you're the only brown kid in a swell of white students.

I can't remember a single thing from any class. Except that Brian was absent. Suspended. Small blessings. The day ends with me at my locker, sighing heavily as I fill my backpack. When I stand, Phil is beside me. He leans forward, like he wants to whisper something, but my withering glance holds him back. Apparently I have the power to freeze-frame people midstep.

A single kind word from him and I will fall utterly to pieces. What I want is for him to flash me a brilliant smile, to take determined strides toward me and kiss me in front of everyone. What I really want is to do that myself. I block the scene so when we kiss, faces around us blur, a filtered lens diffuses the light, and a smoke machine blows gauzy wisps of gray across the floor. And when we stop, I tell him my parents have changed their minds. I'm going to film school. I'm leaving for New York, and he's coming with me. Then he draws me close, and we kiss again as "The End" flashes across the screen.

In real life, he turns and walks away.

VIOLET AGREES TO JOIN me at my parents' clinic so I can document the aftermath of the crime. Filming calms me. I said before that my camera is my shield, but when I'm hiding behind it, I'm also in control.

There are a couple police cars in front of the office along with a brown van with white letters reading GLASS DOCTOR parked at the curb. The large plywood board that last night covered the broken window now leans against the brick wall.

I hand Violet my mini-cam. "I'm going to take my good camera. Maybe you can help me get a few establishing shots?"

Violet nods. I wait for her usual comment, something pithy or flirtatious. I mean, the handsome, gum-chewing, Captain America-esque Officer Jameson is just feet away. But nothing. A nod is all I get, then a slight smile that doesn't find its way to her eyes. Violet rubs my shoulder, then turns, camera in hand, to quietly honor my request.

I raise my good camera to my eye. From a distance, I film my father speaking to the window repairman. He slumps as he talks. The gray hair at his temples seems more prominent.

I approach the broken window, slowly panning across the yellow crime-scene tape that stretches the length of the one-story building. Through the window frame I focus on the slivers of sparkly glass that escaped the vacuum.

My father looks up, sees me with my camera, and narrows his wary eyes. Then he just nods. Probably too tired to argue with me about this not being the right time or place to film. But what he doesn't get is that it is exactly the right time to film.

I walk into the waiting room, camera on. I greet Rose, the receptionist who's been with my parents' practice since the beginning. She looks up and smiles into my lens and then pretends to engross herself in her work. But what could she possibly be doing? My parents aren't seeing patients right now. They can't. The office is still closed. Maybe it's habit. After years of watching me film,

Rose is happy to play along, to star or cameo. I've promised her a shout-out if I ever win an Oscar.

I'm not even exactly sure what I want to do with the film. Right now, I'll take as much raw footage as possible. There's maybe a short doc in all of this, one I could even enter in a student film festival. Something positive has to come of this senselessness.

My mom walks into the waiting room with the same drawn face she's worn since yesterday. "Maya, why are you filming? We don't need memories of this . . ." She trails off; her voice has run out of batteries.

"Maybe the footage will be helpful for the insurance company?" It's a feeble excuse, but she nods, anyway, and then heads toward the back without another word. Maybe she's right. I don't need to document the last three days; I need to delete them from existence.

Outside, my dad, Violet, and three police officers surround the open window of Officer Jameson's squad car. The radio blasts. Violet gestures for me to hurry up and join them. A man's deep voice rings over the car's speakers.

"It's not him. It's not him," Violet repeats as I jog up to the car.

"It's not who?"

"They don't think the Aziz guy is the terrorist. It's not him."

I put my hand to my chest to catch my breath. I squeeze my eyes shut. My mind's camera rolls. The newscaster's words emerge from the radio in three dimensions, hanging in the air in block letters:

TRUCK RENTAL LINKED TO SUSPECT WITH POSSIBLE WHITE SUPREMACIST TIES . . .
AZIZ CLEARED . . .
CITIZENSHIP—HIS AMERICAN DREAM . . .
POLICE EXECUTE SEARCH WARRANTS

My mouth hangs open. I should be more relieved that a Muslim isn't responsible, but all I can think of is the carnage. Over a hundred people are dead, and there have been dozens of attacks on Muslims in retaliation for a crime no Muslim committed. My father and the police stand at grim-faced attention until the station breaks for commercial.

Officer Jameson turns down the dial. "Let's hope this curbs the threats from our neighborhood vandal. I'm going to check with the chief. I'm sure he'll want police detail to stick with your family at least another day."

My dad nods, his mind clearly elsewhere. "Thank you. If you'll excuse me, I need to tell my wife the news." He doesn't say a word to me. He hurries toward his office without glancing back.

VIOLET TAKES ME HOME. We raid the fridge. She grabs a couple leftover *samosas* and tosses them into the microwave. I pour us glasses of chilled mango juice.

"I wish I had vodka to spike those," Violet says.

I have to laugh. It feels good. "Yeah. That would go over big with the parentals."

"I'm trying to help you relax. You should be psyched it's not the Muslim guy. It's some asshole white supremacist dude. This will all blow over, and your parents will let you go to New York. We should be celebrating."

I shake my head. "That's now how it's going to work."

Violet's impish smile fades. "Why not?"

"Are you kidding? All this stuff happened when they only suspected it was a Muslim. Imagine if the next time it actually *is* a Muslim. Like that guy, someone who just happens to have my last name? Which is actually sort of common. My parents told me all these stories about things that happened after 9/11—people getting beat up or harassed because they were brown—some of them weren't even Muslims. This brick through the window? The Brian bullshit at school? I don't see how my mom is going to recover. Or my dad, by the looks of it." As I'm saying these words to Violet, I suddenly fear that my parents could take a lot more away from me than just NYU. They could take away Batavia. They could insist we move somewhere else and start over.

"Maybe your aunt can talk to your mom?" Violet says softly.

"My mom is still pissed at her for aiding and abetting on the whole applying-to-NYU thing." I slump back in my chair. "I can't ask Hina for anything else. Besides, she has her own life."

Violet takes a bite out of the *samosa* in front of her and gulps down her juice. "I know it's bleak, but don't give up. We'll find a way."

I'm silent. I give my head a little shake.

"What's stopping you?" she demands.

It's a simple question, but there is no simple answer. That infuriates me. I can't do whatever I want. I can't *be* whatever I want. No matter what, someone I love will get hurt.

WGN TV Chicago Local News

As cleanup crews continue the arduous process of sorting through the wreckage of the Federal Building here in downtown Springfield, this surprise from the FBI: Kamal Aziz, initial suspect in the terrorist attack appears to be a victim himself. Initial reports tied Mr. Aziz to a terrorist splinter group, but the FBI now is now calling it a simple case of mistaken identity.

In fact, Mr. Aziz was in the Federal Building that day to take part in a citizenship ceremony. He and fifty others were to take an oath to swear allegiance to the United States, to become our nation's newest citizens, when a suicide bomber cut that dream short. Mr. Aziz was a resident at Memorial Medical Center in Springfield. His parents, local store owners in Dearborn, Michigan, mourn him now as the hundred and twenty-fifth victim of the suicide attack.

CHAPTER 16

Life at home is hushed. My parents and I shuffle around like cordial strangers. Sometimes I can barely even muster cordial. Every time I look at them, all I see in their eyes is fear and worry about the state of their practice and the state of our lives. And they might not acknowledge it, but they must sense the resentment that comes off me in waves. It's like we're all unavoidable reminders to one another of what we've lost.

So I now have one mission in life: avoid my parents. That, and to not think of Phil. Or New York. Or all the opportunities I'm missing. My brain hurts from thinking about all the stuff I swear not to think about.

It's Saturday night. I'm not on the work schedule at the bookstore. Violet is going to a party at our friend Monica's house and wants me to come. She's texted me three times in the last hour. Just what I need, to go to some party and walk in on Phil and Lisa making out. Not that I even know Phil is even going to be there, but still, can't risk it. I can't keep ignoring her, so I text: **too tired** 😴 and turn off my phone.

With nothing to do and nowhere to go, I drive.

I drive through town and the houses that sprouted up overnight where once there were only cornfields. I drive down the dark, empty road behind the grocery store to where Batavia's mythic Lincoln Tree once stood. They chopped it down two decades ago when the tree got sick, but according to old Batavia lore, when the leaves were green and full, the elm looked exactly like Abraham Lincoln's profile. It faced in the direction of Bellevue, the sanitarium where Mary Todd Lincoln was forced to stay for a while in the 1870s. They say that when the summer breeze was just so, the branches of the elm would dip down and give the face the appearance of weeping.

I drive on, unable to weep anymore.

When I find myself at the Fabyan Forest Preserve, it feels almost like an accident. Almost. I kill the headlights and drive along the road that parallels the river. The car creeps along a half mile of crunchy gravel. The pond is the best place to wallow in my wretched state. Why not go to the place that will hurt the most to see how much I can stand? It's why I watch the Sullivan Ballou letter-to-his-wife scene in the Ken Burns doc *The Civil War* over and over—because I'm challenging my own heart to burst. He was a Union officer and probably the most romantic guy ever. That letter is so full of longing and gratitude for his wife being in his life. *My love for you is deathless*, he wrote. He died a week after writing it. She never received the letter.

Their tragedy kills me every single time. Sometimes I think that letter is why documentaries need to exist—to show us the almost unbearable truth about ourselves.

As I drive up to the entrance of the Japanese Garden, I see Phil's car parked in front of the NO TRESPASSING sign.

Damn it. My chest tightens. I clasp the steering wheel, afraid it will take flight. But I barely have time to panic. I do a quick U-turn and skid away. Gravel shoots up behind the car. He's seen me, I'm sure of it. Or heard me, at least. And no one else comes to this place.

The space in the car shrinks, closing in on me. Was Phil there with Lisa? No. No. No. Crap. I don't even try to stop myself from crying. I pound the side of my right fist into my thigh when I stop at the first light.

I've run out of road, so I drive home. The dark house is a relief.

A note on the foyer table in my mom's handwriting reads, *At the mosque. Then going to the Khans'*. Since the bombing last week, my parents have gone to prayers every day. I can understand. It gives them a sense of peace and purpose, a place to belong when no other place feels welcoming. But nothing at home has changed. We communicate mostly by notes now. I know they're scared. I'm scared, too. A part of my heart aches for them. But another part of my heart can't forgive them for reneging on their promise.

I walk into the kitchen and open the fridge. I linger long enough to hear my mother's voice in my head: "Shut the door, Maya; you are defrosting everything." She made *parathas* while I was at work. I slather butter on a *paratha* and throw it into the microwave for thirty seconds. Since I'm eating my feelings, though, buttery flat-bread is not enough. I open the freezer and grab a pint of mint chip ice cream, find a spoon, and head to my room.

In low light, I kick off my shoes and sit cross-legged in the middle of my bed. Giant spoonfuls of ice cream aren't enough, either.

I need a friendly voice. A person who understands without me having to explain. I need Kareem.

We haven't talked since the bombing. We've texted. I'm not sure if I should call. But my entire body pulls me to the phone. He always says I can call him whenever. Hope he means it.

I hold the phone to my ear while I put down my food and settle into my bed. I count the rings. Of course he's out; it's Saturday night. I should hang up. But caller ID.

I ready myself to leave a breezy message, but a breathless female voice answers in the middle of the fifth ring. "H-h-ello?"

"Uh, I think . . . sorry. I must have the wrong number?"

"Who are you looking for?"

"Kareem?"

"He stepped out for a second. He'll be right back."

"Oh, okay. Thanks," I say, trying to hide my embarrassment.

"I'll yell down the hall for him. Can I tell him who's calling?"

"Maya."

"The documentarian?"

"I guess . . . that's . . . me."

"Hang on." The woman pulls the phone away from her mouth, but I can still hear her yelling for Kareem. "Babe. Phone. It's Maya."

There's scuffling, and then Kareem's muffled voice says, "Give me five minutes. I'll be right behind you," and then I hear something like a kiss. Definitely a kiss. "Maya? What's up?" He sounds worried.

"Hey, thought I'd give you a ring, but I guess I caught you at a bad time." I bite my bottom lip. I want desperately to sound coolly detached but not like I'm trying too hard to sound coolly detached—basically Lauren Bacall in *To Have and Have Not* but less insolent and more Indian. (Another movie Hina made me watch.)

"No worries," he says. "Everything good with you?"

"Yeah. Sure. But I don't want to keep you from . . . from . . ." I'm fishing for the woman's name. Obviously.

"Suraya."

"I'm sorry. I didn't mean to interrupt—"

"Chill. It's fine. I've been meaning to call you, to see how things have been since the vandalism at your parents' clinic. How have they been holding up?"

"You should go. You don't want to keep Suraya waiting . . ." A whirling fireball grows in my chest. I have no right to feel this way, but I do.

"Maya, you sound kind of—"

"I'm surprised, that's all. I didn't expect someone else to answer your phone."

"Suraya and I got back together last week."

"Back together?" I gulp.

"Remember, in your backyard, my brokenhearted sob story? Suraya was the breaker."

"And now you're back with her?" I try and sound upbeat and friendly instead of simply confused. I'm fairly certain I'm completely failing.

"Funny how life works, right? The timing wasn't right then . . . we both had growing up to do. Anyway, we had dinner a couple weeks ago, and the whole meal neither of us could stop smiling. We decided to give it—us—another try."

Kareem's happiness sings in my ear. I can't begrudge him. After all, I'm the one who threw us away. I knew then as I do now that we weren't meant to be together. So it makes no sense that I'm hurting the way I am.

"It may seem weird, but Suraya and I—she gets me, you know? We can be together, and it's easy. I don't have to pretend to be something I'm not." He pauses. "You know how when life gets too complicated, it's easy to overthink everything? Intellectualize too much?"

"Please, I'm the president of Overthinkers Anonymous. I'm their patron saint."

Kareem laughs. "Sometimes you've got to be less cerebral and more intuitive. So I figured I'd take a chance, trust my heart, and be less concerned about all the made-up things that were supposedly getting in our way. Cue segue. So how are things with Phil?"

"Don't ask. I think he's back together with Lisa."

"You *think*?"

"Maybe? I'm not sure. Things have been so confusing and messed up the last couple weeks . . ."

"Well, the bright lights of New York City are right around the corner. Plenty of new adventures to be had."

"New York's not meant to be, either." My throat tightens. I can no longer even feign being cool and detached. I am the total opposite.

"Why? What happened?"

"My mom totally freaked, and now my parents refuse to let me go to NYU. I'm going to live with my aunt and go to school in Chicago. I can't even live on campus. It's that or community college and live at home."

He takes a breath. "Holy shit. That sucks. I'm so sorry, Maya. They're still being that way even though they discovered the bomber wasn't a Muslim?"

"Believe it or not, my mom actually argued that the fact that the terrorist wasn't Muslim added to her point. It's too dangerous even when the guy isn't Muslim, so imagine if the next terrorist is."

"And your dad's going along with it? It makes no sense."

"I know. He's totally on her side. No matter how irrational she acts. Obviously, he agrees with her, but he won't say it out loud, just defers to her instead. And without them paying for it, there's no way I can afford NYU."

"Has your aunt tried talking to them?"

"Hina is the one who came up with the idea of me living with her so I can have a semblance of freedom and not have to live with my parents."

"Maya, listen." His voice grows urgent. "Whatever happens, you can't stop making your movies. Promise you won't give up. You've got to fight for what you want."

My eyes begin to sting. "But I'm tired of fighting. I tried to step out of the stereotypical good Indian girl mold—with Phil, my movies, New York—and now my whole life is a dumpster fire. So what's the point?"

I hear Suraya call Kareem.

"Sorry," he mutters. "I gotta run. Listen, if you give up now, you'll regret it later. That I know."

"I'll take it under advisement."

"It'll work out. I know it. I'm here if you need me. Listen to your gut. Okay?"

"Got it. See ya."

If I listen to my gut, I'd be throwing up right now.

Good Morning Springfield TV 7

The authorities have traced the partial license plate and VIN from the vehicle that exploded to a rental agency on the Illinois-Indiana border.

The truck was rented to an Ethan Branson—a nineteen-year-old Indiana resident with apparent ties to white supremacist organizations. Mr. Branson frequently commented on right-wing extremist websites with strong antigovernment rhetoric and attended meetings of the Midwestern Knights of Brotherhood in Indiana.

Materials found in his motel room here in Springfield indicate he acted alone.

CHAPTER 17

Every spring, a few weeks before graduation, the senior class heads to the American Adventure amusement park. I'm not exactly a fan of vertigo-inducing roller coasters, but at least it's a break from the stone-cold, silent tomb of my house. Not to mention a distraction from the incessant prom talk, the bitter icing on the rotten cake of senior year.

It's also the perfect day to film. I'm making Violet a movie of senior year as a grad gift, so documenting our last senior outing together is absolutely necessary.

I take my camera in hand.

Roll sound.

Roll camera.

And action.

Technically, I have no assistant director and no boom operator. And in fact, no boom. But in my head, I like to sound authentic.

"Let's go," Violet urges as she slams her locker shut. When she sees me filming, she immediately flashes a brilliant smile. Violet is always camera ready. "I don't want to get stuck in the front of the bus with the chaperones."

I play my part from behind the lens. "You are way too peppy for this early in the morning."

"We're out of school. The weather's gorgeous, and we get to hang outside going on rides all day."

She's saying what the entire class thinks. Everyone except for me because, number one, I don't want to puke. Number two, I want to avoid Phil.

Violet practically breaks into a run once we're outside. I scurry to keep up, but worry these shots will look like I filmed during an earthquake. "Look, there's three buses, and Phil's probably going to ride with the jocks, so it should be easy to avoid him, and once we get there, we'll steer clear." She knows exactly what's on my mind.

She turns to face my lens, eyes sparkling. "The entire glorious purpose of today is to gorge ourselves on fried foods and experience vomit-worthy g-forces. There's Monica and the boys." She waves and walks in their direction, forcing me to follow.

I stand a little apart so I can capture a medium shot. I'm on the perimeter, the observer as always. Sometimes it feels a little lonely, but at least it's on my terms. Violet hugs Monica, who lets go of Justin's hand to return the embrace like it's been months since they've seen each other and not just yesterday.

Violet turns to fist-bump Justin while Monica adjusts her skirt—there are probably only a handful of girls in our class who would dare to wear something so short. And yes, Violet is another one of them. Mike steps forward, arms slightly extended to try and hug Violet, but she is clearly going for the fist-bump and ends up punching him in the shoulder. Awkward. But oh, so perfect on film.

Mike blushes. Poor Mike. He's my male blushing counterpart. He shakes his head when Violet and Monica turn to head for the bus. I can tell Justin is trying to stifle his laughter. He pats Mike on the back and leads him away.

I pan the camera from left to right, capturing the entire class as they mill around and start to pile into the buses. There's this iconic quality to this scene, like it could've been the same thirty years ago. Kids in the school parking lot, American flag fluttering atop a metal pole, cornfields in the distance, blue skies. Everything is such a mess, and I can't wait to graduate, but I still feel this twinge of nostalgia for my time at Batavia High School as it draws to a close.

Brian appears in my frame. He's staring at me from across the parking lot.

I stop short and drop my camera to my side. I guess his suspension is over. For a second, I don't recognize him. He's shaved his head. He's wearing fatigues and an army green T-shirt. There're dog tags around his neck. Josh and Brandon, his constant companions from the football team, are standing next to him, oblivious. Laughing and talking, like everything is totally normal. It's not cold out, but I rub my upper arms. He doesn't drop his eyes from mine. Finally I look away and head toward Violet and Monica, who are happily chatting by the third bus.

Violet and Monica smile as I approach, but when they see my face, they know something is wrong. Violet shrugs her shoulders up in a question. I whisper, "Brian," and then subtly point in his direction, making sure he can't see me.

Violet sneers. "Ignore him. He'll be on the bus with the other football players, anyway." Monica nods in agreement.

They're right. I take a breath and start filming again.

"I don't get it. Boys are always wondering why girls go to the bathroom in groups, and yet the entire football team travels in a pack—even off-season," Monica observes.

And Phil's the alpha.

I don't see Phil anywhere. When I was panning the crowd, I searched for his face. I don't say it, but I'm disappointed not to see him. Even after last night's drive-by fiasco, my crush still burns bright.

We pile into the third bus—Justin and Mike snagged seats early and are waving at us from the back. Violet grabs a window seat, and Monica scoots in next to her, across from Mike and

Justin. I slip into the seat in front of Monica and Violet, then get up on my knees and pivot around to film my establishing shots.

Students pair off and take their seats. Sun pours in the windows on the right side of the bus and casts splotches of light on people's hair and faces. Through my lens, for a moment, this worn-down old bus is beautiful. I zoom in on a couple whispering to each other. The boy tucks the girl's hair behind her ear and—

Phil steps into the shot. And he takes up my whole frame. "Mind if I take that seat?"

"You're not on the jock bus?" Monica pipes up from behind me. She asks what we're all thinking.

Phil shakes his head, just slightly, not taking his eyes from my lens.

I lower the camera and nod. While Phil eases into the spot next to me, I throw a quick, wide-eyed glance at Violet and Monica, clear my throat, and brush the hair out of my face. I'm not sure if I'm breathing, so I remind myself to do so. I can barely look him in the eye. "Hey."

"Hey," Phil says as he taps his thumb on his jeans to an imaginary rhythm.

I close my eyes. My brain is a tempest. I can't decipher a single coherent thought. It feels like forever since Phil and I have been so close. I've tried to forget how good he smells and how the curves of his biceps extend beyond the short sleeves of his shirt. I've tried to erase his simple, factual hotness. It's all been a failure. He places his left hand on the edge of the seat, an inch away from my knee. Heat radiates off him.

"Hey," I say for the second time and bring my hand to rest on my knee. The space between us grows painfully small, but it might as well be the Grand Canyon.

"Hey," Phil repeats and then laughs. "I guess we've covered the hellos."

"We're experts at establishing each other's presence." I bite my lower lip. Either Violet or Monica knees the back of my seat. My money's on Violet.

"Haven't talked in a while."

"No. Well, it's kinda been chaos on my end, what with the death threats and frantic mother."

"I'm so sorry about everything that's happened to you and your folks. It's unreal."

"My mom's still totally freaked."

"She's probably worried. It's parental."

"She has the overprotective, suffocating-mother skill down to a science."

Phil chuckles. I cast a sidelong glance at his face and the incredibly delicious dimple that every smile of his reveals. "You'll be out from under her grasp pretty soon."

"Not as far as I'd like."

"New York is pretty far."

"I won't be in New York."

Phil half-turns his torso toward me. "I thought they were cool with you going."

"Were. Emphasis on the past tense. When I said my mom lost it after the death threat? She totally tightened the screws on me. My parents won't let me go to NYU anymore because they're too scared something will happen to me out there."

"Maya, that sucks. I'm sorry. Is there anything—?"

"No. Trust me. Do you mind if we change the subject?" I'm sick of everyone apologizing and even more tired of trying to convince everyone that it's going to be okay. It's not going to be okay. But there's nothing anyone can do to make it—my life—better.

Phil has no immediate response. I stare out the window, twirling strands of hair around my finger. I'm sure he can hear my heart pounding in my chest.

"Um . . ." He drops his head and lowers his voice so I have to lean in to hear. "Can I ask you a question?"

"Please don't," is what I want to say. I'm content to simply sit next to him in silence, the air between us still crackling with possibility, but Phil is going to ask, and I know I have to answer.

"I was out at the pond Saturday night. When I was walking by the garden, I saw a car pull up on the gravel. Was that you?" Phil turns to look at me. His eyes are so soft it kills me.

Our faces are close, near enough that the soft exhalations of his breath caress my skin. I can end this conversation if I can muster the courage to arc my body into his, bring my lips to his mouth, let our bodies align while the rest of the world falls away.

But if that girl exists inside me, I fail to coax her out from hiding. "It was. Sorry."

"Don't be sorry," Phil whispers in my ear. "Why'd you tear out of there? You saw my car, right?"

"I didn't want to disturb you. I know it's your spot. I should never . . . I'm sorry. I was presumptuous." I long for grace under pressure, but I simply can't conjure it.

"It's fine," Phil says in a voice so gentle and kind I might cry. The tips of his fingers graze my jeans, searing imaginary marks in my skin. "I took you there because I wanted to show it to you. Besides, I don't own it or anything."

"You're kind of squatting, though."

Phil grins. "I'm so edgy. But didn't you want to . . . at least say hi?"

"I thought you might be there with someone else." My cheeks redden.

"Who?"

I keep my voice low. Phil's making me spell it out one painful, humiliating syllable at a time. "Lisa. I thought maybe you were there with her, and I didn't want to be in the way."

"I told you I've never taken her there. I've never taken anyone there but you."

The earth stops spinning. I raise my eyes to his. I shouldn't speak. If I don't speak, this moment will exist, preserved in the amber of my memory forever, exactly perfect.

I do speak, though, because when have I ever been silent? "Then why have you been avoiding me?"

"*I've* been avoiding *you*?" Phil looks at me like I'm speaking in tongues.

I nod.

"I tried talking to you. I wanted to. I thought maybe you didn't want to have anything to do with me after that crap with Lisa's friends. And last week when I was talking to you, the dean came in with that cop. I texted you and didn't hear back."

I take a long, slow breath. "I guess— I couldn't deal with the drama. And Lisa seemed happy, like you two were back together."

Phil looks into my eyes. I don't turn away. "I was trying to be a friend, and she took it the wrong way. Apparently subtlety is not my thing."

"So you're not . . . back . . . with—"

"No." Phil grazes my shoulder with his. I let my hand rest on his forearm.

The bus stops.

Phil slides out of his seat. "I'll talk to you later?"

I smile. It's my first truly spontaneous smile since the bombing. It feels good to know I can still smile like that.

True Crime TV Profile: American Terrorist

The authorities are still piecing together the scraps of what appears to be the tragic and broken life of America's homegrown suicide bomber, Ethan Branson. Here's what we do know about this deeply disturbed young man: The FBI raid on the motel room that Branson stayed in the night before the bombing yielded only a handful of items—a copy of Timothy McVeigh's letter to Fox News written in 2001 shortly before his execution, and a novel that is said to have inspired McVeigh's actions, The Turner Diaries. The Diaries describe a violent Aryan revolution in the United States that over-throws the government and seeks to take over the world.

The FBI also found an envelope placed squarely on the otherwise empty motel room desk. The standard inspections for trace elements of toxic substances came back negative, and the only finger-prints appear to be those of Branson. It was Branson's last letter to the world. Two brief sentences in his scratchy handwriting:

Tell my mother I died for my country. I did what I thought was best.—John Wilkes Booth

CHAPTER 18

Optimism is a funny thing. I swear I'm walking on clouds.

After lunch, I duck out of more roller coasters because I've had enough g-forces for one day, thank you very much. Also because all through lunch, Phil was smiling at me from across the food court and I was smiling back, and I'm secretly hoping that he ditches his friends to come find me. Of course, it's not so secret because Violet made sure to announce a loud, "See you, Maya! Have fun filming by yourself!" as she left the food court with Monica and the boys. Real subtle like.

I'm glad she did.

I'm still wearing my post–Phil conversation smile as I film the park before I head back to the deserted food court. There's a drinking fountain and bathrooms in a small courtyard surrounded by a hedgerow. When I walk out of the bathroom, I blink against the sun's brilliance, but I know I'm glowing from the inside. I turn my camera on again. Walking up the path, I film the light dancing on the brick wall outside of the bathrooms.

"What are you smiling at?" Brian snarls at me as I step into the front courtyard. The light falls from the bricks; it falls from everything.

I lower my camera, grasp it tightly in my right hand, keeping it running. "N-n-nothing. The light and . . ."

I look left and right. Josh and Brandon stand a few feet behind Brian, flanking him, effectively cutting off my only exit. If they weren't with Brian, I probably would've walked right by them. They both have these expressions that look more clueless than menacing. Sort of blank, I guess. They haven't joined Brian in his shaved-head-and-fatigues look. But clearly they're along for the ride.

I swallow and try not to let fear consume me. *Think. Be cool. Figure it out.* A hard pit forms in my stomach. I need to get out of here. "Are you guys having fun?" I try to make my voice sound confident, but it squeaks out of me. I'm buying time. Hoping someone passes by.

Brian looks at Josh and Brandon; they laugh. "Fun's about to start," he says.

He turns back to me. In that moment, I see what happened. Brian snapped after the bombing. It's more than the creepiness I felt when Phil and I ran into him at the bookstore. It's the eyes. I've never seen his eyes so cold and dead. His hands tremble, he's amped up, jittery.

I take a step toward my right, looking over their shoulders, past the entrance to the courtyard and the park beyond. I don't see anyone, but all I need to do is walk a few feet, and maybe I could make a run for it.

Brian steps in front of me, closer now, menacing. He cuts off my path. The world around me comes into deep focus. My heart pounds in my ears, and each hair on my arm rises in warning. Tiny leaves on the hedges ripple individually, distinctly in my peripheral vision. Beads of sweat form at Brian's hairline, and one trickles down the side of his face. I can hear the entire cycle of his breath—inhalation, exhalation.

His face tightens into a scowl. "Where do you think you're going?"

"I'm meeting back up with Violet and Monica and everyone. They should be in the food court any second," I lie, trying not to let my inner frenzy bleed into my voice. *Breathe*, I remind myself. *Talk your way out of it.* But my lips are frozen, and my body is leaden as if earth's gravity has tripled in the very spot I'm standing.

"Doubt it." Brandon speaks for the first time. "Justin and Monica are making out by the kiddie rides."

Brian's stare is unwavering. He chuckles. "You know, Maya, you really are a tremendous pain in the ass."

I hover between fear and rage. I clench my left hand in a fist; my right grips my camera even tighter. "Back off, Brian."

"Back off?" Brian and his friends laugh. "Pretty ballsy for someone who's cornered."

"Look." I take a tiny, hesitant step back as Brian moves closer to me. "I'm sorry you got suspended. I didn't ask for that—"

"And I didn't ask you to come to our country."

"But I was born here . . ." I let my voice fade. There is no point in responding or trying to be reasonable. It's safer if I keep my mouth shut. Every muscle in my body twitches. I'm afraid my knees will buckle.

"I don't give a fuck where you were born." Brian's face twists in anger. "My brother lost his leg in Iraq because of you . . . people."

I shake my head. I can see his pain. My breaths are short and fast. "I'm . . . sorry that happened to him," I whisper, and I am.

"Yeah, you'll be sorry." The veins in Brian's neck bulge. He steps closer to me, his beady eyes in my face. Then he seizes my right arm, hard.

"Ow!" I scream. "Let go of me!" I squirm, try to get out of his grasp. Fear turns to panic. He squeezes my upper arm tighter. His grip is a vise. My hands tingle, but I hold onto my camera like it's a lifeline.

"Come on, Brian. You said you wanted to scare her," Josh says. Brian doesn't turn his gaze from me. "Now you're hurting her."

I catch the shadow that passes over Josh's face. He's wavering. It gives me the tiniest speck of hope that this could still end here.

"That's the point. She has to pay," Brian spits back.

If Brian has doubts, his face doesn't betray them.

"This is bullshit. I'm outta here, man." Josh slinks out of the courtyard.

I turn to Brandon, wide-eyed, pleading. He lowers his head and hurries after his friend. I'm alone now.

"Brian, please. You don't want to do this." Hot tears splash down my cheeks. I want to scream, but I can't hear my voice anymore, and I have no idea if any sound escapes my mouth.

"Yes. I. Do. I want to hurt you."

I look beyond Brian—if I can break his grip, I can make a run for it. It's a few feet . . . if only . . . Brian yanks me closer to him. He grabs my face and squeezes my cheeks so I can't speak.

The ground pushes up against my feet, compelling me to move. I kick Brian in the shin.

"You bitch." He slaps me and throws me to the ground. I hear a crack as my left elbow slams into the pavement. I taste blood. Brian's handprint stings my skin. I try to push myself up. Brian stomps on my left thigh. I scream as the pain pierces to the bone. He clenches his right fist above me. I raise an arm to shield myself.

I'm frozen—until Brian stumbles forward, pushed from behind. Phil.

When Brian turns around, Phil punches him in the stomach. Brian clutches his front with one hand and swings wildly at Phil with his other. Phil strikes Brian's face. Blood spurts from Brian's nose and mouth as he falls backward to the ground, groaning.

Phil looms over him. "I should've done this a long time ago," he says, raising his right fist to punch Brian again.

"Stop," I yell.

Phil eases himself back, breathing hard, his eyes fixed on Brian—who covers his face with his hands, blood dripping between his fingers.

Finally Phil turns to me. His jaw slackens. The rage in his eyes is replaced with worry. I'm still on the ground, clutching my knees and sobbing. He kneels, wraps his arms around me, and speaks softly. "Maya, are you okay? Are you hurt?"

"Uhh . . . my arm . . . how did . . . where did you come from?"

Holding me to his chest, he strokes my hair and kisses the top of my head. I cry into his shirt; my entire body shakes. The frames in my mind fast-forward, rewind, fast-forward without pause, and it's all out of focus.

I'm not sure how much time passes. Seconds or minutes. When I finally look up, the courtyard is a jumble of people and voices. I see the dean and Ms. Jensen with Josh. Violet rushes into the courtyard with Mike and is followed by staff from the park. It's all spinning with me at the very center, trying to hold on.

Phil makes space for Violet, who crouches beside me, her eyes crinkled with concern.

"Can you help me get up?" I ask. "I want to go wash my face in the bathroom."

"Sure, honey."

Violet helps me stand up. I hold my left elbow close to my body, my right hand still fastened around the mini-camcorder. I limp over. My leg throbs. Every muscle coiled, wound too tight.

In the bathroom, I clutch the edge of the sink, trying to balance myself. Violet places a comforting hand on my upper back. "Try splashing cold water on your face. That might help."

I hand Violet my camera and do as she suggests, wincing as I move my left arm. I dry off and breathe deeply a few times. My fingers shake, but it's hard to believe that this is real.

"I caught part of it on camera," I say.

"What?"

"I mean . . . my camera was running the whole time. I'm not sure what the picture looks like, but I probably got the sound."

"At least you'll have evidence."

"For what?"

"If Brian lies. He assaulted you. You can press charges. And you know, with him maybe being involved in the incident at your parents' office and the whole hate-crime thing, he could be in serious trouble."

"I didn't . . . I hadn't thought of . . . I don't want to tell my parents."

"Maya, that's not an option," Violet says. "You're limping. Your left arm is swelling up—you need to go to the hospital. The dean's probably called your parents already."

In the distance, I hear sirens.

THE LITTLE COURTYARD BURSTS with people.

Just beyond the hedgerow, park security guards are talking to Dean Anderson. One of them barks at the buzzing crowd outside, "Make some room, people." A police car pulls up, trailed by two ambulances. Blue-and-red lights splash across the pavement.

God. One of those ambulances is for me.

Violet helps me hobble out to the center of the courtyard. I strain to look for Phil, but I don't see him in the crowd. Justin, Monica, and Mike rush up to us, full of questions. I look at Violet and slowly shake my head. She pulls our friends to the side and gives them the story so I don't have to. I watch the flurry from outside myself. I'm inside the plane of focus, sharp and defined and totally still. All around me, my friends, the cops, they're out of the plane, a blur, a fast-moving spiral. It's dizzying.

I see Phil. And everything stops.

He's talking to a policeman who is writing things down in a spiral notebook.

Two EMTs help Brian onto a stretcher. He's holding an ice pack to his nose. I know it's horrible, but I want him to be in pain. I want him to disappear off the face of the earth. When they move him away, I see splotches of blood on the ground.

Violet reappears at my side as the dean escorts an EMT over to us. "Maya, this is Rachel. She's going to examine your arm and leg and see if you have any other injuries, and the police will need to talk to you as well."

"That can wait till we get to the ER," Rachel says.

"The hospital? But . . . I . . . ." I whisper. I don't want to go to the hospital, but like everything else lately, it's out of my hands.

"I've notified your parents," Dean Anderson adds. "They'll meet us at Community General."

The dam bursts on my river of denial.

"Can I ride with her in the ambulance?" Violet asks.

"Fine with us," the EMT says and looks to the dean, who nods.

The EMT gestures for us to follow her. Violet takes my good elbow. I search for Phil's face again. Did I thank him? I have to thank him. I can't find him anywhere.

"Watch your head," Rachel says, as she helps me step into the back of the ambulance. Another EMT joins her. They put an ice pack on my swollen, bruised arm, take my blood pressure and heart rate, and examine my leg.

"Violet, where's Phil? Can you check?" I'm worried. Why has he disappeared?

"Back in a flash."

"Is he the young man who stepped in?" Rachel asks while scrutinizing my injuries.

"Yeah."

"Brave kid. He your boyfriend?"

I shake my head no.

The EMTs wrap up, ready to take me to the hospital against my wishes. Violet ducks back into the ambulance and sits down but doesn't look me in the eye.

"Did you find him?" I ask.

"Not exactly," Violet says in an uncharacteristic whisper.

"What do you mean?"

"He's with the police. They're charging him with assault."

The little boy with dark curls knows how to make himself invisible.

One rainy day, with his mother shut in her room, he occupies himself bouncing a ball against the living room wall. He hears his mother's rhythmic prayers from behind her closed door, and he loses himself in her voice and the soft thud of the rubber ball against the wall. Startled when he hears the front door slam, he misses the ball and watches it bounce in slow motion as it knocks down a small vase full of fake flowers that his mother keeps on the end table.

Too late to disappear.

Dammit. I've told you a million times not to play in the house. You're going to pay for that, boy, the man yells as he loosens his belt and wraps it a couple times around his hand to get a tight grip.

The mother runs out of her room, pleading.

The boy takes the first blow standing up and then falls to the ground, hoping playing dead will make the man stop.

But he forgets to cover his head, and the buckle strikes hair and skin and bone.

CHAPTER 19

"Maya, *beta*!" I hear my mother's voice before my parents even enter the curtained-off examination area. My father looks grim. My mother immediately bursts into tears upon seeing me. She clutches me in a death grip.

"Mom, I'm okay . . . but . . . you're hurting me," I say, trying to nudge her away.

I study my parents. They look beleaguered. It's like they've aged another decade since this morning. My mom's face is completely ashen. I have a strong urge to move and let her lie down in my place.

My doctor walks back in, saving me from a parental conversation that might be even more painful than my elbow. He details my various injuries: hairline fracture in my left elbow, a deep contusion in my thigh, and various other minor bruises and scrapes.

My mother rubs her temples, and while the doctor outlines what he expects to be a quick recovery process, Dean Anderson enters—along with one of the police officers that I saw talking to Phil. Chief Wickham from the Batavia PD follows. They shake hands with my dad and nod at my mother. We all stare at one another.

Chief Wickham disrupts the charged silence. "Maya, this is Officer Russell. He's with the county sheriff's office. He wants to ask you a few questions. The amusement park is in his jurisdiction, but he's letting me sit in because of the ongoing investigation with the incident at your parents' office. Are you up to it?"

I nod, my throat too dry to speak.

Officer Russell steps forward. He's shorter than Chief Wickham, more barrel-chested. When he smiles, it's natural. Friendly. Not like the chief, whose smile feels like he watched a YouTube tutorial on how to seem friendly. I answer Officer Russell's questions. The memory feels fuzzy, like I'm looking through a soft-focus filter, but I give him every detail I can remember about what Brian did.

But then Officer Russell starts asking me about Phil. When he arrived, what he said, how many times he hit Brian. Then he uses the word *assault*. And it's not Brian he's accusing.

"Phil didn't assault anyone. He prevented Brian from hurting me . . . more." I shouldn't have to say this. And it makes me feel sick that I have to.

"Unfortunately, Brian has a different story." Officer Russell looks at me. "He claims you two simply exchanged words and that you were injured in the scuffle with Phil. So we're looking at two possible assaults."

"He's lying." I want to scream, but my voice is a scratch.

"We'll sort it out, but for now it's your word and Phil's word against his."

"Wait. My camera. I almost forgot. I had it recording the whole time. There's probably no decent picture, but I'm sure I got audio."

Officer Russell nods. "That could help us get all of this straightened out."

"And my daughter's safety?" my mom asks. "When she goes to school? Who is going to be protecting her from this . . . this . . . ?"

"Both of the young men will be suspended from school and—"

"Both? Why is Phil suspended? That's not fair." I start rising out of my bed, but my father places a gentle hand on my shoulder.

"Fighting has consequences. It's school policy."

"But Phil didn't pick the fight—"

"Maya, let the dean decide what is or isn't fair," my father says.

I collapse back against the pillows.

"We'll take a look at any footage you might have caught, miss, and share it with the DA's office," Officer Russell says.

I motion at my mom, and she pulls the camera out of my bag and hands it over.

"The county will be working with Batavia on this, so I'll make sure it's returned to you, Maya," Chief Wickham promises.

The policemen leave, but Dean Anderson hesitates at the door. "I don't expect to see you at school tomorrow, either, Maya. Take as much time as you need. Stay at home and rest up. Get a little TLC from your parents. Dr. and Dr. Aziz, I know how frightening this must be for you. You have my assurances that we will do everything in our power to ensure that Maya is safe at school."

Tears well in my eyes. My head pounds. I barely hear the doctor give my parents my at-home care instructions—a sling, a prescription, and physical therapy starting next week.

BACK HOME, I HALF-HUG my mom and then shut my door. I pull down the blinds and draw the curtains. Using only my right hand, I brush, splash water on my face, and fumble-strip down to my underwear, leave my clothes in a pile on the floor, and climb into bed, cell phone in hand. I dial Phil's number. I don't want to text. I want to talk to him. I get his voicemail.

"Phil . . . it's me . . . Maya." My voice is raspy. "I wanted to make sure . . . are you . . . okay? I'm so sorry. I gave the police my camera . . . I got footage of Brian cornering me. It should help explain how you helped me. I don't know what else to say. Except . . . thanks."

I let my phone drop to the floor and curl up under the duvet on my bed.

It's warm outside, but I'm cold and numb. Even under the covers, I shiver. Sleep pulls at me. I'm fatigued to my bones, but I fight my heavy eyelids for one second more. Images from the day animate themselves, jumbling in my vision. The shrieks and sharp turns of a roller coaster. The slits of Brian's eyes as he glowers over me. Phil punching Brian. Bright red drops of Brian's blood falling to the pavement. The purple and black of my swelling arm. The barely there sensation of Phil's fingertips on my leg. The dimple in his smiling cheek. Phil holding me in his arms, stroking my hair.

"BETA, WAKE UP. YOU'RE dreaming."

My eyes flicker open to my mother's face leaning over the bed. The curtains are drawn, and light streams into my room.

"Wh—what happened?" To my ears, my voice sounds gravelly and low. I clear my throat.

"A nightmare? You were screaming," my mother says, her face as gray and voice as unnerved as it was last night. Maybe more. She hasn't slept at all. "Was it about that boy who did this to you?"

I blink the sleep out of my eyes and look at my mother. "N-n-o. It was . . . one of those *jinn* stories that I heard in India."

My mom nods, willing to accept the fib, if only to lessen her own worry.

"What time is it?" I rub my face with my palms, still groggy.

"It's almost twelve-thirty," my mom says, coming to stand at the foot of my bed.

"What? I've been asleep . . . since . . . how can I still be tired?"

"It's from the pain medication. Do your arm and leg hurt very much?" A fresh wave of panic crosses her face as she asks me.

"Not really," I lie again. "Where's Dad?"

"He went to the office on his own. The patient load isn't too big today."

"Mom, you could've gone."

"How can I leave you like this? Alone in the house?"

"I'm not a baby."

"You are still our daughter, and after yesterday . . . oh, my *beta*, if anything would have happened . . ."

She starts crying. Again. A part of me feels like I should console her, tell her it will be okay. That I'll be okay. But I'm not even sure I can convince myself of that right now. And honestly, I just want to be alone.

"Mom. Mom. I'm hungry. Can you make me something to eat, please?"

With the mention of food, my mom perks up. She hurries out and downstairs to the kitchen.

I ALMOST MANAGE TO get through the omelet she prepares without a word. Almost.

"Violet called this morning while you were asleep. She was so worried about you. She said she will check on you after school."

I nod, shoving the rest of the food into my mouth and dropping my fork on my plate. I wince with the pain. The medicine dulled the ache, but it's still there, and my elbow screams at me whenever I forget.

I'm not in a chatty mood. I'm not much in the mood for anything.

My mom doesn't get the hint. "I want to talk to you . . . Your father and I were discussing this last night, and we want to drive you to school and pick you up. We'll adjust our patient schedules so it won't be a problem, and you can study in the back office of the clinic until we finish for the day."

I shake my head. "I can't go to the clinic with you every day. I have work and—" I pause to catch my breath.

"You will have to quit your job."

"I'm not quitting anything."

"Don't be ridiculous. If you want to buy something, we can give you the money."

"That's not the point. I love working at the Idle Hour. Anna and Richard count on me. It's part of my life, and I won't let you take that away from me, too."

She steps toward me. "You talk like our home is a prison. Haven't we always let you have what you want?"

My mom's magical thinking allows her to believe that I have total autonomy over my life. My exasperation boils over. Everything in my life is a fight right now, and it's exhausting. My parents' fears shrink my universe to the four walls of this house. The world outside paints us all as terrorists. I'm blamed for events that have nothing to do with me. And all I want is to make movies and kiss a boy.

My mother sits down across the table. "Try to understand, *beta*. What happened to you yesterday was serious. God forbid, it could have been worse. And it's too dangerous for you to be alone. When your father comes home, we will discuss the plans for next year—"

"I thought everything was settled for Chicago and living with Hina." The option I protested vehemently against is now my only lifeline to freedom.

"Your father is thinking maybe we should reconsider . . . and have you stay at home."

I rise from my chair. "Stay at home? And go where? To community college?"

Before she can answer, I run to my room and slam the door. Fury twists me into knots. I press my fractured elbow, grimacing through the pain, then grip it harder still to see how much I can bear.

The phone rings. Moments later, my mom shuffles to my door. There's a quiet knock. Usually she barges in, but I know that in this instant, she doesn't dare. She's too afraid of setting me off. "Maya, open the door and talk to me like a normal person."

"I'm changing," I lie.

"Your dad called. I need to go in. Emergency tooth extraction. Will you be okay?"

"I can manage."

"If you need anything—"

"I'll call, and you'll rush right home."

My mom bites her tongue on the other side of the door. It's a sea change. An ominous one. I hear her deliberate and heavy steps as she walks away and down the stairs. There has to be a clever way to turn the tide, but to my besieged brain there's only one way out: the front door. I stare at the ceiling, my neurons on rapid fire.

Later, I text Violet telling her I need rest and will see her tomorrow. I call my dad's cell. I know my mom is with a patient, so this is my best shot. "Dad? Yeah, yeah. Everything's good. Listen, I'm going to spend the night at Violet's. It'll be fine. Yes. Her dad's there. I . . . I want to relax a little, to take my mind off things . . . and . . . I don't want to fight with you guys anymore. I'll call you tomorrow, okay? Thanks, Dad. *Khudafis*."

I slip the phone into my pocket. I smile, a plan taking seed.

Ethan was a quiet kid. You'd see him playing in the yard and so forth, usually alone. Always looked kinda . . . blank. Felt sorry for him with a dad like that. You'd hear him shouting at the boy and his mom. Stumbling from the car to the door, drunk. Never seen a man so full of hate.

One time, it was fall. I guess Ethan was late coming home for dinner, and the dad locked him out of the house. Kid couldn't have been more than eight, nine years old. He was crying and knocking at the door. The dad yelled at him to cut it out, that he needed to learn his lesson. Show some respect.

That boy just sat there. Probably a few hours. A neighbor brought him a blanket and a sandwich. And someone must've called the police because when a couple squad cars came to the house, the dad stormed out. Yelling at the police to get off his property. That they were trespassing. Screaming at the neighbors to mind their own damn business. Then he turned around and walked right up to his own son and slapped him so hard the boy fell over. When the police tried to subdue him, he took a swing at an officer. They had him handcuffed and in the back of a squad car before the boy was even up off the ground.

They moved away the next month.

CHAPTER 20

I duck out of the backyard and through the neighbor's lawn and onto the street, my elbow wrapped tight in a cloth bandage. My hair is tucked into a baseball cap; my old-school Wayfarers cover half my face. Resting my left hand on the handlebars, I grimace through the pain. Pedaling down Main Street, I figure I'm in the clear when I take the turn onto Old Route 72, heading straight to the Fabyan Forest Preserve. A few cars whiz by. I gulp the air as the breeze hits my face. Despite my loaded backpack, I'm light, free from gravity's anchor. I cycle faster into my freedom, tiny beads of sweat popping up on my upper lip and brow, first hot, then cooled by the wind. I try not to think about what will happen when my parents discover I'm gone.

My whole life is thinking. I don't want to think anymore. I push ahead, pedal harder. The wind blows off all my old, scorched feathers, and my new wings let me soar.

The NO TRESPASSING sign in front of the Japanese Garden eases me to a stop. I walk my bike around the skeletons of dead trees and desiccated vines onto the dirt path into the woods.

Coming up on the stone cottage, I inhale the mossy loaminess, and my muscles relax for the first time in weeks, maybe months. I approach the entrance slowly. The door creaks on its hinges, opening to a dishearteningly empty room. I came here to be alone, but was secretly hoping I wouldn't be.

It's early evening. The inside of the cottage is dusky as the fading light rests at the tops of the trees. I fling my backpack onto the La-Z-Boy and pull out its contents—a towel, my swimsuit, dry clothes, the sling for my stupid arm, a couple sandwiches, a book, charger, disposable contact lenses and saline, my glasses, a toothbrush, toothpaste, antibacterial gel, and my meds. But no camera. The police still have my mini-cam, and the other one adds too much weight.

Sweaty from the bike ride, I dare myself to a quick solo swim. My arm throbs as I undo the bandage on my elbow and struggle into my bikini. The woods are more menacing than I remember. Of course they are. I've never been here this late before. Or alone.

Tiny waves flutter over the surface of the pond. Phil's little blanket of beach awaits me. I leave my towel and sneakers on the sand and wade in up to my waist. Besides the slight stirring of the wind through the leaves, there are no sounds. I'm alone. Literally. Metaphorically. And in all the other ways I don't know quite how to name. I inch forward, urged on by the pond's lovely coolness against my bruised and tired skin and a curiosity to see how far I will let myself go. The water ripples in arcs around my body as I creep forward. Swimming isn't an option with an injured elbow, but I might be able to float with my left arm resting on my stomach. I shouldn't drown. I'm ninety percent sure the odds are in my favor.

With the water chest high, I push myself up and onto my back, my right arm bobbing at my side. Letting my neck relax, I open my eyes. I float in the delicious stillness of the world around me, briefly forgetting every moment that brought me to this one.

A branch cracks in the distance. I pull myself to standing. Goosebumps cool my skin. The encroaching gloam calls me to shore. As I rush back to the cottage, the towel pulled tight around me, an imagined series of newspaper headlines appear in the air in front of me, light bulbs flashing and popping like in a 1940s black-and-white crime scene, Humphrey Bogart smoking in the background.

I run into the cottage and shut the door. No lock. Dripping across the warped wooden slats, I search the small back utility room for something to jam against the door. The old boards that Phil apparently uses for firewood aren't long enough to wedge between the doorknob and the floor. I scan the room; my eyes fall on the recliner. It's the heaviest thing in the cottage. I put my shoulder to the footrest of the chair and heave, grunting as I push the chair toward the door. With only a few feet to go, I look up and pause.

Bathroom. Damn it.

I pull a few tissues out of my backpack and step outside. In a matter of minutes, it will be completely dark, and once I secure the chair against the door, I can't imagine walking back out to pee, and I'm not about to go the Laura Ingalls Wilder nighttime bedpan route. So I go around to the back of the cottage, though no one is there to spy on me. I pull down my bikini bottom and squat, forcing myself to sing, so I can relax enough to go. I allow myself a chuckle at this absurdity. Already missing the wonders of modern plumbing, I walk back to the cottage.

Before I lodge the chair against the door, I pull the lever at the side to set it at full recline. The chair will be my desk, lock, bed, and entertainment center for the night, so I want to make it as comfortable as faux cracked leather allows. Using only my good arm is awkward, but I stack firewood on the sills of the two windows that are missing their panes. With my rustic security system in place, I change out of my wet bikini, dry off, and pull on a T-shirt and yoga pants.

The cottage is dark, but I find my way to the flashlight Phil keeps on the mantle. I hunt for the lantern and matches I spotted in the back room. The lantern is actually battery operated. I'm going to alternate between the lantern and the flashlight to conserve power. I light the candles above the mantle. If Phil were here, flickering candles and dancing shadows might be romantic, but I struggle to picture this place as anything but menacing.

Though the evening is balmy, I shiver, overtaken by a slight chill. I throw on a hoodie over my tee and unroll the sleeping bag Phil keeps in the corner. I unleash dust and a mustiness scents the air, but my thread count options are limited, so I unzip the sleeping bag, spread it over the chair, and then inflate the camping pillow. Using the mirror from my half-empty compact, I remove my contacts and push my glasses onto my face. Stepping into the middle of the room and looking around, I'm pleased with my handiwork.

My arm stings, my shoulder aches, the bone bruise on my thigh is now an ugly purple-black, and I'm hungry. I take a painkiller with a tiny swig of water and scarf one of my peanut butter and jelly sandwiches while standing in front of the fireplace watching the candlelight flicker against the glass of the votive holders. I figure the candles have an hour or two of life left. Yawning, I head to the recliner, placing the lantern at my feet and pulling the sleeping bag around me.

Drawing my legs to my chest, I rest my chin on my knees and begin to cry. A montage flickers in the darkening room. Brian. Phil. The dream-crushing rules of my parents. Kids in senior hall, leaning together, whispering. The pitying stares. I take off my glasses, wipe my palms across my eyes, and let them close, grateful the painkillers will dull all the aches with sleep.

THE GOLDEN MORNING LIGHT enters the cottage through the crevices in the piles of wood I'd stacked on the window ledges. I rub my eyes and move my head from one shoulder to the other, stretching my stiff neck. The lantern faded out in the middle of the night. Using my right hand, I pivot the recliner away from the door in time for me to run out behind the cottage to pee. This time, I don't need to sing to distract myself, but I know an extended stay at the cottage will be impossible from the plumbing standpoint alone. I'm tempted to call home, but my phone is dead. Apparently chargers are useless without actual electricity.

For breakfast, I devour the other PB&J from my backpack along with a can of peaches from Phil's stash. I switch into shorts and a T-shirt and sit in the recliner, thinking. The good daughter in me knows I should head home. Maybe I still have a chance to slip back, unnoticed. But I don't want to.

Guilt digs its claws into me, but if I go home, confessing my lie before figuring out some astonishingly clever next steps, I'll be under total house arrest until I turn eighteen in June. And the great American emancipation of eighteen offers few alternatives for me. There's no way around it; I'm totally dependent on my parents for college tuition. Even if I work full-time all summer and with the money I've already saved, I won't have enough to live on in New York for three months, let alone pay for school. I can't go home. Not yet. Not without a plan. But right now, I need more supplies. Like food. Especially potato chips. Because nothing tastes better with stress than salt.

There's an old garage station and mini-mart a mile farther down Route 72. My parents never go there. It's 9:00 A.M. I'm too afraid of wiping out on my bike with the groceries. If I walk, I can be there and back in an hour, and then I can stay put in the cottage. Once my parents realize they've been duped, there will no doubt be an all-out search. They'll probably call the police. I fled yesterday because I didn't want to think anymore. In retrospect, further thought might've been helpful.

THE ONE-PUMP STATION FEELS ominous. It looks like the gas station in *The Birds*. I'm even eyeing the old man in the red plaid shirt at the counter with suspicion. If I see a canary in a cage, I'm running.

I scurry up and down the aisles, piling things into a red plastic basket. I dump my supplies onto the counter: travel-sized toothpaste, shampoo, soap, a big bag of salt-and-vinegar potato chips, a can of Coke, a liter of water, two Snickers bars, a loaf of bread, peanut butter, strawberry jam, Twinkies, gum, batteries, an apple, and a plastic rain poncho. The man slowly rings up each item on an antique cash register and then places it in a paper bag. I tap my foot impatiently while I peer out the plate-glass windows, scanning the sky for seagulls.

"Be careful, dear," the man says as I step out, the bells attached to the door jingling. I feel guilty for painting him with my paranoia.

With half a mile to the cottage, the skies open up. By the time I walk in the cottage door, water permeates my bones and a pain pierces my thigh. I heave my backpack onto the counter, unload it, and scarf down some food. The chips are mostly crushed, but the burn and tang of the salt and vinegar sates me as I gulp down the Coke. I inhale half the bag. My hunger allows me to temporarily forget that my left arm is on fire.

I find a shake-activated ice pack in Phil's first-aid kit and hold it against my left elbow. When Phil shared his desire to be an EMT, it seemed strange to me then that he would ever have to hide a part of himself. But we all have secrets, hopes that stay locked deep inside, trapped by our fears of the world's judgment.

The cold pack makes me shiver, and I realize I should have changed out of my wet clothes before eating. Slipping them off with one hand, I leave them to dry on the mantle.

Dressed only in my bra, underwear, and flip-flops, I step

outside to let the water wash away the dirt, pain, and bitter disappointment that courses through my body. I close my eyes to the sky; the rain falls on my face, each drop pushing the only possible answer to my question deeper into my skin, into my muscle memory, so my courage won't falter when I need it most. I have to face my demons, and I can't do that from a cabin hidden in the woods.

The rest of the afternoon unwinds in slow motion. I wrap myself in a towel and crawl onto the chair, draping the sleeping bag around me. The rain slows, and beads of water collect in the palms of green leaves in the trees, trailing to the edge of each leaf and plopping onto the roof. My heart beats in tempo. I close my eyes and drift off.

IT'S LATE AFTERNOON WHEN I wake; the sun emerges from the clouds, highlighting the tender greens all around the cottage. The shadows from the trees shift in the soft light, and the smell of wet earth infuses the air. Without my camera or a functioning phone, I look out the door, etching the scene in my mind. An impulse draws me to the pond. Not bothering to change into my swimsuit, I hurry along the path, hoping to edge out dusk.

Leaving my shoes on the sand, I creep into the pond up to my shoulders, my bra and underwear sticking to my goose-pimply body. The storm has churned up thick, dark water. Mud oozes between my toes, and I visualize a million leeches crawling up my legs and digging their suckers into my skin. I make a beeline for the shore. *Gross.* I brush away my illusory bloodsuckers.

I speed back to the cottage, resolving to face my parents. It's the only choice. But the horror movie suspense-buildup scene I've manifested distracts me. A girl walking through the woods, alone, half-naked, as the late afternoon sun plays with the light, twigs and branches cracking in the distance. No one is here. I'm alone. My thoughts don't reassure me. But soon, for better or worse, I'll sleep in my own bed and use a real toilet. Parental authoritarian rule comes with creature comforts.

The cottage door is ajar. I stop. Every hair on my body stands on end. I'm sure I closed the door, but maybe I didn't. My brain feels fuzzy, my thoughts thick. I can't remember what I did before leaving for the pond. A part of me wants to run, but the other part, which envisions sprinting down the road in nothing but a wet bra and underwear, decides the wind pushed the door open. My heart thuds against my rib cage. I stand at the threshold, listening to my own breathing. Closing my eyes, I recount Wes Craven's rules for surviving a horror film. Maybe being a virgin is going to pay off after all. Virgins always survive. I place one clammy palm against the grain of the door and push.

The creak of the rusty hinges startles me even before I can react. I have an intruder—

"Phil?" I gasp.

"Maya. Jesus. Are you okay? Half the town is looking for you." I've never seen Phil's face look so drawn before—his eyes are dull with dark circles under them. He tries to smile, but it doesn't reach his eyes.

I take a few hesitant steps toward Phil, who stands at the fire-place. "I know . . . I . . . I'm fine . . . I needed time . . . Phil, I'm sorry . . . for everything."

This could be a perfectly fine freeze-frame ending.

Except it's not.

So I watch the scene unspool. I'm the audience, staring at the big screen. Phil takes three steps toward me, wraps his right arm around my waist, and pulls me to him. His left hand cradles the side of my face, and his warm lips kiss mine in a frenzy. I hug his neck with my right arm and balance on tiptoes to reach his lips. The worn weave of Phil's jeans rubs against my naked thighs. I picture us in a black-and-white movie. Lovers about to be separated by war and continents and the *rat-tat-tat* of machine guns. My lips part as they graze Phil's. Every blood vessel under my skin expands, throwing off heat and warming the space between us. Phil brings his hands to my hips and pulls me closer still.

"Ow," I gasp, breaking the seal of our lips and taking a half step away.

"I'm sorry? Did you not want—"

"No . . . I mean . . . yes . . . It's my arm. It still hurts from, you know."

"Crap. I'm sorry. I wasn't thinking. I was mainly doing." Phil glances away, and a faint red appears on his cheeks.

"I'm the blusher, remember?"

"You kinda are blushing . . . all over." Phil eyes all my exposed skin, and I'm suddenly aware of how little I'm wearing.

"Oh, my God. I forgot—" I snatch my jeans and hold them to my chest. "Can you turn around?"

Phil grins but complies. "You know, I've actually already seen you in your underwear."

I quickly slip into the last of my dry clothes. I quietly walk back to Phil and run my fingers from his shoulder down his arm into his hand. He closes his fingers around mine, raises my hand to his lips, and kisses my palm.

Phil moves his face closer to look into my eyes. "I've been wanting to do this for a very long time. But the timing . . . I kinda screwed that up. And your parents. I'm guessing they wouldn't exactly approve?"

"I would pretty much be facing deportation to India."

"Speaking of them, your mom's frantic. We need to get you home."

"I know, but . . . can't we stay? Please help me ignore reality a little longer."

Phil finally pulls apart from me. I shiver in the sudden cold. He walks over to the chair, takes the sleeping bag, and spreads it over the damp pine floor, then lies down. I take my spot next to him, resting my head on his outstretched arm.

"I like what you've done with the place," he says. "But why did you come here?"

I shrug. "I didn't have anyplace else to go. I guess it was stupid. But I couldn't be at home anymore. I couldn't breathe. When I woke up yesterday, my mom told me I have to stay at home and commute to school. No way. I can't. It's not even . . . Brian attacked me, and someone vandalized their office, but I'm the one facing the consequences."

"That was Brian, too. He confessed—to everything."

My breath catches. "What? He . . . how?"

"That video you took while he was harassing you was enough to show that he lied—that it was more than words, that it was assault. It pretty much saved my ass, too."

"But why would he—?"

"I don't know the whole story yet. My dad talked to the lawyer this morning, and then the police came by the house. I guess they're still sorting it out, but I'm off the hook."

I turn on my side to face Phil and draw my arm across his chest. "I'm so sorry you had to go through all that because of me. If I had only—"

"No. None of it is your fault. At all. If anyone is responsible for not stopping him sooner, it's me."

"What do you mean?"

"I've been meaning to tell you this. I should've told you before . . ."

My pulse pounds. I don't know what he's going to say, but I kind of don't want to hear it. I just want one perfect moment, but this isn't going to be it. I take a breath, put my hand on his arm, and give him a little nod to continue.

"You know how he was being all weird with you at the bookstore and at school?"

"Yes, if by weird you mean an asshole."

"Pretty much. And remember how I told you he'd been that way since the end of the football season?"

"Since he got benched? Right?"

"It wasn't about getting benched. He was benched for behavior, not skill. His brother served in Iraq, and he came home around halfway through the season. He lost a leg over there—IED—and—"

"And he blames me. I know, he said."

"It's not that. I mean, his brother came out to talk to the team one day about leadership and loyalty and counting on each other. He is this total stand-up guy. He wasn't blaming Iraqis or Muslims, more like the facts of war . . ."

"And . . ."

"And I said something to Brian about how his brother was an American hero. I actually said those words. Because it's true. But Brian got pissed about it, shoved me off. I didn't make a big deal about it or get into it with him. It's his brother. Not my situation. But then the next day, I heard him talking to Josh and Brandon after practice. They thought they were alone. And Brian said some really awful things . . ."

"What did he say? He said some pretty horrible things to me, too."

"No. It was worse. What he joked about doing. The words, some of them, one of them. I've never used that word in my life. And I should've stepped up, said something right then, and called Brian out. I'm the captain; that's part of the responsibility. I should've talked to Coach. I mentioned it to Tom. He brushed it off, said I should forget about it. Just Brian blowing off steam. You know, locker room talk, Tom said. But that kind of talk— it's not okay anywhere. I should've known better. I did know better. And I did nothing. And now . . . look what he did to you. What he . . ."

I feel like I've been punched in the chest.

Phil can't look me in the eye.

"How did you know that I was in trouble, anyway?"

His voice is strained. "I saw you walking toward the food court when I was on the Demon, so I ditched the guys after and headed back to find you, to talk to you. Then I heard you scream."

My eyes are wet with tears. I see now that Phil's are, too. "I don't know what I would've done if you hadn't shown up. I tried to fight him off—"

"I could've ripped Brian's head off when I saw him hurt you. I should have. I probably would've, too, if you hadn't stopped me. I could've prevented it—stopped this whole thing from happening."

"That's doubtful."

"I can't get the image of him trying to hurt you out of my mind."

"That makes two of us."

Phil clears his throat and wipes his eyes. "I'm sorry, Maya."

We're quiet for a while. I'm wrapped in Phil's arms. I feel like I have so much to say and also nothing to say. Like I'm full and sort of hollow at the same time. Endings. Beginnings.

Phil kisses me on the forehead. A tear rolls down my cheek and onto his arm. He rubs the tear trail on my face with the back of his index finger. He kisses my neck. I move closer to Phil, and he gently pulls me on top of him. My hair falls across his face. He sweeps it to the side and traces his fingers over my lips. Phil kisses me, his lips hesitant. I kiss him back, deeply and softly.

I'm not sure what is real anymore.

I want the world to fall away so I can live in this exquisite moment. Where I don't have to think or hurt—where I can simply feel the heat of our bodies and breathe in the sweet smell of his cologne until I pass out and wake in the fairy tale where reality bends to me and where this is our happily ever after.

Ethan Branson races home from school on a sunny spring afternoon clutching a story he's written for seventh-grade English class. He runs, panting, into the kitchen and hands the paper to his mother. A gold star decorates the top right next to a large "A." Stapled to the page is a note to the boy's parents: Ethan's story is wonderful. His best work this year by far. His creative writing shows tremendous potential.

Ethan's mother hugs him and strokes his wavy black hair. For a moment he is her little boy again. She puts the paper up on the fridge with a magnet. She blinks back tears as she reads the note from the teacher over and over.

Ethan is in his room when his father comes home. He hears his parents talk. His mother shows the paper and the note to his father. His raised voice and slurred words tell Ethan what will come next. Potential? Potential for what? That kid is going to amount to nothing and no good. Biggest regret of my life.

Ethan opens his bedroom window and slips out as he hears his father's footsteps approach.

CHAPTER 21

An impressive number of emergency vehicles surround my house; red-and-blue lights splash across the lawn and down the street. It's nearly midnight. My parents' humiliation at this very public display must be gnawing at them like a vulture picking flesh off bone. As Phil pulls up to the driveway, the cadre of cops parts, letting us through. My mom bursts out of the house, running at full speed toward us, her unbraided hair wild in the breeze. I've barely stepped out of the car when my mother throws her arms around me, crushing me against her chest.

"Thank God. Thank God," she repeats, tears running down her cheeks.

"Mom . . . my arm . . . remember?"

She steps back, blinking, and then a blast of words explodes from her lips at full volume. "What were you thinking? How could you? We were worried sick. We thought . . . we thought you were dead."

"Mom . . . I'm sorry, please . . . I'm sorry. I know you were worried."

She walks away, fuming. I edge my way to the front of the car, closer to my father and Chief Wickham—and Phil, who is explaining where he found me. The censored version.

I get the death stare from my dad. He doesn't make a single gesture toward me. I was prepared for his wrath, but the cold shoulder stings more.

"Maya," he begins in a formal tone, "why would you run away? You nearly killed your mother with worry, and half the police department was searching for you. You owe the chief an explanation and an apology after everything they've done for us."

I look up at their inquisitive faces. "I'm sorry. It was wrong of me . . . I know I caused a lot of trouble. It's that . . . I was scared." The excuse slips off my tongue almost before I'm aware of it. Obviously, I can't tell the whole truth, so I go with it. "I didn't know what to do. I was afraid that Brian was going to try and hurt me again. Or would do something to you guys."

My dad's eyebrows knit together in confusion. No idea if he is buying this explanation, but the chief nods along. And in a way, what I'm saying is true. Sort of.

"Did any of those boys threaten you again?"

"No, Chief. It wasn't that . . . I basically wigged out. I'm sorry."

"Why didn't you tell me or your mother that you were scared? Your mom wanted to stay home with you."

I wanted to tell you. But I was afraid. You and mom were too blinded by your own fear to see me standing in front of you, almost broken. That's what I want to say. That's what I should say. But I don't.

"You're right, Dad. I'm so sorry. It wasn't smart of me. It all feels so . . . hazy."

Chief Wickham nods like he understands me, but Dad just gives me a slow, judgmental shake of the head. He turns away to escort the chief back to his patrol car, no doubt apologizing for the public spectacle I've caused.

I only now notice that Hina is here. She helps my mom back into the house. I wave at my aunt; she gives me an encouraging smile.

"Are you going to be okay?" Phil asks.

Suddenly we're alone in the center of the driveway.

"They'll probably want to send me to a boarding school in India, but I'll manage." I want to kiss him. I inch closer, and Phil raises his hands to grasp my arms and then pulls them away. I smile again, for real. "Thanks again for talking to my dad."

"I gave him the G-rated version of finding you."

"Which is why you and I are both still standing right now."

"This . . . us . . . isn't going to be easy, is it?"

"No. But I've gotten pretty good at sneaking out, and since I'm probably grounded for life, that skill is going to come in handy." I drop my voice to a whisper. "I wish you didn't have to leave. I wish I could leave with you."

"Me, too, but under the present circumstances—"

I hug Phil. I don't care if my parents see us. I'm tired of hiding all the important parts of myself.

My father walks back up the driveway after the last of the police cars have pulled away. He extends his right hand to Phil. "Thank you for bringing Maya back home. And for helping her. We are indebted to you."

"Sir, it was nothing. I'm glad Maya's safe."

My dad nods at Phil and then walks past. He pauses and turns his head back. "Maya, it's very late. You should come inside."

"I'll be there in a second, Dad."

Phil waits for the front door to shut. "I don't suppose I can kiss you now?"

"I guarantee it's a drive-in movie at my front window."

"I'll take a rain check, then."

Phil gets into his car and eases out of the driveway, waving as he pulls away. I try to shake the foreboding sense that this is the end of something instead of the beginning. I try to grasp at the spark of optimism I felt at the amusement park before Brian attacked me. But it feels beyond reach, and that makes me more anxious. I walk into the house, steeling myself for the inquisition.

My aunt is alone at the kitchen table. Hina rises to hug me and says, "Your mom is in bed. Your father is with her. It's been . . . a lot."

I begin to open my mouth to respond, but Hina puts her hand on my arm and says, "It's late, and everyone is tired. Let's talk about this tomorrow?"

Guilt surges through my body as my aunt speaks, but so does defiance. "They're forcing their fears on me."

"Running away didn't exactly assuage their concerns."

"I know. It was stupid. But I was going to explode if I stayed here one more minute."

Hina smiles and cups my cheek in her hand. It's a maternal gesture that I'm much more willing to receive from her than my actual mother. I know I should want this comfort from my mom, and sometimes I do. If I'm being honest, I know I push her away because I can't be the daughter she expects me to be and still be what *I* want to be at the same time. On some level, I know she's listened to me, but she never really heard what I was trying to tell her. Maybe there's more to it than that, but that's all the truth I'm willing to face right now.

"So this Phil seems . . . like a lucky young man." As always, Hina knows when to change the subject

"Is he? It's like I'm watching my life through a double fog filter. Nothing is clear."

She laughs softly. "Knowing you, I doubt that. Maybe you know what you want to do, but you're scared to do it. Isn't that why you ran away—to clear your head? To figure it all out?"

I pause. Hina is right. The choice is my dreams or theirs. In that way, it's not a real choice at all. It's an imperative.

PBS Frontline Documentary: The War at Home

For days after, weeks even, there was paper. It fell from the sky after Ethan Branson drove his truck through the doors of the Federal Building in Springfield, exploding the heart of the country.

Scraps of paper, driver's licenses, receipts, grocery lists, drawings in crayon and colored pencil, school pictures. Burnt, charred offerings. Words of the dead, drifting down from the heavens like feathers from birds in flight. Remember me, they whisper.

Amongst them, a singed corner of letterhead and these words:

From our beginning as a nation, we have admitted to our country and to citizenship immigrants from the diverse lands of the world. We had faith that thereby we would best serve ourselves and mankind.[1]

---

1 Judge Abraham Lincoln Marovitz, Nov. 17, 1994 US Naturalization Oath Ceremony

CHAPTER 22

"No. That's the final answer. End of discussion." My dad sits stone-faced at the kitchen table. My mom stares into the four cups of tea at the counter, entranced by the little milk eddies she stirs up in each one. The air is heavy with the smell of fennel seeds, cardamom, and panic.

"I'm not asking you for permission; I'm informing you of my decision. I am going to New York in August." I'm unusually calm and direct, which is almost the most shocking part of this entire scene. I don't know if it's the silent strength emanating from my aunt at my side, the soft underbelly of denial, or plain guts, but maybe for the first time, I face my parents with a kind of composure that feels adult—at least to me. Which doesn't mean I'm not also terrified.

"This is ridiculous. You're a child. You can't talk to your parents this way. Ordering us around as if we're you're servants. We didn't bring you into this world to treat us with such disrespect."

"Dad, I'm sorry. But I'm not a child anymore; I'm going to be eighteen in a few weeks. I'll be legally emancipated, and I have a right to live my life how I want."

"Emancipated? Rights? Now you talk as if you're a lawyer? This is not how we raised you." My mom lifts her eyes from the tea, her voice trembling.

"And how will you pay for school? Will you work in the school cafeteria? That won't even pay for your books. Then you will realize what you've done."

"*Bhai.*" I can tell Hina is making an effort to keep her voice relaxed.

"Last night I offered to help Maya financially if she needs it, and—"

"First you hide Maya applying to school in New York, and now this? Paying for our daughter to defy us? You have no right to do this." My mother's rage permeates the space around us.

"*Aapa*, I know you're her mother. I know you love her. But Maya deserves a chance to pursue her dreams. I can help her do that. I can't stand by and watch Maya be pigeonholed into a life she doesn't want. And actually, yes, I have a right to spend *my* money as I deem fit."

"No. No. No! Don't you dare lecture me. I stood by you when everyone criticized you. Becoming a graphic designer. Living in Chicago on your own. Not married at your age. I'm the one who defended your choices, but I won't have that life for *my* daughter."

My family implodes before my eyes. Whatever we really mean to one another feels so lost and far away.

"Stop it!" I scream. I don't even try for calm. I have no calm left. "This isn't Hina's fault. It's my choice. It's my life, and I have a right to do what I want."

"You have a right? You have a right? If we were in India, you would never defy us this way. You would be a good girl who listened to her parents. And now look at you." My mom's hands shake as she steps behind my dad, grasping the back of his chair for support.

"Even if we lived in India, I would still be who I am and want what I want. Geography wouldn't have changed that."

My father shakes his head. "This is our karma for raising you with these . . . these American values."

"Can't you see, Maya?" My mom's voice softens a bit, trying a different tack. "Look what happened after this bombing. We'll always be the scapegoats. Even though it was one of their people who did this. See what happened to us and to you. We don't belong here."

"Yes, terrible racist stuff happened, but we're part of this place, and it's a part of us. And we can help make it better by being here and living our lives and being happy. We can be . . . We *are* American *and* Indian *and* Muslim."

"And what will people think? How will we explain this to everyone?"

"Mom, can't you for once care what I think? You and dad came to America—you left your parents back in India because that's what you wanted for yourselves. You took a chance. That's what I want, too."

"And what if you fail in this . . . this . . . making movies? Then what?"

"Then I pull myself up by my bootstraps and start over. You taught me that. You came here, started with almost nothing, and built your practice. I know how hard you worked. Please, you have to let me at least try before you decide I'm going to fail."

My dad has been quietly rubbing his palms for the last few minutes, not saying a word. But now, he brings his fist down on the table, rattling the cups and spilling his tea. "Maya's right."

"I am?"

"She is?" The blood drains from my mom's face.

"She will be eighteen next month, and in this country she is an adult and can make her own choices." The edge in his voice gives way to fatigue. "Maya, we can't stop you from going to New York. But we have made our opinion clear. So now you must choose— your parents or New York."

Gauntlet thrown.

For a second, I think of Kareem. I know what he would say. Carpe diem. "New York." The words squeak out, barely. But I've said them. They are real.

My father pushes back his chair and stands up. "You've made your decision and now understand mine. As a daughter, you are dead to us. When you turn eighteen in June, you will leave this house."

My dad's words are like a punch to the gut. He can't mean them. This can't be real.

"But Dad, school doesn't start till September, and—"

"You want to be emancipated. So be it." He turns without looking back at me or waiting for a reaction and walks through the kitchen into the backyard.

I brush away tears with the back of my hand.

My mom's jaw is taut. She looks at my aunt. "Leave my house," she says, her voice barely audible. Then she directs her whisper to me. "You have broken your parents' hearts." She lumbers out of the kitchen and up the stairs.

I can't move. I sit at the table, stunned.

Hina wraps her arm around my shoulder and clears her throat. "They'll come around—maybe not right away, but someday. Consider what this means to them. They feel like they've lost their daughter. They love you, even if they don't show it the way you want them to. But you ran away. You scared all of us. And now you've told them you've chosen New York over them. It's an awful lot to handle. Give them time. I know you've made the right decision for yourself—even a courageous one—to pursue your dreams and the life you want. Don't lose faith. Your mother forgave me after all, even if she doesn't show it."

"Forgave you for running away?"

"Forgave me for taking care of you."

"She told you to leave the house."

"But she didn't say it was goodbye. Trust me, I know my sister. And trust yourself, you're braver than you know."

I don't feel brave at all. I feel scared. No camera. No filter. Just my life, totally unscripted.

Michigan Public Radio, WDBN Dearborn

We're joining the funeral service of Kamal Aziz, one of the victims of the suicide bombing in Springfield. Originally mistakenly identified as the bomber, Mr. Aziz is being laid to rest by well over a thousand community members of all faiths here in Dearborn, Michigan. Now we take you live to the eulogy delivered by Michigan's first Arab-American senator:

On a beautiful spring day, Kamal Aziz went to take an oath to support and defend our Constitution and this nation, to follow in the footsteps of so many immigrants who came before him whose work and vision have stitched together the fine fabric of our country. From his volunteer work at a youth basketball league here in Dearborn to his goal of becoming a doctor and bringing quality medical care to poor neighborhoods, Kamal embodied the very best of America.

Tragically, his dream was cut short by an act of hate. It falls to us to pick up the mantle, to live by Kamal's example and ensure that his life is not forgotten and that his death was not in vain. We must build bridges, conquer hate with love, and meet intolerance with a renewed commitment to education and open-mindedness. From many, we are one.

CHAPTER 23

"So you're disowned for going to college?" Violet hoists herself into the hammock in her yard while I take a seat on a wrought-iron bench under the shade of a maple.

"For going away to college," I correct.

"And you're kicked out of the house?"

"I believe that falls under the terms of disownment."

"You can stay here," Violet offers.

Violet's house never smells like onions. I noticed that right away when I first came over freshman year. Honestly, I don't think I've ever seen Violet or her dad use the stove. Maybe that's why Violet loves my mom's cooking so much. There are no tchotchkes, either. And the bare minimum of furniture.

But Violet's room is the exact opposite of the rest of her house—a beautiful mess of strewn clothes and starry lights and a tangle of chargers under her desk. Often there's a plate of pizza crusts or a half-eaten carrot sticking out of a bowl of hummus. Basically a germophobe's nightmare, but somehow cozy and welcoming, too.

"My aunt said I could stay with her. Anyway, don't you have to ask your dad first?"

"He'll be cool with it. We have the space, and it's only a couple months. My dad's going to be in Switzerland for most of July, and when he's home, he's constantly at the lab—he'll barely notice the difference. I mean you're here all the time, anyway."

"Seriously? That would be amazing. Like a summer-long slumber party. Also, it might be easier to see Phil . . ." I give Violet a little grin, the kind she used to give me before this all happened, when she flirted with everyone.

"Super easy, especially since he's on his way here now."

"You did not."

"He texted because he was worried that it was going to be World War Three at your house, and I might have mentioned that you were coming over and that it would be okay if he came by . . ."

I don't need to tell Violet I'm happy Phil's coming over. The emoji heart eyes popping out of my head say it all.

"Look at you. A couple months ago, you could barely imagine talking to Phil, and now you're planning on summering with him after macking, half-naked, in a secret cabin in the woods. I'm so proud." Violet dabs away fake tears.

"Ha, ha. So glad to meet with your approval."

I hear a car pulling up in the driveway. I hear a door slam. I hold my breath.

"We're in the back," Violet yells. She leaps out of the hammock and whispers, "I feel a sudden compulsion to do homework." Giving me a hair toss and a wink, she hurries into the house.

My pulse quickens, my hands get clammy, my body hums in anticipation. Phil turns the corner of the house. And he's his beautiful, dimpled self again. The dark circles are fading away, and his smile, the real one, reaches his eyes once more. And that makes me happy.

"Hi. How's it going?" Phil asks, his hands pushed down into his jean pockets. He glances around, puzzled, looking for Violet, then smiles at me. I beam back, curling my fingers around the edge of the bench, trying to prevent myself from leaping into his arms.

"Hey." I'm still smiling, showing off every one of my child-of-dentists well-aligned teeth. I flush a deep red, self-conscious of my joyful lightheadedness. I scoot over to make some room for him on the bench.

"Sorry about your parents." Phil clasps my hand. I act casual, but cartoon birds tweet around our heads, encircling us with garlands of paper hearts.

"I guess I expected it, but it's still unreal, you know? My aunt tells me they'll get over it eventually. But I don't know—I've never seen their faces like that."

Phil leans over to kiss me. His lips are as pillowy as I'd remembered. He kisses the top of my head. "Your hair smells so . . . so . . . clean."

I laugh. "I have been known to shower occasionally."

"I mean . . . you smell good."

As I straighten my head and shake the hair from my face, I see a curtain in the house swish into place. I point to the window.

"I was wondering where Violet was," Phil says. "Shall we continue the show?"

I shake my head. "Indian modesty complex." I ease out of Phil's lap. "But I have a feeling she's going to be really engrossed in her physics homework for a while."

Phil changes the subject. "So listen, prom is next week. And I want to ask you, but there's that stupid promise I made Lisa."

"As Amber and Kelsey informed me, remember?"

He nods, and the corners of his mouth turn down. "Look, I want us to go and have a great time. But I'm not sure if it's worth the drama. I shouldn't have made that promise, but Lisa was so angry. And I had no idea if you even liked me."

"It's okay. Don't worry about it."

"No. It's not okay. I want to take you. It's the end of senior year. It's tradition. It's cheesy, but there's no one I'd rather be cheesy with."

The secret cheese-loving part of my heart melts. "Seriously, Phil, it's fine. I'm not exactly traditional."

"I know. That's one of the things I love about you," Phil continues, apparently oblivious to how a single word makes me come undone. "So will you go to a nontraditional prom with me?"

"What do you mean?"

"You have to answer first. Is it a 'yes' or a 'no'?"

"Yes. Of course. Now what is it?"

"I'm making it up as I go along. It'll be good, though. Saturday night. Can I pick you up at your house?"

"Definitely not. I'll be over here helping Violet get ready for the dance."

Phil squeezes my hand. "I love planning surprises for you."

All he has to do is ask, and I will go to the ends of the earth with him. Defy my parents' expectations, even my better judgment for the perfection of Phil's arms around me. If only we lived in a vacuum.

He leans over, taking my face in both his hands. When we kiss, my body swells with anticipation. Then I'm the observer again—watching a girl being kissed by a boy, spring sun glistening around them, lighting their bodies in halos.

Then I'm myself once more, and the warmth of Phil's skin seeps into mine. My thoughts and emotions tangle—longing and confusion and uncertainty, but beneath the chaos in my mind, the tender reeds of hope take root and grow inside me. I no longer have to document it all from the perimeter. I am *the girl*, and this *is* my story.

A.M. Chicago Interview with Jessica Fields, classmate of Ethan Branson

He was quiet. Not a lot of friends. I think he sat with some of the skinhead kids at lunch. No one took them seriously—in terms of them being racist or whatever. I mean, there weren't even any black kids at our school. Or Jews. I guess we all thought they were losers who drew swastikas and smoked in the parking lot and wore black hoodies.

I had one class with Ethan, American lit, junior year. He sat in the back doodling in his notebook most of the time. Never wanted to talk in class, not even in group work. It was kind of weird, though. It was like he knew the answers, but didn't want to be bothered answering them or, like, even speak.

But this one time we were studying Walt Whitman and his feelings of being helpless or the futility of life or something. And the teacher called on him to read this poem. He started out reading real slow, but by the end he seemed kind of into it. He even answered questions about it. Mr. Bradley was floored. We all were. I don't think anyone had ever heard Ethan speak so much.

After class I remember him kind of hunched over with the book in his lap. I saw him tear out the page and stuff it into his pocket.

CHAPTER 24

"You look gorgeous. Poor Mike's going to have no idea what to do with all that skin. I can picture him fumbling around, trying to figure out where to put his hands." Somehow despite all the sheepish grins and blushing and quiet crushing, Mike seized his moment and asked Violet to prom. Probably no one was more surprised than him when she said yes.

I grin, almost blushing on Violet's behalf, as I pan the length of her body, allowing my camera to assess her black satin dress, which is short, backless, and tight—and worn with absolute aplomb. "You'll have to be careful when you're dancing, or your ass will pop right out of the two inches of material that are holding it in," I tease.

"That pic would totally make the yearbook." Violet smirks.

"I would love to catch that moment on film." I sigh.

Violet smiles at me. "You look amazing. I mean, that dress. I'm psyched you're embracing your hotness this way." She pushes me in front of the full-length mirror. Then she whispers, "Trust me, your night is going to be epic."

I lower my camera. I smile at my reflection. I look good in the short, peacock-print chiffon dress I chose. The beaded straps form a V-neckline that leads to a ruched bodice and pleated skirt. Violet gave me a blow-out earlier, so my hair is the silkiest it's ever been and falls in loose layers that frame my face.

"Oh, and before I forget, here." She hands me a small backpack.

"What is it?"

"Phil asked me to put it together for you. Don't sneak a peek."

"This better not be full of condoms."

"Maya Aziz, what a dirty little mind you have."

I film as we head into the backyard to take photos. Posing under the trees, on the bench, in the hammock, I balance my camera on various garden objects to get full-length shots of us together. Then we take every imaginable variation of selfie until we hear a car pull up in the driveway. Mike meets us behind the house. He's sweating a little, and I can't tell if it's from being so near to Violet or the actual heat. I shoot footage of Violet pinning a boutonniere on his lapel and Mike handing her flowers. It's terribly corny, but it's sweet in a *Pretty in Pink* way, too. Like, perfectly sentimental. A lump grows in my throat. The last dance. I missed them all.

IT'S NOT QUITE THE magic hour, but the spring light is still flawlessly cinematic. Its warmth perfectly frames Phil as he walks up the path to Violet's house to meet me at the door.

"They're beautiful," I say as he offers me a small, tight nosegay of calla lilies so purple they're almost black.

"You're beautiful."

He's dressed in a slim-fitting black suit that accentuates his broad shoulders, a black shirt, and no tie. Hair perfectly tousled, as ever. Skin tan. Green eyes sparkling. He's The Guy in every ad in every magazine.

"You look good," I say, reaching up to kiss him. Apparently, all my adjectives are lost in this haze of wonder I'm floating around in.

Phil points to my pack. "Did Violet give you that bag?"

"Yes, and she was quite secretive."

"You peeked?"

"I was tempted."

"I can understand temptation." Phil's lips graze my jawline. I shudder. I blush. Those words, still gone.

Phil takes my bags and sticks out his elbow so I can slip my arm through as he escorts me to his car.

We settle into our seats. I notice he's cleaned the interior for the occasion. "One more thing. Close your eyes, please?"

I comply, and Phil slips a soft cloth over my tightened lids and ties it behind my head, taking care not to tangle my hair. This is not what I was expecting.

"Hey, what—" I tug at the blindfold.

"No. Don't. I want it to be a surprise till we get there."

"Fine." I squirm in my seat. "As long as we're not going to a bondage club. This is not my dominatrix outfit."

Phil laughs. "I hope I get to see it one day." Then he leans in and kisses my awaiting lips.

Phil cranks the music, a best of the '80s movie soundtrack playlist personalized for me that begins with Flesh for Lulu, turns to Simple Minds, and brings it home with The Psychedelic Furs. So it's pretty much the most perfect retro-prom-but-not-really-prom playlist ever. I reach over, and he pulls my hand into his.

I try to keep track of turns, but Phil meanders around a bit, clearly trying to throw me off the scent of the trail. Honestly, though, there are not a lot of options around here, and I'm guessing he's not making a mad break for Vegas for a quickie wedding. Still, I love his thoughtfulness.

"Don't take the blindfold off yet."

"I'm getting antsy."

"I wouldn't have guessed from all the foot tapping. Hold on." Phil parks, then gets out of the car and comes around to the passenger side. He opens the door and scoops me into his arms.

"You're carrying me?" Normally, I would be irritated, but I'm so out-of-my-brain ecstatic, it amuses me.

"Don't worry. I won't drop you. I got your bag, too."

Phil shuts the car door with his knee and walks with me in his arms. I rest my head against his shoulder. The familiar smell of woods and grass and the silence, broken only by birds chirping and tiny twigs breaking underfoot, reveals the spot even before my blindfold is off. A door creaks, and then Phil puts me down and unties the blindfold. I blink a few times. The cabin was high on my list of possibilities, but it doesn't look anything like the cabin I'd holed myself up in.

The entire room is lit up with candles and little white fairy lights. A huge vase of fuchsia peonies are set into the fireplace. A table in the corner has two place settings and a bouquet of white gerbera daisies. Drapes hang from the windows, covering the empty panes. Area rugs hide the uneven floor. Music wafts from speakers in the corners. I turn to Phil, my mouth agape. "It's magical. How did you—?"

"I borrowed a generator from my dad for the lights and the stereo, and my brother helped me set up."

"No one's ever done anything like this for me before." I step closer to him.

"I wanted it to be perfect." Phil takes my chin in his hand and gently lifts my face to his. There aren't just sparks between us, there's a giant flame leaping back and forth, engulfing us.

I step out of the kiss and take in the room again. "Best. Prom. Ever," I say, sliding my hand into his.

He smiles. "I'm so glad. Now let's eat." He gestures to the table.

Phil helps me into my seat, then wanders into the back and reappears with two heaping plates of food and places them on the table. Cold pasta salad tossed with sun-dried tomatoes. Thick slabs of roast beef with mustard. Skewers of roasted vegetables. We eat, avoiding any conversation about the situation with my parents, or going off to school in the fall, or definitions of what we are. Instead, we laugh, recalling awkward moments and embarrassing attempts at flirtation and our earliest memories of each other. Phil brings out chocolate cupcakes and a bowl of fresh strawberries for dessert.

When we finish eating, Phil switches the playlist on his iPod. Our prom theme song fills the room: Eric Clapton's "Wonderful Tonight." Which is a million years old, because you can think classic rock was left in the last century, but it sneakily took up residence in Batavia. But like everything tonight, it's gorgeous.

Phil puts his hand out. "May I have this dance?"

I slip my hand in his and let myself be pulled into the center of the room. Melodious tones warm the cabin. For all I know, the song is on repeat, because this moment is liquid amber. I'm keeping it forever. A part of me wishes I could capture this moment on film, a memory of something good and true in my life.

Phil holds me tight. I rest my cheek on his chest. He twirls me out of his arms and brings me back, his green eyes smile as he looks into mine. We continue to dance without words, clutching each other, spinning around the room, while time slides lightly by.

PHIL SNEAKS US INTO the Fabyan Visitor Center, and by sneak, I mean entering through an unlocked back door. Apparently, they're not concerned about thieves stealing all the visitor maps at night.

I take my bag and dash into the restroom. It's heaven to slip into a pair of jeans, T-shirt, and cardigan, and out of my uncomfortable heels. I rifle through the pack and find a toothbrush and a little bouquet of new lip glosses tied together by a silver ribbon. Violet thought of everything. I also find a note with a condom attached: *In case of emergency, rip open. Have fun! XOXO.* I shake my head, then comb my hair back into a ponytail and layer on lip gloss.

Phil's changed into a pair of jeans and a fitted thermal Henley that perfectly follows the curve of his biceps. He looks like his everyday self. His best self.

We drop our bags at the cabin and head directly to the pond. The last time I'd walked this path, it felt like the setting of a horror movie. But in the warm night air and with Phil's hand around mine, it's a gorgeous romance. As the woods give way to the clearing, I see paper lanterns hanging from tree branches, illuminating the pond. A red flannel blanket covers our little square of sand.

There's no scenario I could've imagined that would have ended in this moment of perfection. I blink back a couple tears. I don't want to cry, not tonight, not even if it's from joy. I pause and take in the entire scene. I'm not filming, but I'm etching this into my mind forever.

Phil kneels next to a cooler and a small grill and starts building a little fire. He turns to me and smiles, then motions for me to join him. He reaches into the cooler and hands me a skewered marshmallow and produces a Tupperware full of dark chocolate and graham crackers. He nestles into the spot next to me as we roast our marshmallows. The gooey alchemy of s'mores draws us closer together. We devour them, trying not to burn our tongues. Chocolate dribbles down the side of my chin. Before I can be mortified, Phil swipes it up with his finger and puts it in his mouth. The darkness is a relief; it cloaks my face that blooms half a dozen shades of red. After a few more s'mores, we lie next to each other on the blanket, holding hands, gazing up beyond the fluttering leaves into the canopy of stars.

Phil kisses me on the forehead.

I huddle closer to him; he wraps his arms around me. The warm spring night has given way to a slight chill, but the heat radiates from Phil's body into mine. I inhale deeply, tracing the hard lines of his jaw with the tips of my fingers, pondering the winding paths that life presents—ends leading to beginnings and back again.

Some love stories are tragedies—epics, spanning years, and built on dramatic irony, wars, Russian winters, and hours of film. Others are romantic comedies, a meet-cute ruined by mishaps and bad timing, finally leading to a kiss atop a tall building—the metropolis glimmering in the background, moon rising, love song playing over the credits.

But other romances, like this one, are simply short-subject documentaries—lacking traditional narratives and quippy dialogue. Everyday people lying next to each other on a makeshift beach, the mottled spring light passing through the dense trees before softly surrendering to dusk.

O Me! O Life!

Oh me! Oh life! of the questions of these recurring,
  Of the endless trains of the faithless, of cities fill'd with the foolish,
  Of myself forever reproaching myself, (for who more foolish than I, and who more faithless?)
  Of eyes that vainly crave the light, of the objects mean, of the struggle ever renew'd,
  Of the poor results of all, of the plodding and sordid crowds I see around me,
  Of the empty and useless years of the rest, with the rest me intertwined,
  The question, O me! so sad, recurring—What good amid these, O me, O life?

Answer.
  That you are here—that life exists and identity,
  That the powerful play goes on, and you may contribute a verse.

Walt Whitman, Leaves of Grass, *1892.*

EPILOGUE

"Chapter thirty for next time. And don't forget there's a screening of *Meet the Patels* tonight at the Cantor Film Center," the professor calls as my fellow students and I gather our notebooks and backpacks.

I loop a green silk scarf around my neck and lift my bag onto my shoulder.

"Are you walking back to the dorm?" Rajiv, another film major in my class, asks in a British accent so lovely and warm it could star in its own rom-com.

"Actually, errands. Also I'm headed to the campus store to get my parents some school gear before I head home for Thanksgiving."

"Ahh, yes. The American holiday celebrating colonialism with a bland, dry bird." He grins at me as we walk out of the building together. Rajiv lifts the collar of his jacket to block the wind.

"And the British are such strangers to colonialism and bland food?"

"I can at least take up the food issue with the queen."

"Yes, please do." I nudge Rajiv as we reach the corner.

"So are you thinking of going to the film this evening?"

"Planning on it."

"Would you like to attend . . . with me, perhaps? Together?"

I look at the curly-haired young man in front of me, sporting the exact right amount of stubble and charm. "A documentary about desi matchmaking with a desi. That's not awkward at all." I grin at him and nod.

"Well, I'm Hindu, and you're Muslim; obviously we're star-crossed. I'll pick you up at your dorm tonight, say seven? We can grab falafel at Mamoun's first."

"Perfect. See you." I'm smiling wide, like the American I am, showing off every tooth.

"Cheers," he says, then gives me a quick kiss on the cheek before heading off.

I suck in my breath. It was just a peck, but no one's kissed me since Phil and I said goodbye. Though it wasn't a goodbye, exactly, since we refused to say that word. I'm still not quite sure what it was. The greatest "see-you-later" kiss of all time?

WE'D JUST GONE FOR our last swim at the pond, the summer sun warm through the canopy of leaves. Unlike before, it dried our wet bodies as we walked back to the cabin, silently, hand in hand. We didn't go in.

Phil gently drew me into his arms and bent down to kiss me. I was crying before I knew it. I pulled away to wipe tears from my cheeks, but he took my face in his hands, smiled and said, "We'll always have the pond."

I laughed. "You actually watched *Casablanca*? I thought you said you hated sappy, black-and-white movies."

"*Casablanca*? Nah. That was a reference to an old *Star Trek: Next Generation* episode I saw with my dad."

I laughed through my tears. I kissed him again, then turned to go. I wanted to leave first. I didn't think I could bear to watch him walk away from me. But I glanced over my shoulder and saw him there, face lit by the afternoon. "Here's looking at you, kid," he called.

He was smiling, but his cheeks glistened with tears, too. He knew what I knew: there was no tomorrow for us if we were going our own ways, to different places and different futures.

That was the moment. Our final scene, unadorned.

THE FLEETING WARMTH OF Rajiv's lips on my skin brought it all rushing back—Phil's touch, *his* lips, *his* fingertips and a feeling that is not so fleeting after all. My body remembers what part of my mind wants to forget—because there are times when I struggle to reconcile what I gave up to be here, in this very moment, despite how much I wanted it. How much I do want it. The past may be prologue, but it's with me, every day.

I walk through Washington Square Park, pausing to watch a group of young acrobats perform for tourist tips. The wind kicks up, whirling leaves into little whirlpools. I shiver. The days are growing shorter.

I wonder how my parents will react to the NYU swag. We've agreed to a family Thanksgiving at Hina's house. It was all Hina's idea. She even bought me the ticket home. I was reluctant, but I owe her. More than I can ever repay. I'm hoping it's a good sign that my parents are coming. I guess I sort of owe them this, too. My mom even texted me asking if I wanted her to bring my favorite winter hat to Hina's so I would have it for school. It's not my favorite. It's this bubblegum-pink knit beanie with a white pom-pom on top that she bought me three years ago. But her text broke my heart a little. So I replied with a shouty caps: YES! PLEASE! ❄ 💚 I'm sure that made her happy.

I know now that I can never really understand how much I hurt them or how bewildered they must've been when I left, pondering what they'd done to deserve what they see as a betrayal.

The fact is they didn't do anything wrong. I see that now. They are my parents. I am their daughter. And the world between us cracked because of the difference in how we understand that fundamental bond. But if my mom can extend a peace offering, so can I.

Even with uncertainties at home, I'm excited to go back, trade stories with Violet in person. And see Phil, whatever we may be to each other.

There's time before the movie, and I possess a strong desire to put off my errands and homework, so I set off on a long walk through the city—a habit that's quickly become a favorite pastime since I arrived in New York, my camera always at the ready.

Today, I walk up West Fourth Street, then turn onto West Tenth and head for the river. West Fourth is one of those odd streets that break the New York grid, at least my newbie understanding of it, where streets normally run east-west and avenues north-south. Except in New York parlance where "north" and "south" are "uptown" and "downtown." And then there's the funny way you give an address, always with the cross streets. Like everything else in New York, geography has its own culture.

I head west on Tenth Street, passing trendy boutiques with only a dozen clothes displayed on the racks, a tea shop, a French café, a vintage store, a very expensive florist, bars opening for the afternoon, Federal-style townhouses with grand doors, ivy-covered brownstones, even an apothecary shop. I walk under the barren branches of trees and wonder about the generations of starving artists and writers who once pounded this same pavement, but had to flee when rents rose and heftier pocketbooks moved in. From time to time, I raise my fingers to the silver ginkgo leaf pendant Phil gave me as a goodbye gift. I wear it every day. As a reminder. As a talisman.

Right before Tenth Street emerges onto the cacophony of the West Side Highway, I stop to get a latte, wrapping my cool hands around the cup for warmth. As soon as I cross into

Hudson River Park, the traffic din dies down, giving way to the sloshing of waves against the piers that jut out into the river. I love the unruly water that gives the Hudson its personality. On chilly afternoons, the park is mostly quiet, except for a few bicyclists and people walking their dogs. As I stroll far out onto the pier, I savor the sweetness of having a corner of New York all to myself.

At the end of the wide dock, I gaze down the open river corridor to the Statue of Liberty far in the distance, beyond the pile field of submerged logs that once supported the old piers. I breathe in the salty air—thinking of the first deep breath thousands of immigrants once took as they sailed into New York Harbor, dreaming. Even my own parents, though they arrived by plane from India, first stepped foot on American soil in New York. They stayed with family friends in Queens for a week before their onward journey to the Midwest. An old framed photo on my mother's bureau pops into my mind: My parents standing on a tour boat against white rails, close but not touching. The Statue of Liberty in the background. My mother is graceful and thin with a sari draped over one shoulder and pulled modestly like a shawl around her back. My father, bushy haired and smiling, squints in the sun. The hopes and ambitions they must've had, newly married and in love. How impossible it would've been for those two young people to envision where their lives would lead them. I want to walk into the picture, take their hands, and say that there will be incredible and heartbreaking changes ahead, but that their lives here will be good.

The wind chaps my cheeks. I glance down at my watch and start toward my dorm. At the next corner, I pause, setting up a crane shot for the movie in my mind:

The sky darkens as people brush by The Girl. Her green scarf flutters on the screen as the overcranked motion eventually slows around her. She turns to smile at the camera overhead, the vibrant resonance of New York swelling, as the edges of the frame fade to black.

AUTHOR'S NOTE

I wrote this book out of hope.

I was a New Yorker on September 11, 2001. My old apartment in New York City's East Village once had a clear view of the World Trade Center. During the years I lived there, on the anniversary of 9/11, I would stare out of my big picture window at the two bright shafts of light beaming up to the heavens. Toward those we lost. Mothers and daughters, fathers and sons, brothers and sisters, friends, lovers, wealthy and working class, old and young. Americans. Tourists. Those who chose to make this place their home; those born here. Muslim and Jew. Christian and Hindu. Buddhist and Atheist. Every race. Every creed.

All of them, human beings.

To those of us who live, who bear witness, the Tribute in Light shines as a beacon and reminder, that though we are many, we are one.

I wrote this book out of love.

Raghead. Terrorist. Paki. Illegal. I've been called lots of names that aren't my own and it stings every time, forever burned in my memory. But my experiences of Islamophobia and bigotry are mild compared to the violence many others have faced, will face. In recent times we've seen hate emerge out of dark corners, torches blazing in the night. We've witnessed so-called leaders not merely casually accept cruelty, but engender it. Worse, we've seen horrific violence. But all around us, we've seen people rise up, not merely against the forces of hate, but for equality and justice. Bigotry may run through the

American grain, but so too does resistance. We know the world we are fighting for.

And for those who bear the brunt of hate because of the color of their skin, or the sound of their name, or the scarf on their head, or the person they love; for those who are spat upon, for those who are told to "go home" when they are home: you are known. You are loved. You are enough. Let your light shine.

I wrote this book for you.

ACKNOWLEDGMENTS

This book you are holding in your hands exists in the real world because my amazing agent, Eric Smith, liked a tweet in the virtual one. Eric, thank you for being a fierce advocate, for believing in my story, for DM'ing at all hours, and for breaking your mouse to like that tweet. I owe you a new one and so much more.

Daniel Ehrenhaft, my brilliant, eagle-eyed editor at Soho Teen, saw the things I could not see and challenged me to make my story shine on the page. His unwavering belief in my ability to do so steadied my hand and calmed my nerves. Dan, you totally rule.

Bronwen Hruska, publisher, champion, took a risk and embraced Maya's story and for that I am eternally grateful. The fabulous publicity/marketing team at Soho fashioned wings for this book and made it fly. Abby Koski, Paul Oliver, Rudy Martinez, I know ice cream and stickers and 6-foot-tall Maya only touch on the brilliance of your work. Consider this an official requisition: please send cardboard Maya to me at the end of her journey. I'll make her a star of Maya-camera hands pictures for years to come. Janine Agro designed the striking interior and worked with Cannaday Chapman to bring Maya to life and create this stunning cover, which is now permanently referred to in my home as The Precious. Rachel Kowal brought a sharp eye, kindness, and much patience to the editing process. Shveta Thakrar, my copy editor, graced every page with her love and forgave me for my tenuous grasp of English grammar rules. Juliet Grames, Steven Tran, and Monica White were always at the ready to roll up their sleeves, offer encouraging words, and help make Soho feel like home.

To dear friends and fellow writers who inspired and raised the bar high and believed: Sara Ahmed, Harvey "Smokey" Daniels, Dhonielle Clayton, Aisha Saeed, Heidi Heilig, Sarvenaz Tash, Nicole Pointdexter, Lizzie Cooke, Gloria Chao, Sangu Mandanna, Franny Billingsley, Ronni Davis Selzer, Hebah Uddin, Jonathan Levi, Amy Adams, Tiffany Schmidt, Sona Charaipotra, Adam Silvera, Beth Hahn, Claribel Ortega, Kat Cho, Rena Barron, and Anna Waggener. I am eternally grateful for your eyes and ears and wisdom and love.

Team Rocks, thank you for the laughter and tears and medicake. Waterfall glory forever!

I've been fortunate to meet many wonderful, supportive folks online. The KidLit Authors of Color group, you remind me every day why our stories are worth fighting for. Fight Me Club, you are warriors; thank you for having my back. You have my sword, always. My fellow Electric 18s, may our stars burn long and bright. To my tweeps, especially all the indie booksellers (looking at you Rachel Strolle and Katie Stutz), teachers, and librarians, thank you for being guardians of childhood and defenders of our cultural lighthouses.

My family provided enough fodder to fill ten books. To the top six and bottom six, thank you for your endless *sharaarat* and *hangama*. May your condiment packets and yogurt containers never run out and may the perfect sheets always line your suitcases. Special shout-out to Raeshma Razvi who tutored me on film terms and listened to my endless *bakwas*.

In many ways this book is a valentine to my hometown of Batavia, Illinois. To childhood friends, I hope you found something to smile at in these pages. The Lincoln Tree may be gone, but my love is forever. Go Bulldogs!

To my sisters, Asra and Sara, thank you for your encouragement and for putting up with the Baji treatment all these long years. We're still the winningest sister trio in Batavia High School tennis history (this may not be technically true, but I write fiction so, yes, yes, it is).

To my parents, Hamid and Mazher, you filled our shelves with books and encouraged us to always ask questions. Nearly fifty years ago, you came to this country with your dreams, and you paved the way and built a community brick-by-brick from the ground up and are beacons of light to all those around you.

Lena and Noah, your smiles make me believe in magic. Watching you grow and learn and discover who you are in the world is the greatest honor and privilege of my life. I hope always to endeavor to deserve you. Know that my love for you is boundless.

And to Thomas, my co-creator of this wondrous, improbable life we are writing together. No love, but this proof of love: your belief made this possible.